ZIPPED

Laura and Tom McNeal

Alfred A. Knopf   New York

THIS IS A BORZOI BOOK PUBLISHED BY ALFRED A. KNOPF

www.randomhouse.com/teens

Library of Congress Cataloging-in-Publication Data
McNeal, Laura.
Zipped / Laura and Tom McNeal. — 1st ed.
p.   cm.
SUMMARY: At the end of their sophomore year in high school, the lives of
four teenagers are woven together as they start a tough new job, face family problems,
deal with changing friendships, and find love.
ISBN 0-375-81491-4 (trade) — ISBN 0-375-91491-9 (lib. bdg.)
[1. Interpersonal relations—Fiction. 2. Stepfamilies—Fiction. 3. New York (State)—
Fiction.] I. McNeal, Tom. II. Title.
PZ7.M47879365 Zi 2003
[Fic]—dc21
2002002781

Printed in the United States of America

March 2003

10 9 8 7 6 5 4 3 2 1

First Edition

For Hank
And in memory of Bert Rhoton

With thanks to the following for inspiration and expertise: Susannah Duckworth, Miryam Hernandez, Cynthia Hunt, Bill Jennings, Barbara Kalisuch and her students Vicky, Sally, and Araceli, Thomas Ross McNeal, Jane Morris, Master Sgt. Joe O'Gallagher, Dave Persch, Eric Portigal, David Suggs, Dale Wight, and Maggie Wittenburg. For hospitality near Jemison, we are indebted to Sorayya Khan, her family, and the whole Williams clan. And with gratitude to those who made the manuscript a book: George Nicholson, Joan Slattery, and Jamie Weiss.

PART ONE

Sing a song of sixpence,
A pocket full of rye;
Four and twenty blackbirds
Baked in a pie.
When the pie was opened,
The birds began to sing;
Wasn't that a dainty dish
To set before the king?

CHAPTER ONE

Baked in a Pie

It wasn't a normal Thursday, but all day long it had seemed like
one, so when the final bell rang, Mick Nichols did what he normally did. He walked from Jemison High to Melville Junior High
by way of the athletic fields, fast-walking at first, but then, as he
neared the muddy grass where the girls' field hockey team was
collecting for spring practice, he settled into something closer to
a purposeful stroll.

He hoped he wasn't too early, and he wasn't. Lisa Doyle was
there—he caught a flash of her coppery red hair through the
shifting shoulders and sticks, and suddenly everywhere and all at
once a strange prickling sensation began spreading across his
skin. She bent down to pick up her stick, and when she happened
to flick a glance in his general direction, Mick's face went
wooden. He kept his eyes directly forward and walked stiffly on
without another look her way. Beneath his old bomber jacket,
beneath his khaki T-shirt, a cool bead of sweat coursed down his
rib cage. Dink, he thought as he reached the chain-link fence
that marked the boundary of the high school. Dink dink dink.

Melville Junior High was located just across the street to the
east of Jemison High, so by this time of day Jemison's shadow
already reached across Melville's front lawn. Mick cut through

Melville's parking lot and wandered down to the art room, where his stepmother, Nora Mercer-Nichols, was cleaning up after a day of what she liked jokingly to call "teaching art to the artless." She was stuffing dirty wool into black Hefty bags. When she saw Mick she pushed her sandy blond hair up with the back of her hand and said, "Hello, Maestro!" Then, "Hi, Mick."

Nora Mercer-Nichols was in her early thirties, but she seemed younger. She'd married Mick's father four years before. The first time Mick had met her, she and his father had come in quietly behind him when he was playing the piano in the living room. He'd thought he was alone, and when he finally got through one of Bach's Inventions without a flub, he leaned back on the piano bench and exultantly shot a fist into the air, which drew sudden laughter from Nora and his father. Mick had swung around, surprised and embarrassed. When his father introduced her, he said, "Nora, this is my son, Mick," and she'd smiled and said, "Well, I think I'm going to have to call him Maestro," which she still did. Mick had heard a lot of Bad Stepmother stories, but he liked Nora. He never thought of her as his mother or even his stepmother. She was just Nora, and almost any room was more interesting if she were in it.

Today, standing just inside her classroom door, next to a cabinet lined with bird's nests in clear Plexiglas boxes, Mick read for probably the hundredth time the English and Latin labels he'd helped Nora make one night last fall: BLACK-CAPPED CHICKADEE (*Parus atricapillus*). HOUSE SPARROW (*Passer domesticus*). CHIPPING SPARROW (*Spizella passerina*). A few of the nests held faintly tinted eggs, some freckled, some not. Nora had been asked about the eggs so often that she'd made a small sign that said DON'T WORRY, YOU BIRD LOVERS YOU, I ONLY COLLECT ABANDONED NESTS.

3

Mick found himself staring at some faintly freckled eggs, which made him think of Nora's shoulders in summer, a thought he tried to shake off.

"So," Nora said. "Gimme the daily Doyle report."

Mick shrugged. "Brief visual contact."

"Really? Well, did you smile back?"

"Not exactly."

They both fell silent. About three weeks ago, while driving home with Nora, Mick had told her in a matter-of-fact voice about "this kind of weird effect" that the sight of Lisa Doyle had on him. A laugh had burst from Nora. " 'The heart is the tyrant who spares no one,' " she recited.

"Who said that?"

Nora grinned and nodded toward a small, red ceramic devil that she'd recently set on her dashboard. "Probably little Beelzebub," she said. "Either that or some dead white guy."

Mick didn't know why she called the figurine Beelzebub. All he knew was, he didn't like the little guy. At first it just seemed like a toddler in a devil sleeper, but it always seemed to be peering at you with its black, curious eyes.

"Where'd you get that thing anyway?" he said.

"School," Nora said. "On desktop treasure trading day."

Mick stared at it for a second or two. "It's kind of grimy."

Nora chuckled. "The word I'd use is 'puckish.' " Then, after a block or two had passed, "Weren't we on the subject of one Lisa Doyle? What do you and Lisa talk about?"

"That's kind of the problem," Mick said, and felt his face color slightly. "I haven't actually ever talked to Lisa Doyle."

Nora shot him a look of surprise and then became serious. "Okay, Maestro. Here's the deal. You've been smitten. It may be

4

a foolish infatuation or it may be the real thing. What you have to do is get to know her, and vice versa, which means something more extreme than hockey field walk-bys. You need proximity. If she's on the debate team, join the debate team. If she plays tennis, buy yourself a racket." They were at a stoplight and Nora had fixed Mick with her winsome smile. "If she plays pinochle, take up pinochle."

"I hear she's Mormon," Mick said.

Nora had laughed. "Then say your prayers, and make sure they're good ones," she had said.

The wool they were bagging this afternoon was surprisingly dirty, snagged with twigs and seeds and even clusters of what looked to Mick like sheep dung. He broke a silence by saying, "This stuff's pretty disgusting. What's it for anyway?"

"A new enrichment class." Nora pointed at the near bulletin board, where in large letters it said WOOL: FROM SHEEP TO SWEATER. She laughed again. "You'll be happy to know it's open to students of both genders. The early colonists taught all their children to spin, including boys."

Mick said, "So this class would be a serious opportunity for any guy who might want to be a colonist when he grows up." He hoped this would be good for a chuckle from Nora, and it was. Then he said, "Well, maybe Dad or me'll get a sweater out of it." This was a joke. Although Nora had been working on something that was supposed to be a sweater, she wouldn't say who it was for or what it was supposed to look like, and more often than not she seemed to be unraveling it to correct a mistake.

"Ha," said Nora. "That'll depend on who does the supper dishes."

The drama teacher, Mrs. Van Riper, poked her head into the

art room, gave Mick a cheery hello, and then said to Nora, "You coming to the curriculum committee, sweetie?"

"Oh, God," Nora said. "I forgot completely." She turned to Mick. "I'll be pretty late. Wanna wait?"

He glanced up at the clock—3:32; the city bus had already left—then shrugged. "It's okay," he said. "I'll just walk."

He was at the door when Nora said, "Oh, wait! I've got something that might interest you." She pulled open her desk drawer and presented him with a bright yellow flyer that said

Attention
Reliable Self-Starting Youths
Ages 14-19!
Saturday & Summer Employment
Outdoor Entry-Level Positions Open
Wage Plus Bonuses
Apply At The Village Greens Seniors' Community

Interviews and orientation were scheduled for this Saturday. The contact person was a Mr. Blodgett.

Mick said, "Since when did I strike you as a reliable and self-starting youth?"

Nora was gathering materials from her desk, but her mood was still perky. "Always saw you that way," she said. "Always. Never faltered."

Mick started to put the flyer back on her desk, but Nora took it, folded it, and tucked it into his shirt pocket. "You should apply for this job," she said, close to him now and looking him in the eye. Her breath smelled minty. "Take my word for it, Maestro."

*   *   *

It was a cool, pale blue afternoon. Jemison was a village-turned-suburb of Syracuse, New York, and April was mud season. The air was warm sometimes, but you couldn't trust it. The ground was visible, finally, but you couldn't trust that, either. Mick had once done a report for his science class that tracked annual snowfall (nine and a half feet, on average) and rate of soil absorption. Today it looked like ten feet of snow had melted, eased its way in, and then frozen again.

Mick kept his hands jammed in the pockets of his jacket, a faded brown bomber he'd bought from a store called Plan B with most of the hundred silver dollars his father had given him for Christmas. He'd returned to Plan B four times, trying on the same coat each time, before he finally made the purchase. Now it was like his own little room, snug but portable.

For a while, Mick walked past rich people's houses—Georgian this, Revival that, long spreading yards behind fieldstone walls— yet even these looked slightly dazed to him, as though they, too, were standing in ice water. He was always happy to cross Chestnut into his own neighborhood, where the houses were tattered and closer together, but friendlier.

It had always been Mick's nature to come to ideas slowly, turning them in his mind this way and that before either accepting or rejecting them. Today as he made his way home, he began mulling the job deal. There were a bunch of pluses. He didn't mind working outdoors. It would be actual job experience. And it would be actual money. The only minus was that it meant he wouldn't spend the summer hanging out with Nora, which was what he'd pretty much done the past two summers, and which, to be truthful, he was looking forward to doing again.

But maybe Nora wasn't.

7

Maybe that was why she was trying to find him a job.

Maybe she was trying to get him out of her hair.

Mick began absentmindedly running the zipper of his inner jacket pocket open and closed, then abruptly turned up Morris Avenue, away from home and toward his father's shop. He turned west on Brook past O'Doul's and Twelve Brothers grocery (Nora had preferred to call it Dozen Brothers before finally shortening it to Duz-Bro), then cut through a vacant lot to Central and crossed the street to Shammas Auto Repair. He picked his way through a small parking lot packed with Volkswagens, Mercedes, and BMWs. The shop was owned by two brothers, Essa and Hana Shammas, who had both emigrated to Jemison from Lebanon and promptly set up shop fixing German cars. Their card said IF YOU'RE HERE AND YOUR CAR'S GERMAN, YOU'RE IN THE RIGHT PLACE! Today Essa and Hana were in the near repair bay sitting in a squatting position drinking thick black coffee from small cups, an afternoon ritual Mick had seen before. "Hello, Mister Mick," Essa called out. Essa was the outgoing one; his brother was handsome and shy. Both, according to Mick's father, were crackerjack mechanics. "You want good coffee?" Essa said.

"Maybe next time," said Mick, who'd tasted their coffee.

"Then please have soda. Plenty of sodas."

Mick said thanks and went to an old, grease-smudged refrigerator that was always stocked with just two varieties—Hires Root Beer and Mr. Pibb. Mick popped open a Mr. Pibb and wandered down to the far repair bay, where his father was working under the hood of an old Mercedes and whistling absentmindedly. *Zip-a-dee-doo-dah, zip-a-dee-ay*. When he glanced up and saw Mick, his face broke into a broad brimming smile. "Well, here comes the Mick."

8

Mick grinned and glanced into the dark and mysterious recesses of the Mercedes motor. "What're you doing?"

His father shrugged. "Just a tune-up, and I'm almost done."

Mick took a sip of soda. "Nora wants me to apply for a Saturday and summer job doing yardwork at some old folks' place."

His father was bent over the engine and didn't look up. "Yeah, she told me when we talked at lunch."

Mick had thought maybe she had. It was the reason he'd swung by the shop. "So why do you think she's all of a sudden so gung-ho on me finding a job?"

From under the hood his father's voice came out in muffled grunts. "You know . . . Nora . . . she's death . . . on idleness." With two more low grunts, he ratcheted something tight, straightened himself, and while wiping his hands on his shop rag shot Mick a grin. "Course with Nora you always got to take into account the possible ulterior motive."

Which might be getting me out of her hair, Mick thought. "Like what?" he asked his father, who just shrugged.

"Got me," he said. Then, "Want to start it up for me?"

Mick slid inside the car and carefully did all the things his father had taught him to do. Set the brake, depress the clutch, put the transmission in neutral, turn the ignition. After it started, he climbed out and stared again at the motor while his dad throttled up the rpm's. Over the din his father yelled, "How does it sound?"

Mick yelled back that it sounded pretty good.

His father nodded and cut the engine. "Yep. That's it exactly. Pretty good." He gave Mick a wink. "But not perfect." He pulled out a box wrench and went back to work.

Mick said, "See ya for dinner."

As he was walking away he heard his father beginning again

to whistle quietly the zip-a-dee-doo-dah song. His father had always been a quiet whistler, but there had been different phases. When Mick was little, his father had whistled happy songs like "Zip-A-Dee-Doo-Dah" and "We're Off to See the Wizard," but then when Mick's parents had all but stopped talking his father started whistling sad-seeming songs, and the songs got even sadder after his mother left to take a temporary job in San Francisco and a few months later divorce papers showed up in the mail. Then he'd met Nora and the songs turned sunny again. He'd mentioned this once to his father, how the songs had changed from one phase to another, and his father had shaken his head. "Had no idea," he said. Then he grinned at Mick. "Most of the time I don't even know I'm whistling."

When he got home, Mick checked the crockpot (pot roast, his personal fave), bolted down a twin pack of Twinkies, then grabbed a handful of popcorn from a big bag in the pantry. He carried the popcorn into the garage, where a lean, angular black dog leaped up from sleep and began bounding frantically around Mick in canine bliss. Mick began tossing kernels of popcorn, which the dog snapped frantically from the air. Mick laughed and said, "This is why we call you foolish, Foolish." Foolish was a black Irish setter who had followed Mick home from the park one day and never left. "You name him, Nora," Mick had said, and once she had, Mick knew his father would never turn the dog out.

Mick grabbed the leash and walked Foolish down the hill to Roosevelt Park, a vast swath of grass that completely lacked the one element that, in Mick's opinion, you needed in order to call a park a park: trees. Mick unleashed Foolish, then tossed the Frisbee in a long sweeping arc. Foolish tore after it and, catching

10

up, leaped high and snatched it out of the air. It was a beautiful thing to see. When he trotted back with the Frisbee in his mouth he seemed to be grinning.

Back home, Mick untied the English laurels that circled the foundation of the house. In October he and Nora had gathered up the loose-hanging laurel limbs and bound them into what she called sheaves in order to prevent breakage from winter snowload, but the snows were probably—hopefully—past. He checked, too, to see if the forsythias were budding. Nora always brought armloads in and waited while the house worked as an incubator and the buds popped into blossoms. Mick fingered some branches and found some swelling but no real buds yet. He went inside, practiced the piano, then decided to finish revising the second draft of his U.S. History paper (due tomorrow) so he could watch TV with Nora and his father later on.

The family computer was set up in a nook near the head of the stairs. Mick checked for e-mail, but got only a disappointing no-mail quack. Mick double-clicked first on his U.S. History file, and then on Dem Muckrakers, which is what he called the file containing drafts of his essay on the early-twentieth-century journalists who became famous for exposing corruption by corporations. But there was something wrong. His first draft was there, but not the second. It should've been the other way around. He'd meant to trash only the first. He looked everywhere for the second draft, but it was gone.

Mick tried to fend off his rising panic. He leaned back from the computer, gave Foolish a scratch, and said, "Okay, what're the possibilities here?"

He suddenly remembered that he'd e-mailed the second draft to his mother in San Francisco in hopes she would proofread it, but after five days she'd sent a two-sentence return message: *Well done! I'll bet no 14-year-old has ever made muck so interesting!* Mick had read it and said to the screen in a low voice, "In two months I'll be sixteen, Mom." Then, in a quick fit of spite, he'd deleted it.

He kept coming back to Nora. He'd taught his stepmother how to use the computer for e-mails and research, but she was, as she herself put it, technologically impaired. Mick wondered if maybe she'd somehow stashed his draft somewhere without really knowing it. He went through her files quickly—there was nothing resembling muckrakers—then pulled the cursor lower right to the trash icon, and double-clicked.

There were twenty-one items in the unemptied trash. Most of them were Nora's—letters, recipes, something called the Dead File—and a few were Mick's. One by one, he dragged his own out of the trash and opened them. Nothing but the discarded first draft. So, a little guiltily, he started on Nora's. The first was a boring letter to an aunt in Iowa, in which she described Mick and his father as "the lights of her life." The second was the address of a wool shop in Ithaca. The third file that he removed from the trash was the Dead File.

It was a series of e-mails.

The first one said, *Dear Miz Schoolmarm, let me tell you last night you taught me a thing or two I never even dreamed of knowing. —a.*

From Nora came this reply: *And vice versa. Ready for the next lesson? —Miz S*

Affirmative on that. When & where?

Nora: *Same time, same station. Park a ways off and make sure nobody sees you.*

Mick felt himself closing up. It was as if he'd been an open

12

hand and was now a tight fist. The nook felt closed in and hot. His heartbeat seemed to throb in his ears.

Round 4 of wild & woolly tomorrow same time same station? —Miz S

Yes mam, miss Schoolmarm. I could go there and do that depending if you promise to wear that certain something. Did I mention that you, Miss Marmschool, are strangely vivifying. —a.s.

Mick was both repulsed and transfixed. Why had she saved this stuff into a regular file, and why had she then thrown it away? Why would anyone do that?

He scrolled down.

A.S. you outdid even you. Those were the mustiest dustiest lustiest doings i ever done did. When's next?

And: *Hey A.S. i've got a hankerin to take you down from the naughty shelf. tomorrow same time same station?*

And: *Tomorrow i wear a dress with sixteen buttons all of which will need undoing. —Miz s.*

And: *Want to know something? 15 seconds after I saw you I knew my poor life wouldn't be complete till I'd been done and double-done by one alexander selkirk.*

Mick felt the first hint of sour bile surge into his throat. He closed the file and hurried down the hall to the bathroom, where he bent over the toilet and vomited up a combination of Hostess Twinkie, cafeteria nachos, and Mr. Pibb. His whole body felt wet with sweat. His hand, when he stared at it, was trembling. He took off his jacket, washed and dried his face, put his jacket back on. He stared in the mirror. The more he stared, the less he seemed to look like himself.

Who was Alexander Selkirk?

He walked back to the study. He didn't reopen the dead file, but he moved it to a green floppy disk, which he ejected. He didn't label it. He slid it into the interior pocket of his jacket, and zipped the pocket closed. Then he moved the cursor to the trash file, and emptied the trash properly, just as he had taught Nora to do.

Downstairs, the opening of the front door was followed by his father's muted whistling. Mick shut down the computer and tiptoed to his room. He could hear his father moving around downstairs and knew what he was doing: shuffling through the bills, checking the crockpot, and grabbing a Coors from the refrigerator before heading upstairs to shower.

"Mick?" His father, calling up from below.

"In my room," Mick yelled. He felt so different that he was surprised his voice sounded so much like his own.

He heard his father's heavy footsteps on the stairs. Mick pulled the covers up around him. The door eased open and his father peered in. Mick's room was dim, and the backlighting from the hall turned his father into a huge silhouette. "Jeez," he said. "What's the matter?"

"Nothing really," Mick said. "I think it's something I ate for lunch. I kind of threw it all up."

With a flip of the light switch the silhouette became his father. He looked worried. "Got a fever or anything?" He put down his unopened can of beer and lay his big hand across Mick's forehead. He smelled pleasantly of grease and gasoline. "You don't feel hot."

"I'm fine," Mick said. "I think I just need to rest a little. Go ahead and take your shower."

But his father stayed. "You don't want to take off your jacket?" he said.

14

"No."

"You want some bread and soup? I could bring up some bread and soup."

Mick closed his eyes. "I think I just need to lie here for a while." When he opened his eyes, his father had gone to stand by the window. He didn't look like a loser. He wasn't fat. His hair was still black and curly and kind of cool. For a middle-aged guy, he was pretty decent looking, like a friendly fireman in a kids' book. But maybe that's what got left out of kids' books—that the decent-looking friendly firemen had good-looking wandering wives.

For these few moments his father had been standing so still at the window that Mick was slightly surprised when he suddenly moved. "Okay," his father said, taking up his unopened can of beer. "I'm going to take my shower. Yell if you want something."

Every night after work his father took his cold Coors into a hot shower, drank the beer, then washed his hair. He'd told Mick it wasn't so much to get his hair clean as to get the grime from his fingernails. "Nora hates the greasy fingernails," he'd said, grinning, and Nora, throwing an arm around Mick's father, had said, "I'm a sucker for a just-scrubbed Mr. Goodwrench."

In the shower tonight, his father was whistling, but quietly, so Mick couldn't get the tune. A few minutes after the water stopped, his father was again looking in on Mick, who pretended to be asleep. His father eased shut the door and went downstairs. He was whistling again. It was a happy song, the zip-a-dee-doo-dah song.

Mick, after faking sleep, actually fell asleep and was awakened some time later by a faint tapping at the door. A soft voice said, "Mick?"

It was Nora.

15

Mick was lying on his side, turned toward the wall in the darkness. He didn't answer.

"Mick?"

He hardly breathed.

She waited a few more seconds then went away. He switched on the bedside lamp, checked the clock—6:30 P.M.—then lay on his back and stared at the ceiling, which was painted with a Union Jack. One day last summer Nora had discovered him up on a ladder sketching it with a pencil, and she'd suggested blocking the lines out with masking tape instead. Instead of asking why in God's name he wanted to paint a Union Jack on his ceiling, she'd helped him cover the furniture with sheets and mix up the paint. They worked on different sections and listened to oldies on the radio, and in three days they were done. He'd been sorry, in a way, to finish.

Another light knock on the door. "Mick?" Nora said softly. "It's me. I've brought some soup. May I come in?" She waited a few seconds. Then she said, "I see your light's on."

"I'm not hungry."

Nora waited a few seconds. "How about chamomile tea then? That always helps settle my stomach."

"No, thanks," Mick said. He didn't say it very loud. He didn't really care if she heard him or not.

She said, "What?"

This time Mick spoke up in a hard voice. "I said I don't want anything at all right now!"

Nora stood outside the door for a few seconds without speaking, then went away.

Nearly an hour passed before Mick heard the heavy ascending

footsteps of his father. When he got to Mick's room he simultaneously knocked and pushed open the door. "How's the Mick doing?"

"I've done better," Mick said.

His father laughed. "Yeah, I remember that cafeteria food."

Mick made a murmuring assent.

"You okay though?" his father said.

"I will be."

A silence followed, then his father said, "You made Nora feel a little bad there. Not letting her in."

Mick said, "I didn't not let her in. I just didn't want anything to eat."

His father waited a few seconds, seemed to want to say something, but didn't. Finally he said, "Is this something about your mom?"

Mick shook his head, though it did in some weird way seem connected to his mom, or at least to his mom's leaving them. He said, "I'll be okay. It's just something I ate, is all."

A second or two passed and his father said, "I got food poisoning once. At a Country Kitchen in Casper, Wyoming. I lay in bed for two days thinking I was going to croak." He laughed.

Mick let out a little laugh, too. "I'm not planning on doing any croaking."

Another silence. "We're all set to watch TV down there. Wanna come on down? You can have the whole sofa."

Mick shook his head. "I think I'll just lay low."

His father took a step back. "You don't want to take off your coat and put on pajamas or something?"

"I might do that, yeah," Mick said, but he didn't.

CHAPTER TWO

Three Selkirks, No Alexanders

When Mick awakened the next morning he was still wearing his Levi's and bomber jacket. He'd slept a deep dreamless sleep, and for a second or two he felt normal. Then he remembered and felt his insides closing into itself like a fist. He put his hand to the inside pocket of his jacket and felt the green floppy disk zipped inside. And then the name slammed through his nervous system: Alexander Selkirk.

Mick had more than once said he hated someone or something—a teacher, say, or TV show, and once he'd even told his mother he hated her—but that was just talk. The hatred he felt for Alexander Selkirk wasn't talk. It was the actual way he felt, and what he felt was not just intense dislike—it was combined with malicious ideas. Whoever Alexander Selkirk was, Mick wanted him to go away forever and for good. Dropped by a massive heart attack would work, for example. Or maybe dissolved by a terrible flesh-eating disease.

He didn't see Nora that morning—when she knocked, he said he was still feeling bad and thought he'd better stay home. If he felt better, he said, he'd go to school later on. After both Nora and his dad left the house, Mick showered, dressed, and walked to school. It was a grim day. He'd forgotten to study for a vocabulary quiz. About an hour after lunch, it began to rain, which made Lisa Doyle's field hockey iffy. Last period he had to tell Mr. Cruso that he'd lost the second draft of his muckraker paper and hadn't had time to finish the final draft. Mr. Cruso was nice about it, giving him a week to finish, but Mick was dreading going anywhere near it again. And though it would turn out field hockey practice wasn't canceled because of the rain, he assumed it was, so he didn't sight Lisa Doyle all day.

After school, he bypassed the art wing and took the bus home, sitting by himself in the back. There, as he had at private moments all through the day, he slid his hand inside his jacket and confirmed the presence of the green floppy disk. But this time, when he thought of Alexander Selkirk, he tried to use something he'd learned in journalism class. His teacher, Mr. Clucas, had said that to get to the bottom of any story you always start with The 5 W's and an H—Who, What, When, Where, Why, and How.

Okay, Mick thought. Who was Alexander Selkirk? What was he doing messing around with Nora? When and where was he messing around with Nora? Why was she letting him? And how had they kept it from his father?

Mick stared out the trickly bus window. So he had the questions, he thought. That and a buck would buy you a Whopper. What he needed were the answers.

At home, out of habit, Mick grabbed a Twinkie twin pack from the pantry, but as he broke the seal its smell made him faintly nauseated, and he threw it into the trash. There was a break in the rain, so he took Foolish to Roosevelt Park and tossed him Frisbees zombielike, without really watching. He threw and he threw and he threw. Finally Foolish trotted back, stopped well short of Mick, dropped the Frisbee, and lay down in the wet grass panting, something Mick had never before seen him do. "Sorry," he said. "I wasn't counting."

No one was home when he returned. He went upstairs, flipped on the computer, and checked for e-mails. Nothing. He snooped in the trash—nothing there either. But that was the real why question. Why did Nora *save* the e-mails to begin with? And then why did she dump them in the trash?

Mick pulled the phone book out of the drawer. There were three Selkirks, but no Alexanders. He dialed the first number and hung up when he got a machine. A woman answered at the second number. "Hi," Mick said. "I'm a student reporter from the *Jemison Tattler* and I'm trying to get hold of Alexander Selkirk."

"Who?"

Mick repeated the name.

"Well," the woman said, "this is the Selkirk residence, but I don't know any Alexander."

An older man answered the final number. He said, "There is no Alexander Selkirk at this number. But as an alumnus of Jemison High School, may I ask why the student newspaper is after him?"

Mick, flustered, said he wasn't at liberty to say and hung up.

When Mick's father opened the front door an hour later, he brought with him the smell of pizza. Mick was on the sofa, half watching a "Simpsons" rerun, a good one, the one where Bart's father eats a blowfish and thinks he has only twenty-four hours to live, but Mick's mind kept wandering. "Pizza man," his father announced and when Mick glanced up, his father said, "Vegetarian okay?"

A joke. His father knew Mick hated vegetarian.

Mick came over to the table, lifted the cardboard lid, and eyed the pizza—pepperoni and sausage. Mick said, "Guess they're adding new foods to the veggie column all the time."

His father grinned, pulled out his can of beer, and brought out the milk for Mick. "Dive in," he said.

Mick was still on his first piece when he said, "Where's Nora?"

Through a mouthful of pizza his father said, "Third Friday. Teachers' night out."

They ate for a while in silence. When Mick pushed aside his second slice of pizza only half eaten, his father said, "Still feeling not quite right, huh?"

Mick nodded. "Guess not."

His father stopped chewing for a second. "Might be flu."

The phone rang. It was evidently one of the Shammas brothers, because his father said sure, he could come in for a couple of hours in the morning, and then fell into listening.

While his father stood with the phone to his ear, Mick found himself looking at him in that strange way again, not as his father but as a man Nora had first chosen and then, for some reason, lost interest in. He was wearing a T-shirt and jeans and work boots. Mick calculated his age: forty-four. He looked sturdy. Mick's friends' fathers looked fleshier, weaker, somehow. But they also, Mick realized, looked like they had more money. The way they dressed was part of it, but it was also the way they walked and talked and, he didn't know, *carried* themselves. Tonight, when his

21

father hung up the phone and reseated himself at the table, a sentence formed in Mick's head. Have you heard of somebody named Alexander Selkirk? Mick even half opened his mouth.

"What?" his father said, evidently sensing Mick had been about to speak.

Mick blinked. "Oh," he said. "I was just wondering when Nora would be home."

"Late," his father said. He beamed Mick a big smile. "Which means we could go down to O'Doul's and play some foosball."

Nora telephoned while his father was upstairs.

"Dad's in the shower," Mick said.

"What?" Nora said. She was almost shouting. Even through the telephone Mick could hear the din behind her. It sounded like a restaurant or bar or something.

"Dad's in the shower!" Mick said louder.

"Wait a second," Nora shouted. "I'll call you right back."

Thirty seconds later she did. "That better?" she said.

"Yeah."

"I'm outside on somebody's cell phone."

"Whose cell phone?" He wondered if it was Alexander Selkirk's.

Nora laughed. "I'm not really sure. One of the teachers just handed it to me. So, where's Mr. Goodwrench?"

"In the shower," Mick said.

"And how are you feeling?"

"A little better, I guess, but about the same."

"You guys just going to stay home then?"

"I don't know. Dad said something about O'Doul's."

"Well, don't overdo it. You've got that job interview in the morning."

The job interview. Village Greens. Mick had forgotten all about it, and said so.

"So what do you think," Nora asked, "are you up for it?" When he didn't respond, she said, "Take my word, kiddo. This is something the boy Maestro should do."

"I might go if I feel okay," Mick said, and suddenly realized how much he hated the Maestro thing. It'd always been over the top, something he didn't deserve, but now it grated on him because it seemed connected to Nora's bigger bogusness.

"I already called their personnel office, so they're expecting you," Nora said. "I can drive you if you want."

"Sounds like you really want me out of the house this summer," Mick said, but this merely drew a chuckle from Nora. "Trust me on this one, Maestro. I'm looking after your interests here. So should I plan on driving you?"

"It's not that far," Mick said. "If I go, I'll just walk." Then, he couldn't help himself: "Do you think you could stop calling me Maestro?"

Nora seemed shocked. "Why would I do that?"

"Because it's not true. And I don't like it."

"Sure," she said.

There was a long silence.

His father came into the room wet-haired and smelling of soap. He silently mouthed, Who?

"Nora," Mick said, and handed over the phone.

"Hello, missus," his father said in a low pleasant voice. "You staying away from the sailors?"

Whatever Nora replied at the other end of the line made his father laugh. Then in his ever-cheery voice he said, "You'd better think that through, sister."

After his father had hung up, Mick said, "Think what through?"

His father laughed. "Guess the teachers are talking up sailing an outrigger to Polynesia." He winked at Mick. "I've met those teachers. Most of them couldn't sail their way to the deep end of a swimming pool."

He grabbed his grungy green raincoat and said, "I've got to quick re-cover the leak, and then we can go. Be right back." It was raining again—a hard, cold, wintry rain—and there was a leak in the garage roof. Until it could be fixed, his father had been covering it with heavy black plastic weighted with bricks. He left the extension ladder leaning against the roof for ready access.

"I can help," Mick said, more out of politeness than anything else, but his father waved him off. "Not when you're feeling lousy. Besides, it'll just take a second." He pulled up the hood of his raincoat before he stepped out the back door.

The coat was eight years old. Mick knew that because it was eight years ago, in the fall, that his mother had left Jemison to take the so-called temporary job in San Francisco. After the divorce papers came in the mail, Mick's father seemed to walk around in a daze, like this was a bolt from the blue, and then there was the custody hearing. One night Mick's father came into Mick's room and told him he might have to go in front of a judge and say whether he'd rather be with his mother or his father, but then his father's face had contorted like he was going to cry, something Mick had never seen his father do, and his father turned and left the room.

It had rained the day of the hearing. Before his father went into the courtroom he took off the green raincoat—new then—and had Mick hold it for him. Mick sat around outside the courtroom waiting to be called in, but he never was. After a while—

not very long really—his father and his father's attorney came out together. Mick was sitting in a chair with the raincoat laid over his lap, and they walked right past him and stopped with their backs to him maybe ten feet away. The attorney's voice swelled with triumph, but Mick could tell from his father's stillness and rounded shoulders that he was in a serious mood. "My God," the attorney said, "that was an effing piece of cake. She didn't even *show*. In this state, if you're going to win a custody case, you've got to effing show." That was when Mick's father had turned around, and his eyes met Mick's.

"Let's talk about this later," Mick's father said to the attorney, but the attorney said, "You know, given the money she's bringing in, we're gonna get some big-time child support out of her."

Mick's father was still staring at Mick when he said, "No, we're not. We don't need her money. Not one penny." They'd been quiet on the ride home, but after his father parked the car in the driveway, he'd said something. He didn't look at Mick. He'd stared straight ahead, and in a low voice he'd said, "We'll be all right, you and me. We'll be fine." On the console between them, there was a tube of butterscotch Life Savers, his mother's favorites. His father peeled back the wrapper and offered Mick one, but Mick had to look away from it to keep from crying. "No, thanks," he said, and they'd both sat in the car a long time before getting out.

Tonight, the back door opened and his father stepped inside, unzipping the old green raincoat, which was dripping wet. He grabbed his new red one from the hall tree and grinned at Mick. "O'Doul's then?" he said, and Mick said, "Sure, Dad," and followed him out to the car.

Mick had always figured his father's being surprised by his

mother's leaving was because his mother had been quiet about her changing feelings or maybe even sly about them, but now Mick wondered something else. He wondered if it wasn't because his father just hadn't been paying attention.

Usually at O'Doul's, Mick played foosball casually, letting his father win as many as he lost. But that was when things had been normal, and now they weren't. Tonight something funny had come over Mick. From the beginning, he played intensely and not only won every game, but won decisively. He was trying, he realized suddenly, to get his father's attention, to make him play harder, maybe even get a little mad, but his father never did. He smiled through every loss, and when they were done he said, "Well, I guess all it takes is a little food poisoning to turn you into a crackerjack foosball player."

CHAPTER THREE

Older Boys

When field hockey practice ended on Friday, Lisa Doyle and Janice Bledsoe headed for the bus loop to wait for Janice's mother, who was always late.

"I'm sick of field hockey already," Janice said, zipping her parka. "Why do we have to practice in the off-season?"

Lisa shrugged. She was tired, too. And cold. The clouds overhead were dark and rumpled, like the sky in a landscape painting. She rubbed her arms inside her sweatshirt and wished she'd changed out of her field hockey shorts. "So how'd you know to wear a coat?" Lisa asked. "It was sunny this morning."

"Weatherdude," Janice said. "Very watchable weatherdude on CBS."

A fat drop of rain spattered on the sidewalk, then another.

"Mother," Janice said impatiently, jiggling her legs. "Where art thou?"

From the gymnasium behind them came the dull clunk of a metal door. It was a compact, muscular guy wearing baggy pants, a tight, striped T-shirt, and no coat, in spite of the weather. "I think it's Popeye the Sailor Man," Janice said, but Lisa recognized the approaching face.

"It's the wrestling guy from three years ago," she said. "His picture's all over the trophy case."

Lisa looked away, but Janice didn't. She stared frankly, waited until he got within ten feet of them, and said, "Hey, are you the wrestling guy?"

He was handsome, Lisa had to admit. Buff and handsome. But older, maybe twenty or twenty-one. He stopped and, smiling, let his eyes settle first on Lisa, then Janice. He seemed to be chewing something. "I wrestled a little, yeah."

"I never wrestled," Janice said. She was using her zingy voice, the one Lisa knew she saved for serious flirting. "Is it fun?"

The wrestling guy kept his smile and made a slow blink. "Depends who you're wrestling with."

This was smoothly suggestive, and while Janice laughed some emotion quickened within Lisa, but it wasn't a pleasant one.

"What're those?" Janice said, staring down at the stack of yellow papers he held in his hand.

"Job flyers," he said, and peeled off two, one for each of them, and upon looking it over Janice let out a jingly laugh. "We already saw these. In fact, we'd already decided to apply. You going to be there?"

While replying to Janice he looked at Lisa. "Wouldn't miss it." From between his lips a small pink bubble appeared, expanded, and abruptly snapped back into his mouth. Then—it took him a while to free his eyes from Lisa—he said to Janice, "Maybe I'll see you Saturday, then."

The raindrops, which had been fat and scattered, now began to fall in real volume. The wrestling guy turned to walk away, had in fact taken a few steps when Janice said, "So what's your name?"

He stopped and smiled. "Maurice."

A strange nervous chuckle escaped from Janice. *"Maurice?"* she said.

Very calmly Maurice nodded. Rain streamed down his face. "That's right. Maurice."

Janice said, "Well, could we just call you Maury? Or maybe Mo?"

In slow succession Maurice winked, widened his smile, and said in a low, calm voice, "No."

He walked away.

They watched him go.

He got into a customized black Honda.

"Okay," Janice said when he'd closed the door, "that was definitely the closest I've ever come to a hands-off orgasm."

"Ja-nice! Eeee-yew." Lisa squinched her nose comically, but the truth was Janice's blunt talk bothered her. "Besides, that guy is a yikes. A complete reptile."

Janice turned to Lisa with what looked like genuine surprise. "Are you kidding, Leeze? Those eyes could melt butter." Then, looking over Lisa's shoulder toward the street, "Finally—here comes the mother ship."

Down the block, Mrs. Bledsoe's vast brown Electra was idling at the corner, waiting the light to change. Raindrops merged on the pavement and started reflecting the whites and reds of head- and taillights. The Electra began to move, and swung into the far end of the bus loop.

Mrs. Bledsoe's car smelled peculiar, as always, but it was blissfully warm. It was also a mess. To settle herself on the backseat, Lisa had to pick up a Mozart CD on which something pink had dribbled, an empty container of Frappuccino, a copy of *Ms.* magazine, a tape recorder, a pair of sling-back pumps, and a dry-cleaning bag.

"Excuse the detritus," Mrs. Bledsoe said, flashing her familiar gap-toothed smile over her shoulder at Lisa and then flipping on the windshield wipers. She turned out of the bus loop and up Indian Hill Drive, where, a few blocks farther on, she pulled up at a signal alongside a low-slung black Honda. "Popeye," Janice said over her shoulder to Lisa, and nodded toward the car.

Lisa glanced over—the rear and side windows were all tinted—and said, "Mr. Lizardo."

"Who're we discussing here?" Mrs. Bledsoe said.

"Guy in the Honda," Janice said. "He used to be a wrestling jock at Jemison."

Mrs. Bledsoe leaned forward and gave the car a quick study. "And now he expresses his vanity vehicularly."

Lisa laughed, but Janice didn't. She said, "And, let's see, in the world according to Mom, that's some kind of crime?"

The light changed. "Only if he's capable of something more than window tinting." As she pulled ahead of the Honda, Mrs. Bledsoe gave it a last glance. "Okay, I'm going on record here," she said amiably. "Mr. Honda is a bad bet."

"Says the mom who really knew how to choose," Janice said.

Mrs. Bledsoe, who had twice been married and divorced, nodded good-naturedly. "Point to daughter," she said.

No one said anything for a few moments, and through the back window Lisa watched the Honda slowly splash through a right turn onto a side street. What was weird was how slowly Maurice drove.

Up front, Mrs. Bledsoe said, "I have to exchange a bathrobe at the mall. You girls mind riding along?" The mall was in Syracuse, twenty minutes from Jemison. "When we get there, we'll probably have to check in at Starbucks for hot chocolate."

"Yum," Lisa said.

"Hot chocolate," Janice said matter-of-factly. "Very Mormon. Makes Lisa feel at home. Very obliging of the mother ship."

Mrs. Bledsoe grinned and said, "The mother ship will herself partake generously of caffeine."

"Could we look at shorts afterward?" Janice asked.

"Nyet," her mother said. "But we could look at job apps. Dog on a Stick is hiring, I heard."

"Have you even *seen* the uniforms they wear?" Janice asked, and gave Lisa a grin over her shoulder. "We'd look like a couple of doggy dipsticks! Besides, Lisa and I are on to serious job possibilities at Village Greens."

Lisa leaned forward over the backseat to get nearer the heat vents and, trying to dispel the bad feeling about Maurice, said, "Healthy outdoor labor. We're going to be yard girls."

Mrs. Bledsoe studied a chipped red fingernail as they waited for a red light. "Yard girls, huh?" Her tone was definitely dubious.

Janice began to sing, "Greeeen acres is the place to be, Faaaarm livin' is the life for me," and Lisa jumped in with, "Land spreadin' out so far and wide . . ."

Mrs. Bledsoe interrupted. "You two are going to mow lawns at Village Greens? Have either of you so much as touched a lawn mower before?"

"No," Janice said. "But the boys can do that. We'll clip and prune. Rake and sweep. Wave at the old gentlemen."

"What boys?" Mrs. Bledsoe said.

"The yard boys," Janice said. "Tanned, buff yard boys." Then, mock serious, "Hardworking, college-bound boys who would never ever window tint. Which is why we need new shorts."

"What part of nyet don't you understand, sweetness?" Mrs.

Bledsoe said, and even though her tone was friendly, Lisa could tell that she meant it, and Janice seemed to understand it, too, because she let the matter drop. Probably the issue was money—with Janice and her mom, it usually was.

The windshield wipers went *ka-tick ka-tick ka-tick*. For no reason she understood, Lisa found herself thinking of a boy she'd been watching lately during sacrament meeting, only he wasn't really a boy, he was a missionary, which meant he was at least 19, or maybe 20. His name tag said only Elder Keesler—she had no idea what his first name was. Still, once or twice in the past week she'd found herself writing his last name over and over in the same place until KEESLER was impressed in the paper.

Lisa felt the heat on her face and looked out the window at downtown Syracuse. Smith Restaurant Supply. Red turrets like in a gothic movie. Gold brick, gray stone, spires here and there, old concrete, bare trees, wet streets. Elder Keesler was too old for her, Lisa knew, and he was technically off limits while he was an elder, but who else was she supposed to think about? There were no Mormon boys that she liked in Jemison, or even in Syracuse. "Just wait until you get to BYU," her mother said, but what kind of lame idea was that? Wait until *college* for your first boyfriend?

"Penny loafer for your thoughts," Janice said.

"Oh, I was just thinking about something," Lisa said.

"Something or some*one?*"

"Someone," Lisa admitted.

"Gender, please."

Lisa didn't really want to talk about it, but Janice was insistent. "Gender, please," she repeated.

"You could almost say neither," Lisa said. "He's a Mormon missionary."

Janice pounced on this. *"Neither?* So the Mormonoids *neuter* their poor missionaries?"

Lisa laughed, but uncomfortably, and in a mild, mock-warning voice Mrs. Bledsoe said, "Play nice, Janice." Then she said, "I was just reading that Mormons on average live eight to eleven years longer than your comparable standard-issue American. Why do you think that is, Lisa?"

Lisa gave what she supposed was the right answer: no smoking, no drinking, no caffeine.

"Yeah," Mrs. Bledsoe said, "researchers chalk some of the actuarial difference up to that, and also to the interconnectedness of their lives, but some of it they can't explain."

Mrs. Bledsoe's voice trailed off, and it was clear she was lost in her own thoughts.

Lisa stared again out the wet window. No smoking, she thought. No drinking, no caffeine. No boyfriends. No fun.

CHAPTER FOUR

Jeeps

The Village Greens, according to an expensive-looking sign out front, was A RESIDENTIAL COMMUNITY FOR DISCERNING ADULTS 55 OR BETTER. The entrance was marked by elaborate rock columns and ornate black auto gates that were divided by a small, natural-seeming waterfall. Behind the waterfall was a little house right out of *Snow White*, but the person who stepped out of it as Mick Nichols approached on foot was no dwarf. He was a burly older man in a blue security uniform. "Howdy-ho," he said.

Mick said, "Hi," and hoped howdy-ho was not some kind of password.

"You here to apply for one of the maintenance positions?"

Mick said he was, and after giving his name, address, and telephone number, the man asked for some form of ID. Mick showed him his Jemison student card.

"Alrighty then," the man said. "I'll call ahead and let 'em know you're coming." He pointed off. "Proceed to Narragansett, turn left, and head for the maintenance shed. It's got a green roof. You can't miss it."

Mick could miss it, of course, and did. Village Greens was enormous, with pleasant bungalows nestled among oak trees along streets that curved and meandered in all directions. Occasionally the trees and houses gave way to the wide expansive fairways of a golf course. The day had broken sunny and there were quite a few walkers on the streets, older women in jogging gear mostly, and a number of people—also old—moving quietly along in battery-powered carts. Then Mick came to a large, brown-shingled building with a green metal roof. He tried three different locked doors before the fourth door opened onto a good-sized room with maybe a dozen kids scattered out among folding chairs. A man stood up in front of the blackboard talking, but fell abruptly quiet when Mick came in and slid into the back row. The man picked up his clipboard and ran a pencil down the page. "You must be Mick Nichols," the man said, and when he looked back at Mick all the kids turned in their seats to look, too.

One of them had coppery red hair.

One of them was Lisa Doyle.

The rest of the morning passed in a rush. Mick completed an application form, went through a two-minute interview, and was pronounced qualified. Then, along with the others, he was given the Village Greens Younger Employees' Handbook, the Village Greens Injury Prevention Program, and a demonstration on the safe use of such small equipment as blowers, Weed Eaters, and mowers. The man, a Mr. Blodgett, said, "It's all common sense, but Uncle Sam's never happy unless he's whipped up a batch of paperwork," and here he passed out Safety Training Acknowledgment Forms for everyone to sign.

When Lisa Doyle signed hers, she leaned close to Janice Bledsoe and whispered something that made Janice laugh. Except for their own brief interviews, they'd been sitting together all morning.

"Okay," Mr. Blodgett said, "we're ready to break into teams.

The building you're in sits roughly at the center of the community, which, for maintenance purposes, we break into four quadrants"—here he pointed as he talked—"northwest, southwest, southeast, and northeast. Take a look at your Employees' Handbook. In the upper right of the back cover you'll see your designation."

There was a shuffle in the room as everyone found their hand-books and flipped them over. Mick's said NE. Northeast.

A boy in the front said, "Mine says ess double-ewe—what does that mean?" and everyone laughed.

Mr. Blodgett said, "That would stand for southwest. You'll be working in the southwest quadrant." He pointed to four older boys standing against the wall. "I'm going to introduce you now to your crew chiefs. They've all worked here for at least three years and have proven themselves able workers and supervisors. Okay, beginning with the northwest team—"

Mick stared at the four. They all wore work boots and khaki shorts. Their T-shirts and caps were embroidered with the Village Greens logo. They all smiled and looked more or less ruggedly handsome.

This time it was Janice Bledsoe who, red-faced and excited looking, leaned over to Lisa Doyle and whispered something that made her laugh.

"And the leader of the northeast team," Mr. Blodgett was saying, "is Maurice Gritz." Maurice took a half step forward, nodded, and very slightly widened his smile.

Mick thought, He looks okay, I guess.

Mr. Blodgett said, "Alrighty then, the team leaders will go to separate corners, and each of you will join his or her team leader for further orientation."

Alrighty then, Mick thought.

Everyone stood, and most of the kids started moving toward one corner or another, but Mick noticed Janice Bledsoe and Lisa Doyle standing uncertainly, then going over to Mr. Blodgett. They were asking for some kind of favor, Mick could tell by their body language, but Mr. Blodgett just smiled and shook his head no. Then he turned to the room in general and said, "I'm sorry, people, but assignments can't be changed or traded. You must report to the crew leader you've been assigned to."

This seemed to affect Janice more than Lisa. Janice's shoulders drooped. She gave Lisa one last look and headed off to the southwest team. Lisa turned and walked toward the group gathering around Maurice Gritz.

The northeast team.

Mick's team.

Maurice Gritz blew pink gum bubbles while he waited for his new recruits to assemble. When they had, he expertly deflated the bubble, sucked it into his mouth, and led the group outside, where it was quieter. "Okay," he said. "Bad news, good news. The bad is that we've got another hour or so of orientation. The good is that you're now on company time and will be paid for it."

This was met with a general murmur of assent. Mick was at the back of the half circle of kids that curved around Maurice. Lisa Doyle was in front of him, so close that, if he leaned forward, he might smell her shampoo. If she leaned to the side and let the sun through, it gave her hair a coppery aura. Otherwise, he knew no one in his group, although there was a pretty Hispanic girl he thought he'd seen around school.

"Question," Maurice said, and scanned his group. "Who knows what Lilliput is?"

After a second or two, Lisa Doyle said, "Where the Lilliputians live."

Maurice smiled. "And what are Lilliputians?"

Lisa said, "Little people."

Maurice's gaze was now fixed solely on Lisa Doyle. "And where exactly is Lilliput?"

Lisa shrugged. "Someplace in England?"

Maurice slowly separated his gaze from Lisa. "I suggest you all look around, because you're standing in it," he said. "This *is* Lilliput. The old coots you see around here look normal sized, but they're not. They're Lilliputians, and they want their little village to look a certain little way."

Mick had the feeling none of this was coming from the company script. There was a strange suppressed vehemence to Maurice's words.

Maurice gazed beyond the crew for a second, then was looking at them again. "Making Lilliput look a certain little way is what you and I are paid to do, and we're going to do it efficiently and we're going to do it right. Are you with me on this?"

Everyone nodded.

"Okay," Maurice said, "for your first six Saturdays, you guys will be officially known as jeeps, which is hand-me-down service slang for new guys. After that you're normals—those of you who make the grade—and if you're good enough, you'll work full-time during summer. While you're jeeps, you get minimum wage. When you're a normal, you get minimum plus a buck." He grinned. "Which ain't bad, considering."

He went through his roll sheet, using only last names. Doyle, Furman, Gallagher, Nichols, Traylor, and then he stopped. "Uh-oh," he said. He looked at the last new recruit, the pretty

Hispanic girl. "Are you Lizette Uribe?" He pronounced it in sluggish separate syllables: *you-rib-bee*.

She nodded. "Except it's *oo-ree-bay*."

"That's the problem right there," Maurice said. "It's too hard to pronounce. I'm what you might call monolingual, and I don't want to offend you by mangling your name. So how about we go to something easier? Something I can pronounce?" He grinned at Lizette Uribe. "How about if we just call you Gomez?"

One of the boys laughed. Traylor.

Lizette Uribe just stared, as if confused.

Mick thought he ought to say something, but didn't know what.

"Okay, then," Maurice said. "It's Gomez then. I'll just make a note of it."

Lisa Doyle blurted, "Couldn't you just call her Lizette? That's easy to pronounce."

Maurice turned sharply, snapped a quick bubble, and stared at Lisa for a long still moment. "Problem is, Lizette is too close to Lisa. That could lead to confusion, and confusion can lead to safety problems." A sudden grin split his handsome face. "But high marks, Doyle, for looking for solutions." He kept his eyes directly on her. "There's nothing I like better than a good little problem solver."

The hour went quickly. Maurice showed them the men's and women's locker rooms, the time clock, and the sheds where tools were kept and trucks stored. They all climbed into a Village Greens minivan and he drove them around "their territory," the common areas of the northeast quadrant. Mick had taken the seat right behind Lisa Doyle, but by the time the tour was over he hadn't thought of a thing to say to her.

Back at the maintenance shed, Maurice brought out two big boxes of Village Greens hats and T-shirts. "Here's the deal," he said. "You show up every day on time wearing your official three-color Village Greens shirt and hat in good condition during any pay period, and you work all day without leaving early in that pay period, then you get a fifty-cent bonus for every hour in that pay period. So wash 'em, iron 'em, and wear 'em with pride. The half bucks add up." He scanned his grin around the group and let it land on Lisa Doyle. "Okay, the hats are like me. One size fits all."

Everyone laughed because they knew they were meant to laugh.

"The shirts come in five sizes," Maurice went on. "Small, medium, large, extra large, and V.O." He waited a beat. "V.O. is for very obese."

Another weak laugh from the jeeps.

Maurice said, "I wouldn't have said that if anyone here were actually in that category." Another beat. "Wouldn't want to be accused of sizeism."

This time Traylor was the only one to laugh, but that didn't seem to bother Maurice. "Okay, I'm pretty good at estimating sizes, so if you'll allow me."

He gave Mick, who wasn't large, a large. When Lisa Doyle checked her label, she said, "I think small's going to be too . . . small."

Maurice grinned. "Boys wear 'em loose, girls wear 'em small. That's informal policy on Maurice's crew." He was closing up the boxes, putting them away. Mick couldn't help but notice that Maurice was the exception to his own rule. His own T-shirt wasn't tight exactly, but it was close fitting, so you couldn't miss the definition of his pecs.

*　　　　　*　　　　　*

40

The recruits dispersed without talking. The two older boys headed off to their cars. Lisa Doyle headed off to the maintenance shed, probably to find Janice Bledsoe. Mick followed a distance behind, and when she glanced back he swerved toward the driving range, where a row of older men and women were whacking balls here and there. When Mick again looked back, Lisa Doyle was nowhere to be seen.

He started walking out. Lizette Uribe was in front of him, moving so slowly he couldn't avoid catching up. When he did, he said, "Hi."

She glanced at him, but didn't speak.

"Maurice is kind of a donkey, isn't he?"

Silence. This time she didn't even glance at him.

"Okay, I'll see you next Saturday," Mick said, and picked up his pace. But he honestly wondered who would be back next Saturday.

CHAPTER FIVE

Plebes Like Us

Mick was relieved when he returned home Saturday afternoon and found no one there except Foolish. On the memo pad next to the telephone was a note from Nora:

Mick,

Your dad's working all day so I went out. Reece left message, which I saved.

Nora

P.S. I'm dying to know how job interview went!

Winston Reece and Mick Nichols had been friends since third grade when they both would sneak away from recess kickball games and go inside to investigate Mr. Reger's miniplanetarium. Now Mick went to the answering machine in the pantry, hit play, and heard Reece's voice. "Reece's log, Saturday, April 21, 11:30 A.M. I have awakened refreshed and finding no parental units present am now free to roam about the cabin." *Click*.

It was now nearly one o'clock. Mick made himself a sandwich, dialed Reece's number, and counted the rings. Reece never picked up before three rings. On the fourth ring a voice answered in a monotone. "By design or happy accident you have reached the telephonic nerve center of the empire's only Reeceman. At the tone, briefly state your business, please." The voice then made a short beeping sound.

"Hey," Mick said.

"Oh, it's you," Reece said.

Mick said, "So what besides confirming your own weirdness are you doing?" He said this flat voiced. It was one of his standard lines.

"Usual Saturday stuff. Sleeping, eating, and downloading."

"Who?"

"You've never heard of them."

"Yeah, I have."

Reece said, "You've heard of A Geek's Worst Dream?"

"Just did," Mick said, and laughed.

They went on like this for a few minutes more, and then Mick told him about the new job. Reece responded to each of its requirements—being there at 7:30 A.M.; wearing the official three-color Village Greens hat and T-shirt—with an incredulous, "You're going to do that?"

"For a while," Mick said, because that's what he'd decided. He'd stick with the job as long as Lisa Doyle did. In describing the job to Reece, he hadn't mentioned that Lisa Doyle was also among the new recruits, not that it would've mattered, because he'd never told Reece he was interested in Lisa Doyle. Reece was maybe his best friend, but he was a hanging-out kind of friend, not a talking-to kind of friend. The person he talked to was Nora, but that, he suddenly realized, was now a past-tense issue. He said, "I guess I'll take Foolish to the park in a while. Want me to call you when I go?"

Reece said, "That would mean putting on clothes, wouldn't it?"

"Your decision entirely," Mick said, and hung up.

He put his lunch dishes in the sink without washing them, something he knew Nora hated. In the living room, he sat down at the old Chickering upright and played a few chords of the piece his piano teacher, Mrs. Marquart, had given him last week. He knew he should do his finger exercises, then his lesson pieces, then try to finish off his muckraker paper, but he was too tired. He lay down on the sofa, remoted through the TV channels, and turned off the TV. The room was dim—all the lights were off— and he felt tired. He lay on his back and spread his leather jacket across his chest like a small blanket, then closed his eyes and imagined Lisa Doyle in her too-small T-shirt, which didn't help him fall asleep, so he thought of himself lying in a rowboat on a still lake on a sunny afternoon, which did.

He awakened to the tink of the front door latch followed by Nora's quick-clicking steps in the tiled entry. She hung a scarf on the hall tree and peered up the staircase. "Hello? Anybody home?"

Mick said nothing. He expected the sheer force of his gaze to cause her to turn his way, but it didn't. She flipped on the entry light and leaned close to the hall tree mirror. She adjusted the collar of her dress. She stretched her mouth and with the nail of her little finger scraped something from her upper lip. Then she did something odd. She leaned back and smiled at herself in the mirror. Mick thought he knew what she was doing because he'd done it himself. She was trying to see what she'd looked like through someone else's eyes. Even from here, Mick could tell her face had a flushed look.

"You're back," he said.

Nora started and wheeled around. The pink in her face suddenly deepened. "Hi, Maestro," she said, but her voice didn't sound quite like her voice. "Mick," she said, correcting herself.

"You look kind of hot," Mick said.

Nora tried to laugh. "That's your father's line," she said.

Mick just stared. "No, I meant your face looks kind of red."

"Oh." Nora tried to laugh again, but it came out more of a gurgle. "It's the weather. I went to the mall, but I overdressed. It turned so warm out. You live in Jemison long enough and you don't know how to act when the sun comes out."

There was a short silence that Mick broke by saying, "Was it crowded at the mall?"

Nora's eyes slipped away from his. "Not very," she said.

Mick studied her. "What did you buy?"

"What?"

"I just said, 'What did you buy?' "

"Oh. Nothing! It was some kind of personal best! I tried on a zillion things and bought nothing. I'm thinking this'll please your father big time." She made another odd gurgling laugh.

Mick said nothing. A question formed in his mind, but he couldn't bring himself to ask it. The question was, "How was Alexander Selkirk today?"

Nora said, "How come you didn't answer when I said, 'Anybody home?' "

Mick made a slow blink. It was strange how little he cared now what Nora thought. He said, "I guess I was asleep and thought I was dreaming."

This time it was Nora studying him. She gave him a slow, dubious nod. She broke the silence that followed by saying, "I'm going to change my clothes and make dinner. I thawed pork chops."

His father's favorite, they both knew that.

She was three steps up the stairs before she suddenly stopped

45

and turned back around. "Oh, my God, I forgot! How'd the job interview go?"

"Fine."

"You got the job, then?"

Mick nodded.

Nora was grinning her old grin now, the infectious mischievous grin. "Anybody else of interest apply?"

"Not really."

"No redheaded girls?"

"If you mean Lisa Doyle, yeah, she was there."

Nora laughed. "Yep, that's what a little bird told me."

"A little bird," Mick said in his flat voice.

Nora grinned and nodded. "A little bird named Melissa Daley." Mrs. Daley, a math teacher at Jemison High and a friend of Nora's.

Mick said in a sullen voice, "So why didn't you just tell me Lisa Doyle would be there?"

The cheeriness drained from Nora's expression. "You don't seem exactly grateful about this."

Mick just stared.

Nora said, "I didn't tell you because Mrs. Daley posted the flyers, and she heard Lisa say she *might* apply. I didn't want to mislead you." She paused. "I was also worried that your knowing she was applying might scare you off."

"You didn't think I could handle the truth."

Nora said in a soft voice, "That's not what I thought at all."

"I thought the deal was you tell the truth to people you care about."

"C'mon, Mick! I *was* telling you the truth. I told you you ought to apply for this job, and that was the truth. You should've, and you did."

Mick didn't speak. He knew his expression was sullen, but he didn't care.

Nora took a breath and said, "Mick, look. The truth isn't of exact dimensions. It isn't rigid. It can be shaped, made a little bigger here, a little smaller there. But it's still the truth."

Mick blurted, "No! That's not right! The truth is the truth."

His sudden vehemence surprised him and seemed to surprise Nora, too. She looked at her hands for a few seconds, then looked up at Mick. Softly she said, "Is there something wrong, Mick?"

He let a few seconds pass, until he was sure he had his flat voice back. "Not that I know of," he said. "Why? Am I missing something?" He kept his eyes sullen.

Nora remained on the third step. She stood perfectly still for perhaps ten seconds, staring evenly at Mick, then without a word she turned and went up the stairs. Mick listened as she went first to her room, then to the bathroom. The water pipes made a shuddering sound when she turned on the shower.

Ten minutes later she came back downstairs. She was barefoot, her hair was wet, and she was wearing beige denims and a loose blue top. She went into the kitchen without saying a word to Mick.

Mick wasn't sure why he did what he did next. It was just something he couldn't keep himself from doing. He went upstairs to the bathroom and quietly closed the door after him. It was an old door, and locked with an old-fashioned long-stemmed key. Mick locked it. Then he opened the wicker hamper where dirty clothes were tossed. Nora's underwear was on top.

Over the years and without really meaning to, Mick had learned the basic patterns of Nora's underwear use. Normally she wore white cotton briefs and plain back-closure bras, but she had a few sets of fancier underwear she seemed to save for special occasions. What she'd worn today was some of the special-occasion underwear, a black bra with matching brief. Each had fancy lacy scallops at the edges, and when Mick held the bra in his hand he could see right through it.

He stared at the underwear a long time before dropping it back on top and closing the hamper. Then he made appropriate sound effects—flushing the toilet, running water at the washbasin—before coming downstairs. He phoned Reece from the kitchen, where Nora was slicing carrots to go with the pork chops. "I'm taking Foolish to the park now," he told Reece.

"Which park?" Reece said.

"Thornden," Mick said.

He grabbed his jacket from the sofa and headed for the backyard to leash Foolish.

"Dinner's at six," Nora called after him.

Mick pretended not to hear.

Mick had been tossing Frisbees to Foolish for about ten minutes before Reece ambled up. He was a big kid who gave a general impression of looseness. His Nikes were untied, his flannel shirt was untucked, and he'd made slow walking part of his personal code of conduct. "You walk fast, and citizens might erroneously believe you've bought into the system," he once told Mick.

Today he sat on a tabletop with his feet on the bench and said, "So our own Mick Nichols is gainfully employed."

Mick grinned and waited for Foolish to set the Frisbee at his feet.

Reece said, "You know what you are now? Part of the working class. One more lump folded into the buttery batter."

Mick gave a little laugh and tossed the Frisbee in a long slicing arc that ended with Foolish snatching it from the sky. It was hot in the sun. Mick shed his leather jacket and laid it on the table beside Reece.

A few tosses later, Reece said, "What's this?"

Mick turned. Reece was holding the green floppy disk, turning it over in his hand. Mick's first impulse was to say, "None of your business, put it back," but he knew that would only feed Reece's interest. He tried to sound matter-of-fact. "It's the second draft of my muckraker essay," he lied, "which I can't lose, because I already lost it once."

As Mick spoke, Reece studied him closely. "Then why didn't you label it?"

Mick gave the Frisbee a casual toss. "Because I know what it is." Then he turned to his friend. "Also where it is, so if you wouldn't mind zipping it back into the pocket . . ."

Reece was still regarding the disk when something beyond Mick caught his eye. Reece sat transfixed, staring. Finally he said in a low voice, "Okay. Incoming at three o'clock. Two females. Really, really excellent bazongas."

Mick gave the girls a quick glance—they carried heavy textbooks, wore long SU T-shirts over cutoff denim shorts, and were spreading out a blanket in the sun. Mick turned back around. "College girls," he said.

Reece was undeterred. He kept staring. A half minute passed, and then he said, "I urge you to take another look, Mickman."

Mick did. The girls had pulled off their shirts and were sitting now in denim cutoffs and bikini tops. They were putting on sunscreen. Reece said, "Throw the Frisbee over there."

Mick said, "That would be impressive."

Reece stared at the girls fixedly. "Okay. Let's go talk to them."

Mick had to laugh. "They're five years older than us, Reece. And this is not to mention the fact that you and I don't go up and talk to girls of that caliber, ever."

Reece gave it some thought and said, "I read in one of Mr. Reece's psychology books that lots of women secretly crave younger men." Mr. and Mrs. Reece were Reece's joke terms for his parents.

Mick laughed again. "You're not a man, kiddo. You're a Reececake."

Reece said nothing but kept staring. Finally he said, "Okay, I'll go alone."

"You, Winston Reece, are going to go over there and talk to them alone?"

"That's right," Reece said. "In fact, I'm already gone," and he was. He shambled directly toward the girls until he got within perhaps twenty yards of them and then veered abruptly toward the water fountain, where he took a quick drink before returning to the picnic table. Mick was grinning hugely. "How'd that go?" he said.

"You know who that is?" Reece said.

"Lorena Bobbitt?"

"That's rich," Reece said without smiling.

Mick, still grinning, said, "Okay. Who?"

"Myra Vidal and Pam Crozier."

This was news. Myra Vidal and Pam Crozier had graduated from Jemison High two years earlier and had gotten a lot of publicity as "the brainy beauty queens." The brainy part came from their 4.0s, but the beauty part got them the press. In her senior year Myra had won the Miss Jemison Beauty Contest, but wouldn't accept the position unless she could share it with Pam, who'd been runner-up. The contest people, sensing good publicity, acceded, and both Mick and Reece had watched mesmerized as Pam and Myra had stood in minimal swimsuits waving easily from the City of Commerce float in the Jemison Fourth of July parade.

Mick flung the Frisbee, its long hanging trail of doggy saliva reflected in the sunlight. He said, "So Pam and Myra's major-babe reputation was too much for the Reececake."

Reece smiled. "That's correct. Froze him solid. Popsicle City."

Mick watched Foolish trotting back with his Frisbee. Foolish's life was simple. He ate, he slept, he fetched Frisbees. He never read other people's e-mails. He never judged people on the basis of their secret sex lives. He never worried what people thought of him. Mick said, "What would it pay if I went over and talked to those girls?"

Reece gave him a look. "Depends. Zippo, if you're just going to go over there and ask what time it is." Mick had done that once before to collect this kind of bet.

"No. I mean, what would it pay if I go actually talk to them."

Reece narrowed his gaze. "We'd be talking a five-minute minimum."

"Yeah, okay."

Reece began to get interested. "And what's our A.O.? We've got to have an attainable objective."

Mick laughed. "Getting Myra Vidal and Pam Crozier to give plebes like us five minutes of their time is the objective."

But Reece was shaking his head. "Negative on that. Our A.O. is a phone number. You need to go over there and get one of their telephone numbers."

Mick chuckled. "Reece, dudester and good buddy, I hate to be the one to tell you, but this is a reality-based show."

Reece was unfazed. He said, "Here's the deal. Five bucks for a minimum five-minute conversation. Twenty for a phone number." He grinned at Mick. "Okay?"

Mick knew the one thing he shouldn't do was think about this too much. "Okay," he said.

"But you pay me five for a failure-to-approach. Okay?"

"Yeah," he said, eyeing the girls at the far side of the field, "okay. Five bucks for an F.T.A."

He swung his jacket over his shoulder and headed over in the direction of Pam Crozier and Myra Vidal, with Foolish and Reece close behind. "What're you going to say?" Reece said.

Mick didn't answer. He had no idea what he was going to say.

From behind, Reece said, "I mean, aren't you supposed to have . . . you know . . . like an opening line?"

The who-cares-anyway attitude that Mick had set out with was quickly slipping away from him. He began to feel more like himself, and the one thing he knew he wasn't was the kind of person who strolls up to beautiful girls to strike up casual conversations.

His heart began to pound wildly.

Mick's father had a saying for putting problems into perspective. "It ain't my wife and it ain't my life."

It's not Lisa Doyle, Mick thought. It's not Lisa Doyle.

This helped only a little.

He was closer now, within thirty feet, entering the no-turn-around zone. At any moment Pam Crozier and Myra Vidal would sense his presence and look up.

It's not Lisa Doyle, it's not Lisa Doyle.

They looked up.

Mick tried to smile. Sweat seemed all at once to pop from every pore of his body. He opened his mouth and tried to say, "Hi," but his throat had tightened and it came out more like a croak.

Myra Vidal and Pam Crozier stared at the croaking boy. They didn't speak or smile.

Mick was having a hard time breathing. He turned to the one with dark hair and olive skin and said, "You're Myra Vidal, right?"

She nodded. She waited. So did everybody else. Mick could feel it. Suddenly he said, "Do you know Alexander Selkirk?"

Myra Vidal cocked her head quizzically. "Who?"

"Alexander Selkirk."

"Alexander Selkirk," Myra said. She said it slowly, as if searching it for a taste.

Mick said, "The reason I ask is he says he knows you."

Myra said, "Who's Alexander Selkirk?"

"This older guy who says he knows you."

"How much older?"

Mick took a deep breath. It felt good to take a deep breath. It was as if for the past minute or two he hadn't been breathing at all. He said, "Well, he's about my stepmother's age and she's thirty-one."

"And he says he knows me?"

Suddenly, in spite of—maybe even because of—Myra's confusion, Mick began to feel better, almost calm, in fact. "That's right. Alexander Selkirk said he knows you intimately."

Myra stared in disbelief, but Pam Crozier broke into a laugh. "Sister woman! You've been holding out on me! Have you got a cute little old-timer tucked away in a cupboard?"

Mick could see Myra's face moving from disbelief to anger. He himself felt weirdly composed. In a matter-of-fact voice he said, "The reason I came over to talk to you is because when I heard Alexander Selkirk say that he knew you intimately, I had a feeling he was lying. I remembered how nice you seemed and he's kind of a donkey."

Myra's face relaxed. It was a dazzlingly pretty face. "You were right," she said. "He was lying."

Pam Crozier said, "But Myra's not as nice as she seems."

Demurely Myra said, "As a matter of fact, I am. Possibly nicer."

Mick wasn't sure what he was going to say next, but Myra saved him. She said, "Can I throw the Frisbee for your dog?"

Pam evidently didn't like this idea. "My-ra," she said in a low mock whine. "What are you doing?"

"Throwing a dog a Frisbee is what. Making some doggy happiness."

When Myra reached for the Frisbee, Mick glimpsed between her breasts all the way to her flat stomach. "Frisbee's kind of mungy," he said.

"I don't mind mung," Myra said.

She threw the Frisbee in a long graceful arc that Foolish caught up with at the shady end of the field. "Wow," Myra said quietly.

While Myra kept throwing Frisbees, Pam lay on the blanket reading from her textbook—*The Economics of Child Labor in the Industrial Age*—and Mick and Reece stood there not knowing what to do with themselves. Reece kept sneaking glances at one or another set of breasts. Mick tried to focus his attention on Foolish. Finally Pam said, "I guess you guys can sit down if you want."

Mick and Reece both nodded and sat. Myra threw another Frisbee, and Pam turned toward Mick and Reece. She'd shifted onto her side, which had a plumpening effect on her breasts. "So do you guys live around here, or what?"

They both nodded. Mick kept his eyes fixed on hers, but he sensed Reece's eyes were wandering.

"You go to Melville or Jemison?" she said.

"Sophomores at Jemison," Mick said, but he was thinking, Melville? We look like middle schoolers?

Myra sat back down, and Foolish lay down nearby, panting. To Pam she said, "So, what'd you find out about these individuals?"

Pam shrugged. "Sophomores. Carless and clueless."

Myra said, "Oh, I don't know. I adored sophomore year. And eighth grade was even better."

Pam flicked a glance at Mick. "For Myra, eighth grade was a twofer. She had a hot boyfriend and developed mammillation."

Mick made a mental note to look up mammillation.

"We walked everywhere," Myra said. "When you walk, you talk. It was kind of nice." She scanned her smile from Mick to Reece. "So what're your names?"

"Mick Nichols."

Reece pried his eyes from Pam Crozier, who'd resumed reading. "Reece," he said. "Winston Reece."

"Winston?" Myra said.

"After that Churchill guy. My mother thinks Churchill was a big deal."

Pam looked up from her book and said, "Yeah, well, she's right. When the BBC, the *London Times,* and Neville Chamberlain all said, 'Appease Mr. Hitler,' Churchill said, 'Resist.'" She suddenly fixed her eyes on Reece. "You were named after the possibly greatest man of the twentieth century," she said, "but that still doesn't give you the right to keep staring at my mammary glands."

55

A laugh burst from Myra, then from Mick and finally Reece. "Sorry," he said. "It's just that—"

"You're just a hungry boy at the smorgasbord?" Pam said quickly, which drew more laughs at Reece's expense. As the laughter dimmed, a faint partial melody sounded.

Reece's cell phone was ringing, but it wasn't a ring. It was the first few bars of "Strangers in the Night," which, when he'd selected it, had seemed hilarious. Now it didn't so much, and Reece was trying to pretend it didn't exist. From one of his baggy front pant pockets the muted *dooby-dooby-do* notes kept sounding, again and again. Finally Pam said, "Is that your cell phone, or do you have a tiny orchestra where your penis should be?"

Mick couldn't help laughing. Reece's cheeks flamed red for a moment, but then he was laughing, too, and reaching for the phone.

"Yeah," he answered, and when he turned away from the group, Mick knew it was his mother checking up on him. "The park," he said. "With Mick." Long silences followed with Reece now and then murmuring, "Okay." Just before hanging up, he said, "Oh-kay, I'll tell him."

"Tell who what?" Pam said, grinning.

Reece looked sheepish. "Tell Mick he's invited to dinner."

"A dinner invitation!" Pam said. She turned to Mick. "Winston wants to take you home to meet his mother! Do you accept?"

Mick played along. "Depends. What are they serving?"

Pam turned quickly to Reece. "What are they serving?"

"Polish sausage and other stuff."

To Mick, Pam said, "Polish sausage and other stuff."

"Sure," Mick said. "Why not?"

"Good! That's settled. Now, what about us? Are Myra and I invited?"

Reece gave her a brightening look of real surprise. "Sure. Do you want to come?"

Pam grinned. "No. But it was polite of you to ask."

They laughed and then there was a lull, but it didn't feel like an awkward lull. Clouds that had been massing to the east were now directly overhead, and when one of them passed in front of the sun, Mick shivered and wondered if he could put his jacket back on. Myra, evidently following his gaze, pointed to it. "So here's what I want to know. Whose jacket is that, where'd you get it, and what'd it cost?"

Mick said, "Mine, Plan B, and eighty bucks."

"Can I try it on?"

She slipped it on and left it unbuttoned. Mick and Reece sat imprinting the image in their memories. Pam said, "God, Myra, you look like this year's Harley calendar."

Myra smiled and began to take it off.

Mick said quietly, "If you want it, you can have it."

Myra looked at him. She didn't speak, but her look said, *You mean it?*

He nodded. He meant it. He said, "Looks a lot better on you than me." This was true, it did look pretty great on her, but it wasn't just that. If she took the coat, she'd take the green disk, too, and maybe he could just forget it ever existed.

But Myra was shrugging out of the coat. "Nope," she said, and for the first time gave him such a thorough look that Mick thought he could feel it going through him. Then she said, "It's incredibly sweet of you to offer, but nope."

Nobody said anything for a few seconds. Finally Mick said, "Well, it was nice of you guys to talk to us." They didn't say anything, so he said, "I guess we'd better go now."

He stood, and Foolish and Reece stood, too. They'd started to move away when Pam said, "You know, just so you could start getting in the habit of it, you should've asked us for our phone numbers."

They turned. Mick said, "Okay. Would you give us your phone numbers?"

"No," Pam said, "but it was definitely worth a try."

They all laughed and then there was a strangely pleasant stillness among them that ended when Myra said, "But you know what? You guys could give us your e-mails just in case we might want to check up on your progress."

"Really?" Mick said.

Myra found a ballpoint pen. "Here," she said, "write them down on my hand so I won't forget to log them when I get back to the dorm."

Mick knelt and held the back of her hand with his left hand while printing carefully with the other. Her hand was soft, and her body had the pleasant buttery smell of suntan lotion. After he was done, Reece wrote his e-mail address on Myra's hand. He seemed to take his time. When he finally leaned away, his face was flushed. Everybody grinned at parting.

"*Vaya con Dios*," Myra said.

Mick looked back. Myra was smiling. Pam was already putting her shirt back on.

Mick, Reece, and Foolish walked across the grass without speaking until they were safely out of earshot, then Reece spoke in a low, excited voice. "Okay," he said, "when you were writing your address did you see what I saw?"

"Dunno," Mick said. "What'd you see?"

"Nipple! Or the aureole part of it or whatever that's called. It was just barely peeking out of her top."

"Let's consider for a moment your vivid imagination," Mick said.

"I didn't imagine it. I saw. I saw plenty. I saw Myra Vidal's nippleodeon up close and personal."

Mick noticed that Reece was walking faster than normal. He said, "You seem pretty hyped-up about this."

Reece grinned. "Oh, heck, yes. I mean, I was beamed to Bazongaville." They walked a little farther, and he said, "You know what that was? I'm going to tell you what that was. That was the highlight of my sexual career up to now."

Mick said, "Reececake, unless you count certain onanistic practices, you've had no sexual career up to now."

"Yeah, but now I do," Reece said. "I was three inches from Myra Vidal's partially exposed nipple."

Mick laughed. "It's true, only a major stud could've peered into her bikini like you did."

Reece smiled serenely. "Rag all you want. I saw what I saw and I know what I know." He wagged his eyebrows. "The excitable member was in a state."

Mick said nothing more. The truth was, he was feeling pretty good himself. He'd talked to two college girls and found out that besides being really, really pretty they were funny and nice. In fact, he'd realized as they were talking that even though they didn't look at all alike, Myra reminded him of Lisa Doyle, except older and chestier and brown-haired instead of red. But she really did remind him of Lisa. It was something about how friendly her eyes seemed.

As Mick was clipping the leash on Foolish at the edge of the park, Reece said, "Okay, you definitely get the five bucks." He considered it. "But not the twenty. I mean, you came close, but you didn't get a phone number." They walked another block and he said, "I mean, giving them our e-mails isn't the same as them giving us their phone numbers." A half block farther he said, "Tell you what, I'll give you ten. Ten okay?"

"Ten's good," Mick said.

"But you'll have to wait till I have it."

They crossed to the shady side of the street, and when they got to Walnut and Sixth, where he would go left toward home or right toward Reece's, Mick went right. "Okay if Foolish comes?" he said.

"Sure," Reece said. "Mr. and Mrs. Reece have no issues with canines." They walked half a block, and Reece said, "If you want to call Nora and let her know, you can use my phone."

"It's okay," Mick said. "Nora's not there." This felt to Mick as much truth as lie. Nora was there, of course, but it wasn't the Nora he knew. It was somebody else, somebody who sneaked off with some other guy on a Saturday while his father was working and then came home and pretended she'd been at the mall shopping.

On Reece's street, while they were waiting for Foolish to pee in the bushes, Reece said, "So who's Alexander Selkirk anyway?"

The question buzzed through Mick's body like a faint electric shock. "What?"

"Who's Alexander Selkirk? The guy who said he knew Myra Vidal."

"Oh. Him. Nobody. I just made him up."

"You made him up?" Reece tipped his head away, nodding.

"He made him up." He kept nodding. "You are such a stud, Mickster. I mean it. You should have corporate sponsorship. You should have a shoe contract." He gave Mick a mock shoulder punch. "Okay. For making up Alexander Selkirk, I'm gonna go to twelve-fifty. Is that fair?"

"More than fair," Mick said. "Instead of waiting forever to not get ten dollars, I'll be waiting forever to not get twelve-fifty."

"Exactly."

When they turned up the walkway to Reece's house, he said, "Sure you don't want to call and leave Nora a message?"

"Yeah," Mick said. "I'm sure."

Automatically his hand felt inside his jacket. The pocket was zipped and within it he could feel the outlines of the green floppy disk.

CHAPTER SIX

The Wooden Lady's Walnut Tidbits

Late Saturday night Lisa Doyle was at Janice Bledsoe's apartment, sitting at the kitchen table eating Chef Boyardee pizza and talking about boys, or more particularly the boys on the Village Greens crew to which Janice had been assigned. All of them were sevens or eights, according to Janice, except the group leader, whose name was Ned. Ned was a nine. "He was checking me out," Janice said. "Nothing blatant, but there was some definite visual perusal."

Footsteps, and then Mrs. Bledsoe was at the kitchen door with a long folded fax in her hand. She was wearing her glasses low on her nose. She lay down the fax, broke off a piece of pizza, and said, "So who did you say was checking you out, sweetness?"

Janice turned to Lisa. "The momster's got the big ears."

"It's evolutionary," Mrs. Bledsoe said. "You'll develop them, too, when you have a teenage daughter." She smiled at Janice. "Now who was checking you out?"

"Ned," Janice said. "An impeccably moral, college-bound Ned who works at Village Greens."

Mrs. Bledsoe peered over her bifocals. "So the pastures really are greener at Village Greens."

"Not necessarily," Lisa said. She was thinking of Maurice Gritz leering at her and saying, "The hats are like me. One size fits all." Calling Lizette "Gomez." Giving the girls too-small T-shirts.

"We're on separate crews," Janice explained. "I got a bunch of cool guys, but Lisa thinks she got mostly creeps and dinks."

"Well," Mrs. Bledsoe said, turning her smile on Lisa, "creeps and dinks is what the male persuasion mostly is. You might as well get used to it." After the second divorce Genevieve Bledsoe had needlepointed a sampler that said NEVER AGAIN, BETSY. It hung over the fake fireplace of their third-floor apartment.

Now Mrs. Bledsoe ate her piece of pizza standing up and washed it down with mineral water before picking up her fax and scrolling through it. "Okay, gals, tell me what you think of this. 'Coronary care patients who receive prayers without their knowledge' "—here she peered up meaningfully —" 'fare better than those not receiving prayers.' " She looked over her glasses at Lisa and Janice. "That can't be possible. Can that be possible? That somebody can get better faster because, unbeknownst to him, a stranger is praying for him?"

Lisa wanted to say yes, but she didn't know what she could say after that that wouldn't sound like Sister Watts, who got up in fast and testimony meeting every single month and said, "I want to share with you, brothers and sisters, that the Lord hears and answers prayers."

Mrs. Bledsoe shook her head a final time and went back to her office.

"She's doing this long article on health and spirituality," Janice explained. "Which makes absolutely no sense because she's like a practicing atheist or something. Once when she was asked to do the blessing at my aunt's house, she said, 'Hubba hubba, thanks for the grubba.' "

Lisa chuckled.

Janice said, "You laugh, but my aunt didn't. It was pretty awful."

From Mrs. Bledsoe's office came the muted sounds of choral music, which Lisa recognized as Handel's *Messiah*. Without thinking, Lisa said, "I like your mom."

"But then you don't have to live with her," Janice said, laughing, and Lisa laughed, too, but sometimes she wondered if Janice's mom wasn't one reason she and Janice were still friends. They'd been friends forever, since grade school, when they liked exactly the same things: blue Otter Pops, Quick Curl Barbie, and a day-camp counselor named Booth Spinelli. Now it seemed like Janice wanted to try all the things Lisa wasn't even supposed to think about. She was probably becoming what the church would call a bad influence. But she was still Janice, and Mrs. Bledsoe felt almost like an aunt—an exotic, friendly, world-wise aunt. A few weeks ago, when her father had for the umpteenth time asked Lisa what she might want to do with her life, Lisa had surprised herself by saying, "I was thinking about freelance writing." Her father had considered it (approvingly, it seemed to Lisa) and said, "Like Janice's mom," and Lisa had nodded and said, "Yeah, like Janice's mom."

"Okay, check this out," Janice said now, and she slipped out a book hidden under the stack of newspapers on the table. *The Nancy Drew Cookbook*. On the cover was a ham steak topped with a pineapple slice topped with a maraschino cherry.

Janice grinned and said, "The cover's just the tip of the iceberg. There's more grossness within." She skimmed the recipes. "Double Jinx Salad. Invisible Intruder's Coconut Custard. And I urge you to consider The Wooden Lady's Walnut Tidbits."

"Let's burn it," Lisa said. "For our country. It's the right thing to do."

Janice laughed. "Can't. It's an artifact from my mother's past. My grandma says little Genevieve loved this book. She even had a rating system for how each recipe turned out." She flipped a few more pages. "For example, the Mysterious Mannequin Casserole got only two stars."

"Two stars too many," Lisa said.

But Janice had become interested in something. "Wow, the glossary's really something." She read silently for a few seconds, then said, "Okay, automatic response. Who would you like to bake beat blend boil broil and chop?"

"Coach Kapsiak."

Janice laughed. "Excellent! Now who would you like to core cube dice fold fry and garnish?"

"The Nancester." Nancy Forster, her ice-queen geometry teacher.

Janice said, "Okay, those were the easy ones. Here's the biggie. Who would you like to"—she slid her voice into a sultry register—"peel simmer and stir?"

Color rose in Lisa's face. She pictured Elder Keesler in his black missionary suit. "Nobody," she said quietly.

"Oh, that's a little fib," Janice said grinning.

"No, it's not. There's nobody I'd want to . . . do those things to."

Janice kept grinning. "Someday, girlfriend, you'll cast aside your weighted chains."

Lisa, who was looking out the back window, suddenly stood up. Was she seeing what she thought she was seeing?

Two guys in white shirts, ties, and dark parkas were wheeling bicycles up the walk of the building behind Janice's. It was Elder Keesler, for sure, and his smaller companion, Elder P-something.

"It's the missionaries," Lisa said. "They just got transferred to Jemison, and I got my mother to invite them to dinner next Sunday. Isn't Elder Keesler gorgio? He's from Boston."

"If you mean the tall one, he seems potentially peelable." She was still staring down at them. "Aren't they kind of young for elders? I mean, shouldn't they be *youngers?*"

Lisa laughed. "No. They're deacons when they're twelve, teachers at fourteen, priests at sixteen, elders at nineteen, and, as my dad's always saying, set in their ways by twenty-one."

"But, God, Leeze, those haircuts—they look like they could be buying at the commissary."

"Yeah, well, they have to knock on people's doors all day and say, 'I have a message about Jesus Christ.' Who's gonna open the door for a Hell's Angel who says that?"

"I might," Janice said, laughing.

Elder Keesler pulled out a key, and Lisa made note of the apartment they disappeared into.

"I bet people think they're gay," Janice said.

Lisa whacked her on the shoulder. "Why?"

"Well, they live together and dress very tidily."

Lisa laughed. "You should see them up close. Half of them wear clip-on ties. I'm pretty sure there's a gay rule against clip-on ties."

Janice said, "How about Elder Keester? Does he wear clip-on ties?"

"It's Elder *Keesler,* you moron. And no, he was wearing this very cool retro tie on Sunday. I'm hoping he wears the same one when he comes to dinner."

Janice flopped back down on the floor and picked up a pizza crust. "So, are there any Mormons on motorcycles? I might be able to go for a Harley Mormon."

Lisa laughed and then fell quiet. She was wondering what

Elder Keesler was doing in his apartment right now. Elder Keesler. Elder Keesler. Elder Keesler.

Janice was quiet, too. Then, a little too casually, she said, "You know, I've been thinking about that stuff you told me about Maurice."

The mere mention of his name made Lisa wary. "And?"

"And that whole Gomez thing kind of just sounds like a bad joke to me. And I'd rather have to wear my shirt a little small than way big, which is what Ned handed to me."

Lisa considered—and rejected—this. "No," she said, "those actions were the first droplets of Maurician slime."

Janice gave this a chuckle. "Okay, class, let's make a note of 'Maurician slime.'"

There was a silence. Lately there had been a lot of silences. Finally Lisa said, "Okay, I'll bet my too-small T shirt that Maurice Gritz is a sleazeball sexist creep."

"Says our little Mormon, who is right this minute lusting after a celibate missionary."

"I left out racist," Lisa said, flushing. "I should've said sleazeball racist sexist creep."

"That's a mouthful, girlfriend," Janice said, laughing.

Lisa forced herself to stop looking out the window and sit down. She didn't immediately look at Janice, but when she did, Janice didn't look mad. She had finished her crust and was looking at the half moon of unbroken pizza.

"Okay," Janice said, "just one more."

"We'll do sit-ups afterward and go for a run."

"Hundreds of sit-ups," Janice said.

"Thousands."

They each broke off another slice.

A bite or two later Janice said, "So what about that one guy who got assigned to your crew, the one who's always following you around?"

Lisa's cheeks pinkened slightly. "Mick Nichols. And he doesn't follow me around."

"Oh, excuse me very much. He just happens to pop up wherever you happen to be."

Lisa didn't say anything. To her surprise, she felt a pleasant warmth moving through her body. She didn't know Mick Nichols, but she didn't mind the idea of him popping up wherever she happened to be.

"So what's his story anyway?" Janice said.

Lisa shrugged. "He's A.P. and doesn't play sports. That's all I know." She could picture him though. He was average sized, but he had dark curly hair, and something about his eyes made him look like he was always amused at something, and she didn't know why exactly, but she liked the way he walked. "He's kind of cute, I guess, and at least he's not rich." He also wasn't Mormon, but who was, besides Thaine Briscoe, and he was about two feet shorter than Lisa.

"I'd trade him something good for that olive complexion," Janice said. "I'll bet he gets tan in about ten seconds." She was quiet a few moments. Then, "He's friends with Weinie Reece, isn't he?"

Alarms rang in Lisa's head. Winston Reece was in two of Janice's classes, and Lisa knew Janice believed in indirect negotiation. "Don't even think about it, Janice," she said.

Janice was grinning. "Think about what?"

"About grilling Winston Reece about Mick Nichols!" Lisa said.

"Let's not call it grilling," Janice said. "Let's call it a few gently probing questions."

"I mean it, Janice!" Lisa said.

"She means it," Janice said, still grinning.

Lisa set down her pizza. "Look, Janice—"

"Okay, okay, okay," Janice said. "Settle down, schoolgirl."

Lisa was wary. "So you promise?"

Janice stopped grinning. They'd made a pact a long time ago. That a promise really would be a promise. "Yeah, I do," she said.

"Do what?"

"Promise not to talk to Weinie Reece about Mick Nichols's interest in one Lisa Doyle."

Lisa nodded and went back to eating pizza and talking about other boys, but her mind kept coming back to Mick Nichols, which was okay, she guessed, and, more often and urgently, to Elder Keesler, which wasn't. Suddenly she set aside her half-eaten slice of pizza. "Let's go for a run."

"It's fuh-reezing out there," Janice said.

"It is not," Lisa said. "Nippy, maybe. Brisk, at most. And that's why God made hooded sweatshirts."

Janice said, "That's why God made cozy little kitchens to stay warm in," but she'd already put down her pizza, too, and was pushing back from the table. "Okay," she said, "what did God do with my running shoes?"

CHAPTER SEVEN

Night Owls

Maurice felt good. It was Saturday night and he was out driving. He'd just finished a two-hour workout at Fizz Ed's Gym—he'd maxed out on the full regimen of bench presses, crunches, curls, and squats—and now it felt as if his muscles were so tightly packed into his body he could almost burst.

He drove his black, heavily modified Accord—low-profile tires, lowered suspension, loud exhaust, tinted rear and side windows—and he loved crawling along Jemison's back streets this time of night, feeling hard and tight and powerful, chewing his gum, blowing slow patient bubbles, driving with one hand on the steering wheel, the other in his lap, leaning back, peering into the houses that were still lighted, heading only indirectly back to his place, an old caretaker's cottage in Village Greens.

Bor-Lan Plastics. Spruce Bough Restaurant. Narrow houses with gold lights in the upstairs windows. A line of freight cars going nowhere. He eased the Accord over three sets of railroad tracks, under a trestle bridge, and up the hill into more prosperous, tree-lined streets. Up ahead two dark figures jogging along the sidewalk passed under a streetlight and again into darkness.

Misses, probably, running in twos like that, but it was hard to tell if they were youthful misses.

Maurice let the Honda creep behind them. They weren't big, and one carried a flashlight. The other had something gripped in one hand, a can of Mace probably. One of them glanced back at the Accord. Misses, he was sure of it.

Okay, then.

He flipped on the Honda's interior lights and accelerated slightly. When he'd caught up with the joggers, he kept the car at their pace, moving alongside until they turned to look at him. They were wearing their sweatshirts hoods up, so Maurice couldn't see their hair, but he stared evenly from his lighted car, just staring and grinning. Then he slowly inflated a pink gum bubble to real size before bursting it and sucking it neatly back into his mouth.

Okay, then. He didn't know those little misses, but now they knew him.

Freezing his grin, he switched off the overhead light and gently eased the Honda ahead. None of that music-blasting clutch-popping tire-squealing teenage shit for him who was Maurice.

He ramped onto the highway so he could let the Accord feel her oats a little before taking Leverwood Road past the Moose Lodge, the Jewish cemetery, Pipsissewa Wood, and a white farm-house to the lilac-hedged border of Village Greens.

When he got to the entrance, he could've remoted himself on through, or even entered the property through one of the mainte-nance gates, but he liked to establish his patterns with the security guards. He wanted them to think they knew what to expect of him. So he did tonight what he always did—he used the visitor lane, pulled up alongside the security kiosk, and rolled down his window.

"How're they hangin', Alvin?" he said.

Alvin was a bald, dapper man who was himself a resident of Village Greens. He said, "About the same as yesterday, I imagine. You get my age, Maurice, and you don't check that often."

Maurice gave this a big grin and changed subjects. "Lots doin'? Any more big-time security breaches?" There had been a couple of break-ins last week with small valuables stolen, what the police investigator had called typical examples of walkaway crime.

"Nope," Alvin said. "All quiet as far as I know. Guess you heard Mrs. Hartwell claimed to see a prowler night before last."

Maurice said no, he hadn't heard that. "Any idea who?"

Alvin shrugged. "Dark-complected male. Afro American, she thought." He shook his head. "That didn't make folks feel any better."

Maurice started to smile but blew a quick golfball-sized bubble instead. It was true, though. Nothing scared the old white folks more than a black dude. "Well, pretty soon whoever it is will go away or get caught and then we'll go back to being our sleepy little village again."

Alvin turned serious. "I'll tell you what, he *better* go away. Or one of these old vets will get out the live ammo."

A laugh slipped from Maurice. He couldn't help it—"live ammo" had a comic flavor to it. Then he said, "Think these old vets can still shoot straight?"

Alvin grinned. "Well, that's another question."

Maurice said, "I'm thinking that with those vets after him, our bogeyman just may be the safest guy in town."

Alvin kept his grin and said, "Then again, you might be surprised."

Maurice didn't believe this but nodded as if he did. He

snapped a bubble and said he'd better keep moving. It was late and he still had Mrs. Kinderman's cats to feed.

"I'll tell the patrol you'll be over that way," Alvin said. "We wouldn't want 'em taking you for the wrong guy."

"No, we wouldn't," Maurice said, and gave a nod before driving on.

Maurice cruised by Mrs. Hartwell's house (new low-sodium lights shone from both porches), then turned down Elysian Lane and let the Accord creep along the street. He pulled his little reporter's notebook from his glove box. Elysian Lane was a good street, in his view, an eight on a one-to-ten scale. Most homes were dark. Within a few houses—and he noted the addresses—a single security light shone, and from a few others you could see the flickering bluish light of a TV (he noted these as "night owls"). But nobody was out. Nobody was out except him. He loved this place when it was dark and fenced and quiet and nobody was out but him who was Maurice.

When he'd finished canvassing Elysian Lane, Maurice took two rights to Fairway Place, cut the lights, pulled into Mrs. Kinderman's driveway, and remoted open the garage door. Mrs. Kinderman was one of the few residents of Village Greens Maurice could think of with anything like affection. Soon after he'd started working here three years ago, on a hot summer day, she'd seen him on the fringes of the seventh fairway working in the sun, trying to get the three-reel mower going again, and she'd brought him iced root beer in a tall glass. When he'd gulped that down, she brought another, this time walking a harnessed black cat on a leash. "This is Harriet," she'd said, nodding at the cat, "and I'm Mrs. Kinderman. Who are you?"

Maurice gave his name and bent to scratch the cat.

Mrs. Kinderman said she had two more cats back at the house, both marmalades, and she invited Maurice home to meet them. Then she invited him to dinner the next week, and even though he didn't like seeing cats roaming the kitchen counters, he'd enjoyed the home cooking and, a surprise, he hadn't minded her company. She was a tiny, tidy woman, with her slacks neatly pressed and her cardigan buttoned to the throat, but what caught him by surprise was how open she was in her conversation. She said that seeing Maurice working on the mower, blowing a bubble and "scowling at that miscreant machine," had reminded her of her son, William, "who loved taking things apart and putting them together again. Or at least trying to." By dessert, Maurice had learned, among many other things, that William had died of meningitis when he was eleven, and though she had two other children, he'd been her only son. Mrs. Kinderman smiled at Maurice. "I thought it was going to kill me. I honestly did. But I had the girls to look after and then my husband got sick and I had him to take care of and strangely enough while he got worse, I got better." After that first meal, Maurice had come to dinner at Mrs. Kinderman's the first Tuesday of every month, but this past winter she'd had a series of small strokes, and her daughters had moved her to a place described by its brochure as "an assisted-care facility." Mrs. Kinderman believed she would be coming back to Village Greens and had asked Maurice to take care of her cats.

Maurice was glad to, and stopped in once a day. What was interesting was how the two marmalade cats scissored through his legs waiting for him to fork out the tin of fishy byproducts, but Harriet, the black cat, always stayed back until the moment he seated himself at the kitchen table, and then she would leap into his lap, more anxious for petting than food. Maurice liked the cat, liked the way, with just a few strokes along her back, she fell into a murmuring purr. When the two marmalades had finished the first tin, and were stationed here and there licking their paws, Maurice always put out a second tin for Harriet before cleaning the cat box and heading home.

As he turned up his gravel lane tonight, Maurice lowered his window, letting the cold come in, and the sound of the rough, rolling crunch of the gravel under the tires. The caretaker's cottage Maurice lived in was separated from the maintenance shed and other outbuildings by a small gully spanned by a footbridge. The cottage had its charms—it was brown shingled and surrounded by ferns and dogwoods—but its interior was nothing more than a large single room with adjoining alcoves for kitchen, closet, and bath. The cottage's three windows were covered with yellowed shades that Maurice kept pulled. The furnishings were mismatched discards passed on by residents of Village Greens—a painted brass bed, a chipped antique chest of drawers, a worn wing chair. A bar heavily weighted with barbells rested on a padded weight bench and stood before a wall covered with mirrored squares that Maurice had installed himself. A rusty wood-burning stove at the other end of the room provided the only heat. The room's single expensive element was a clock given to him by his father on his third birthday, less than a year before his father had died. It was a fine-grained, three-arch mantel clock that rested on a secondhand chest of drawers and at each quarter hour sounded the appropriate fraction of the sixteen-note Westminster chimes. Behind the clock, at the edges of the mirror frame, Maurice had wedged five or six photographs of his father in combat fatigues, his eyes shaded by a brimmed khaki cap.

When Maurice came in tonight, he banked the coals in the

stove and set two logs across them. He took a bottle of Rolling Rock beer from the refrigerator, then went to the bed and pulled a small plastic folder from its hiding place between mattress and box springs. The case folded open to display photographs of eight or nine girls. He flipped over the last of this lineup to see where he'd written ISABELLE SHIFF, along with her telephone number. He sat on the edge of the bed and dialed the number. When a woman answered, he said in a low voice, "Hello, Miss Iz."

"Hi, Maurice."

He said, "Can you come over here right now?"

"I guess so."

"Good," Maurice said, and gently set the phone into its cradle. He lay back on the bed smiling. The clock on the bureau began to chime. It was midnight, straight up, in Village Greens.

PART TWO

The king was in the counting house,
Counting out his money;
The queen was in the parlor,
Eating bread and honey.

CHAPTER EIGHT

Passer Domesticus

It was a Sunday evening. A female bird was building a nest in the small alcove of a missing brick beneath the eaves of Mick's garage. The hoarse, insistent song of her mate could be heard from the kitchen, the living room, the yard, his bed. *Fee-bee. Fee-bee. Fee-bee.* Which turned out to be the bird's name. After scanning Nora's bird books and peering through her binoculars, he decided the bird was an eastern phoebe. As he patched together his history paper for Mr. Cruso, Mick positioned his chair by the window where he could watch the bird's comings and goings.

Nora and his father were downstairs. They'd called Mick down for supper—he'd declined—then Nora had offered to bring sandwiches up, and he'd declined that, too. Now they were down there listening to Dire Straits. The only singers they could agree on were Frank Sinatra, Dwight Yoakam, and Dire Straits, all of which, to Mick's way of thinking, were only slightly better than polka bands.

"Males precede females by a week or two, returning to their previous breeding territories and quickly announcing their arrival by repetitive song," Nora's book said. "Females build the nests, then frequently disappear for up to three weeks before returning to lay eggs."

So the male was making the noise, and the female was making

the nest. Sometimes she came with clumps of moss, other times a twig or snatch of cloth. Once she came with a cigarette wrapper. Mostly she pulled strands from the frayed basketball net that hung from the basket his father had installed in hopes of fanning his interest in the sport. That's where she was now when the music stopped downstairs.

In the silence Mick could hear low voices, low earnest voices. Again.

Mick crept to the head of the stairs. Nora and his father were in the kitchen, and their words were muffled. Mick eased down the stairs until the murmurings turned into words.

"Sugarloaf, listen to me," Nora was saying. "Mick's going through a phase. It's a dark phase, but it's only a phase. It's like a long tunnel. One day he went into it, and one day he'll come out of it."

His father's lowered voice was like a tight whisper. "A week ago we were one unit, all three of us, and then—*bam!*—he's gone. Departed. It's like he seceded from the Union or something. What kind of phase is that?"

"An independence phase," Nora said. She was using her teacher's voice. "He's almost sixteen. He's flexing his muscles."

"But why all of a sudden? What caused it?"

Nora didn't even hesitate. "It could be anything. Some imagined slight. Or something he picked up at school. I can tell you firsthand that parents don't get a lot of good PR in the hallways of Jemison High."

Mick had heard enough. He quietly slipped back upstairs, grabbed his pack and jacket, then came trouncing heavily back down. When he entered the kitchen, Nora and his father had fallen silent. Mick grabbed a can of Mr. Pibb from the refrigerator.

"Going somewhere?" his father asked softly. He looked miserable. It reminded Mick of when his mother had left.

"Just over to Reece's, Dad. We've got a test in English. On intransitive verbs." He could see that his father had no idea what he was talking about. "Anyhow, I've got some clothes, so I'll just sleep over there."

His father didn't say anything. He kept sitting there looking forlorn.

"You cleared all this with Reece's mom?" Nora asked.

In the instant his gaze shifted from his father to Nora, Mick's expression hardened. "Yeah, but you can call and check for yourself if you don't trust me."

His father came slightly back to life. "Hey, c'mon, Mick," he said. "This is us. Nora and me. We're not the bad guys."

Mick turned to his father. "I didn't say you were."

His father dropped his eyes. Nora, who'd been standing, moved close to her husband and began massaging his shoulders. From behind him, she glared at Mick.

Mick stared right back. I see you, he thought. He said, "I smell something. Is something burning?"

Instinctively Nora turned to check the stove, and Mick used that moment to exit.

It was a bad week. Mick didn't sight Lisa Doyle all day Monday, and Tuesday, when he didn't see her with the field hockey team, he stopped to peer through the chain-link fence.

"She's not here!" one of the girls yelled—was that what she yelled? Mick's face burned red. "She's sick!" the girl yelled, and Mick suddenly recognized her. Janice Bledsoe. Lisa's friend. Standing there, grinning at him.

Stiffly, without a word, Mick turned and walked away.

Very impressive.

Lisa Doyle was off the absence list on Wednesday, but it didn't matter. On Wednesdays he had to hustle to get to his piano lesson by 3:30, and anyway Mick was too embarrassed to appear anywhere near the normal sighting places, especially the practice field. Every day after school, he just went home, fed and ran Foolish, checked incoming e-mail as well as the trash for more secret messages (there had been no more), then headed for Reece's, where he would study and spend the night.

"So what's this book blitz all about?" Reece asked Wednesday night.

They were sitting in the Reece basement, thickly carpeted and furnished with leather sofas, a Ping-Pong table, and an upright piano.

Mick looked up from his grammar book. It was true. He had been doing the books full tilt all of a sudden. Nora might screw his father out of his life, but she wasn't going to screw him out of his. He needed his diploma. He needed a few diplomas. "I don't know," Mick said. "I just want to get somewhere, you know? Somewhere different than where my dad is. I mean, look at my mom. She was a minimum-wage filing clerk while she was getting her M.B.A., and now she's got like three assistants and the company sends a limo to pick her up every morning."

After a second or two, Reece said quietly, "I didn't think your dad had it so bad."

There was something different about this conversation, Mick could feel it. It was as if Reece was after something. He said, "What my dad does is all right, I'm not saying that. It's just not what I want to do."

Reece was quiet for a few seconds. "Okay," he said, "I should tell you. Nora talked to Mrs. Reece. She said your dad's freaking out over you. Not talking to them, not eating there, not sleeping there." He waited. "So what's the matter, man?"

"Nothing."

Another silence. "Then why can't you stay at home?"

"Just can't."

Reece grinned and went into robot talk. "Human unit in question may need probing to reveal contents of data bank."

Mick ignored him.

Reece stared at him for a while, very still, then finally shrugged and made an audible sigh. "Okay, chief. You get to make all the big decisions."

Mick went back to his grammar book, but the predicate adjectives and nominatives kept slipping away from him. He couldn't stop thinking of Nora and Alexander Selkirk. He went over to the piano and played a few chords of the zip-a-dee-doo-dah song, quickly at first, but then gradually slowing the tempo, turning a happy song sad.

Nora hadn't dumped any more e-messages in the trash, so Mick had begun trying to get into her e-mail. During the school day he would make a list of hunch words that might be Nora's password—her middle name (Abigail), her mother's maiden name (Bosworth), her favorite vegetable (snow peas)—and then when he got to the house in the afternoon, he would see if any of the words would open her e-mails. None did.

Thursday afternoon, however, Mick himself received an unexpected e-mail. *How's my Frisbee-fetching hound?* it said. *And how is you?*

82

It was from Myra Vidal.

Mick felt the slightest acceleration of his heartbeat.

Foolish as ever, Mick wrote back. *The hound and human both. How about you?* He pressed send and watched the little bar graph fill up—*zing!*—as the letter flew to Myra's dorm room.

He didn't mention Myra's e-mail to Reece that night. He knew Reece. Reece would try to make it into something, and it wasn't anything. It wasn't nothing, but it was close to nothing. So he did his homework in Reece's basement and ate popcorn and played Ping-Pong and for long periods of time never gave a thought to Nora or Myra or Lisa.

Around 9:30, when Reece was talking to someone on the phone, Mick wandered over to the piano and began to play Bach's Invention 13. He kept playing until he heard the door open at the head of the basement stairs. It was Reece's mother, in her slippers and robe, her hair in curlers, holding a coffee cup. "Don't stop," she said. "I heard it from upstairs and it was just so pretty, I wanted to hear it better."

She sat on the steps sipping coffee while Mick played it again.

"It's beautiful," she said quietly when he was done. "Bach, right?"

Mick nodded and laid the cover over the keys. "It's about the only thing I know by heart." It was also Nora's favorite piece, which is why he'd learned it. The day he met her he was playing the 12th and she'd said the only thing better than the 12th is the 13th, which, she said, "had heft."

Reece hung up the phone and turned to his mother. "Hey, I thought the basement was off limits to big pink curlers."

His mother made a wry smile and stood up. "And here I thought it was off limits to filial incivility."

"Fancy phrases, Mrs. Reece."

Reece's mom thanked Mick for his piano playing and went back upstairs.

Later that night, Mick lay in a sleeping bag on the carpet of Reece's room. The house was quiet and the moon made shadows in the room. In his sleep Reece made slow rhythmic nasal wheezes. Mick closed his eyes and at once saw Lisa Doyle, then Myra Vidal, then Nora. He imagined them one at a time, and the longer he imagined them, the fewer clothes they wore. Finally Nora presented herself at the head of the Reeces' basement stairs, completely naked, smiling at him sitting at the piano, saying, "Play that one more time and then—"

Mick blinked open his eyes. His heart was beating fast, and his body was in a state of high agitation. From the floor, looking up through the window, he could see a long bare limb silhouetted by a nearly full moon. Foolish, he thought. It was the name Nora gave a dog, but it was more than that. It was the perfect adjective for him, his father, and his father's dreams, whatever form they might be taking in the buff-colored house under the nearly full moon in a room overlooking a finished, empty nest.

CHAPTER NINE

The Eternal Husband

Reece's family was going to Connecticut to visit relatives for the weekend, so Friday night Mick had no place to go but home. Last period Friday a note was delivered to him in History. It said, *Your father will pick you up at south gate 3:05.*

Brittany Allen, after leaning over his shoulder to see, made a general announcement to the rest of the class: "It's from his daddy. His daddy's driving him home after school."

This played to smirks and chuckles all around.

"At least I know who my daddy is," Mick said, which kept the smirks coming.

Mr. Cruso, the history teacher and Mick's adviser, was popular. He had dark, longish, perfectly groomed hair and a trim black beard. Some of the girls who hung around his class before school called him "the happy bachelor," and it seemed as if he was. He was an easy grader, wore more or less cool clothes, and drove a vintage emerald green Porsche. But mostly he just seemed to like people, students and teachers alike, fat ones and slim ones, smart ones and slackers—they all seemed to amuse him. His chief weapon of classroom restraint was irony, and for this occasion he said, "Civility, children, is the outer garment of inner peace."

"Whatever that means," Brittany Allen said, which drew a few more laughs and a mugging frown from Mr. Cruso. Everyone, student and teacher alike, was glad to be released by the last Friday bell.

Mick shuffled books at his locker, went to the second floor, and gazed out at the playing field—empty—then headed for the windows that gave onto the south gate. His father's optic yellow 2002 was there, parked along the curb. He started to step away from the window and head down to the car, but something stopped him, something not quite right. He looked again. There were two heads in the front seat, not one.

Nora.

It was his father and Nora.

Mick moved away from the window, hurried downstairs to the north exit, and fled the campus by back streets. He wandered around Plan B for a while, went to Bing's for fries and a Coke, then went to a phone booth and looked up "Doyle." There were nineteen of them. He found addresses for three nearby, jotted them down, and walked by each, trying to stare into the windows without appearing to stare in the windows. He didn't see anyone inside any of them.

Finally he walked to the Jemison library and sat down with *The Eternal Husband*, which was on the World Literature extra-credit list. It was by the same guy who'd written *Crime and Punishment*, which Mick had liked even though after the crime it seemed to take an awful long time to get to the punishment.

This one was much shorter, but it was confusing to start with. The narrator was a cranky upper-class guy who realized he was being followed around by a little ordinary man wearing black crepe on his hat, which meant he was in mourning for someone who'd died. But after that it got interesting, and Mick kept turning pages until the lights flickered on and off—the sign that the library would be closing in ten minutes.

Mick walked home in a cold drizzle. Nora and his father were sitting in the living room when he came in. Nora was stiffly holding a pair of knitting needles and counting stitches, which always required moving her lips. His father had his hands wrapped around a full cup of coffee, as if for warmth.

When Nora stopped counting, she said, "We waited for you after school. We thought we'd drive out to the Glassworks for dinner." It was an old-factory-turned-Italian-restaurant his father liked, mostly because you had to drive way out of town to get there. Two-lane country roads were what the 2002 was meant for, he said.

"Sorry," Mick said without a trace of sorrow in his voice.

"You didn't get the message?" Nora said. "No one delivered you the message?"

"You sent a note? How did you send it?"

"School courier."

"Sorry," Mick said again, "but school courier's pretty much a message in a bottle." Nora wasn't buying this, he could tell, but before she could pin him down further, Mick's father said, "Where were you tonight, Mick?"

"Library," Mick said.

"On a Friday night?" Nora said.

He eyed her. "That's right. I was reading an extra-credit world-lit book." He didn't owe her an explanation, but all of a sudden he felt like giving one. "It's a pretty good book. It's about a guy whose wife dies and while going through her stuff he finds love letters to a mutual friend written in the middle of their marriage, so the husband begins following the mutual friend around trying to decide what to do." He shrugged off his wet backpack and pulled out the book. "*The Eternal Husband* by Dostoyevsky. I'm not quite done with it, but I'm hoping the husband whacks the guy."

Nora started moving her needles in and out of the brown yarn and his father sat silent. Finally Nora said, "And that's where you were all night—sitting in the library reading a book by a dead Russian?"

Mick was beginning to enjoy this. "Well, no. First I went to Plan B and looked around and then I went to Bing's and got something to eat, and then I went to the library where I read the book by the dead Russian." He stared at her. "That's the real truth, not that taffy kind you were telling me about that can be stretched any way you want it."

In a sharp voice his father said, "Okay, that's enough, Mick."

Mick looked down. There was a little pool of dripped water where he'd been standing. "I'm freezing," he said. "I'm going to go change."

Mick took a hot shower, checked his e-mails (nothing from Myra), and then quickly tried his new list of possible passwords to Nora's e-mails (no luck) before going to his room. He was reading the last chapter of *The Eternal Husband* when his father knocked gently on the door and poked his head in.

"You real busy?"

"Not really."

His father's progress into the room was tentative, like a stranger's who'd never been there before. He didn't seem to know what to do with his hands or where to sit. Finally he put his hands in his pockets and leaned against Mick's desk.

"I'm not very good at this kind of thing," he began. "But

you're acting real different, Mick." He let his eyes settle on Mick. His eyes seemed old. Mick just waited. His father said, "I know I don't know beans about the things kids go through these days, but I want you to know you can talk to me about anything and I'm not going to be mad."

"Yeah, I know that, Dad."

When Mick didn't elaborate, the room grew dense with silence. Finally his father said in a soft voice, "This isn't anything to do with drugs, is it, Mick?"

Mick couldn't help but laugh. "C'mon, Dad. I mean, it's out there and everything, but that's just not my style."

Again in the soft awkward voice his father said, "You didn't get a girl in trouble?"

Another laugh from Mick. "Jeez, Dad."

"Well, then, what's going on?"

"Nothing." Mick knew that wasn't going to be enough, so he said, "I just think that it finally dawned on me how I'm getting closer to, you know, being out on my own, and how I'm not exactly the brainiest box on the shelf, but I still want to go to college and maybe law school and now's the time to start, you know, kicking butt at school."

He stopped. It had sounded pretty good.

His father was nodding. "Okay," he said. "I can follow that." He pushed himself away from the desk, but he had one last question. "Would it kill you to be a little nicer to Nora?"

Mick looked at his father with the soft, old eyes and said, no, it wouldn't kill him.

His father said, "Nora and I're going up to Tug Hill with the cross-country skis tomorrow. It'd be a lot more fun if you'd come, too."

"Can't, Dad. I'm working tomorrow. It wouldn't look that good to miss my first day."

His father was nodding in agreement. "Work first, fun second." He turned his eyes on Mick and his whole expression softened. "Night, Mick."

"Night, Dad."

But his father didn't leave. He said, "You know how when there was some little problem like a broken water heater or a late mortgage payment, I would always say, 'It's not my wife and it's not my life'?"

Mick nodded.

"Well, I said it that way because I heard it somewhere and it has a nice ring to it, but the truth is, I should've said, 'It's not my life, it's not my wife, and it's not my kid.' "

Mick felt his throat getting tight.

His father took a deep breath. "I know you're reading and everything, but do you think you could just come downstairs and play the piano? I'd like it and I know Nora would like it, too."

Mick looked at his father, then marked his place in his book. "Sure, Dad."

Nora had made popcorn, and Mick took a handful when the bowl was offered. He drank the hot chocolate she gave him. He started one of the Inventions, but then pulled out an old book of ragtime tunes. There was one called "Solace" that he liked because it was slow and sad and easy enough that as his fingers moved, his mind could float. Images appeared of Lisa Doyle's coppery red hair, and of Myra Vidal's breasts, and of the dream Nora standing at the top of Reece's stairs. Mick turned to Nora sitting on the couch knitting something brown and fuzzy, probably thinking of Alexander Selkirk. She was like a replicant in one of those movies, a body inhabited by an alien.

When he finished, Mick's father said, "That was good, Mick." He winked. "Gooder than good." He turned to Nora. "How about you play one of those études?" He made it sound almost like two words. Aye. Tudes.

"Let me get to the end of this row," Nora said, holding the needles closer to her face and slipping their points in and out of the moving yarn. Then she stabbed her needles into the ball of yarn and said, "There." She found her Chopin book, and if it was an alien playing, the alien had Nora's piano style down cold. She played as she always played, impressively fluttery on the trills, impressively massive on the fortes.

Nora finished, Mick and his father clapped lightly, and she turned the page to play one more. She was wearing tight Levi's and a beige, soft-looking sweater. She sat with perfect posture, erect, which made her breasts more pronounced. Tomorrow, Mick suddenly thought. Tomorrow he would actually talk out loud to Lisa Doyle.

Tomorrow.

No ifs, ands, or buts.

CHAPTER TEN

Heigh-Ho, Heigh-Ho

Maurice Gritz grinned at the jeeps huddled in front of him. It was eight o'clock Saturday morning and they'd all been issued flannel-lined Village Greens parkas and Village Greens work gloves, but they all stood before him cold and wooden faced. He took a quick roll—everyone was there—then he snapped a pink bubble and said, "Well, let's just pretend it's balmy and everyone's happy to be here."

Everyone seemed too cold to respond except the boy named Traylor, who chuckled to show that he actually was happy to be there. Mick noted Traylor for a half second—he had a loose-jointed, eager-to-please look to him—then turned back toward Maurice, who had pulled out his clipboard.

"Okay," Maurice said, "let's check the nature of this morning's jeeply fun."

While Maurice silently read through the page attached to his clipboard, Mick sneaked a glance at Lisa Doyle, who stood opposite him in the half circle. She was looking down at her boots, so he was able to let his gaze rest fully on her. She'd dressed for work—her red hair was braided and she'd worn a turtleneck thermal under her T-shirt. She looked in fact like an advertisement for the health benefits of outdoor activity—chopping firewood or cross-country skiing, say—and Mick was lost in thoughts of schussing along a snow trail with nobody but her when she slowly raised her eyes and looked directly at him.

Mick was paralyzed.

He tried to smile, but couldn't—what he was doing with his lips felt more like some kind of weird rubbery facial contortion, something you might do in the dentist's office under the influence of Novocaine. It didn't matter, though. Lisa Doyle was smiling back.

All at once the strangest, pleasantest feeling coursed through Mick's body, expanded, seemed to fill him up. It was like helium— he thought if he kept staring at her, he might float away. He lowered his eyes.

Maurice put aside his clipboard. "Okay," he said. "The first fun of the day is the cotoneaster bank." He pronounced it ko-tone-ee-as-ter. He scanned the jeeps. "Now what do you suppose that is? The cotoneaster bank."

Mick had no idea what a ko-tone-ee-as-ter bank was because he had no idea what a ko-tone-ee-as-ter was, and didn't really care because Lisa Doyle had just smiled at him.

He suddenly noticed the others turning toward him.

Maurice said, "You paying attention, Nichols?"

Mick flushed and said, "I think right then at that exact moment I might not've been."

Snickers from the group.

Maurice stared. "I asked you to tell us what a cotoneaster bank is."

Mick said, "A place where you go to deposit your cotoneasters when you've saved up enough of them?"

This drew more snickering laughs from the other jeeps, but one of the laughs had the smoother modulation of a girl. Maurice shot a glance at Lizette—she was stone-faced—and then at Lisa, whose face was in the elastic aftermath of laughter. Maurice composed a fixed smile and turned back to Mick. "I appreciate your attempt at levity, Nichols." He waited. "But what I notice about funny guys is how often their funniness is meant to hide how little they actually know."

The group fell still, which seemed to please Maurice. "Okay, then. Who can tell me what a cotoneaster bank is without making funny?"

Traylor said, "A bank that has cotoneaster growing on it?"

"Thank you, Traylor," Maurice said. "Now the problem is, we have some other things growing on our cotoneaster bank, and these other things are called dogbane. As you may have noticed, many Lilliputians are pro-poodle. Last year we were sued for not ridding the common areas of dogbane, which a poodle-owning gent claimed had poisoned his little doglet." Maurice grinned and snapped another bubble. "Bad news is, dogbane is also poisonous to jeeps, so wear gloves."

As they dispersed, Mick considered whistling the first bars of Heigh-ho, heigh-ho, but decided against it.

The bank was huge. Maurice led the jeeps over to its base, leaned down, and with a gloved hand snapped off a branch from a woody, low-growing shrub with ruddled leaves. "This," he said, "is cotoneaster." Then he yanked hard on a shrubby, red-stemmed plant beneath it. He shook off its roots, held it in front of him, and said, "This is dogbane. And if you haven't got it by the roots, you haven't got it."

Mick thought Maurice had probably watched a lot of John Wayne movies.

Maurice glanced up at the sky—the faintest mist fell, just

enough to wet every surface—then he began to assign different jeeps to different sections of the bank. "This way," he said, "we know who's been picking 'bane and who's been picking his nose."

He gave Lizette the most overgrown section and Traylor a section that was almost clear. He put Lisa at the bank's east end and Mick at the west end. Mick saw her glance his way as she set off for her section, or at least he thought she glanced his way.

The work was messy but mindless, and Mick floated through the next two hours yanking up thick-stemmed bunches of dogbane, which oozed a milky liquid he half expected to burn through his gloves, and chasing round and round his thoughts about Lisa Doyle. Occasionally some stray troubling thought or image of Nora would interfere, but then he'd quickly reroute back to Lisa. His thinking was this. She'd smiled at him, and that meant she wouldn't mind him trying to talk to her. But if he was going to talk to her, he needed to have an idea of what he might ask her to do, something definitely casual, like maybe studying together at the library or meeting at the mall or something. Or maybe he should just talk to her and wait till next Saturday to ask her to do something. Or, or, or . . .

None of the jeeps talked. Maurice had gone away in the truck without saying when he'd be back, and nobody wanted to be caught talking when he returned. So they all kept yanking and tugging. Sometimes the roots pulled easily from the wet soil and flung mud onto their faces and parkas. It stayed cold—the clouds had packed tighter and darkened since this morning and the mist kept floating down. Occasionally Mick would stand to straighten his back, and once when he did this he saw Lisa standing, too, straightening her back, turned his way. Then they both leaned over again and resumed work.

When Maurice returned midmorning, the bank was nearly done. He walked from section to section scrutinizing the jeeps' work in silence until he got to the area where Lizette Uribe was still working. Nearly a third of her section was still covered with blue-green leaves and red stems. Lisa, who'd finished her section, had moved over to Lizette's. Maurice stood watching the girls bent over and tugging for a few long seconds before he spoke.

"What're you doing, Doyle?" he asked.

Lisa stood and turned. She looked scared but spoke up clearly. "Lizette's area was a lot worse than mine, so when I finished my area I just started helping her out."

"Gomez needed help?" Maurice said.

Lisa said, "Not exactly. She—"

Maurice held up his hand to cut her off. He let his smile move among the group that had gathered nearby. "Two lessons here. First, to Doyle's credit, she did what all of you should do. You jump in to finish the job." He kept his smile fixed on his lips. "And lesson two is that if one jeep slacks off, all the other jeeps pay the price. Just to refresh your memory, your future pay depends on my written evaluation of your work, and nothing on that evaluation is more important than efficiency." He turned now to Lizette. "You know what efficiency is, Gomez?"

Lizette looked confused. "Working hard, I guess."

Maurice smiled. "It's the effect of working hard. It's how much work gets done in how little time." He popped a bubble and kept his eyes on Lizette. "In this case, everyone finished his section with one exception, and that exception is you."

Mick, without thinking, said, "But her area had a lot more dogbane."

Calmly Maurice moved his eyes from Lizette to Mick. "Thank

you for your input, Nichols. In the future please be reminded that when him who is Maurice wants your opinion, he'll ask for it."

The crew stood in frozen silence.

Mick thought, Him who is Maurice? And then he thought, Actually, it should be He who is Maurice.

The mist had increased to a drizzle. Drops beaded on the hood of Mick's parka and dripped to his face. Maurice said, "Now I suggest you all get up into Gomez's section and help her finish."

They clambered up the bank with their barrels and began tugging. Mick kept peering out his parka and worked his way closer to Lisa. When he was within a few feet of her she glanced up. Her hair was wet and so was her face. She looked miserable.

Mick didn't know what to say, but he knew he had to say something. He said, "I'm thinking maybe we assassinate him who is Maurice."

A quick laugh burst from Lisa, which she stifled at once, but it wasn't soon enough.

"Something strike you as funny, Doyle?"

Lisa's face froze. She looked down the bank at Maurice.

He was smiling. "Perhaps you'd care to share with the rest of us."

Lisa stared at him bleakly. She opened her mouth, but no words came out.

Quickly Mick said, "Someone up here passed some pretty rich gas, is all. I asked for the air freshener."

Maurice eyed Mick, then Lisa. "And that struck you as comical, Doyle?"

Lisa said, "I guess it did, kind of."

Maurice nodded and smoothed out his smile. "Well, it's nice to know what kind of thing can tickle a redhead's fancy," he said, and looked into her as if he was saying one thing and thinking another.

The drizzle was turning to rain. Maurice looked up at the sky and widened his smile. "You're in luck, jeepsters. What we've got here is perfect weather for fertilizing." He looked beamingly at the crew. "This is how we make green pastures greener."

For the next hour the jeeps were fertilizing front lawns on both sides of five different streets. Mick's job was to keep the spreaders filled with fertilizer so that the other jeeps would have a full one waiting when they returned with an empty. The chemical fertilizer came in sixty-pound bags. He cut them open and poured the white crystals into the next spreader. The rain had soaked through his parka and his pants, and what wasn't muddy was now dotted with white fertilizer stains.

Mick was wet and he was cold, and he knew everyone else was, too. The only good thing was that Maurice had left and he could say something to Lisa every time she came back with her spreader empty. Once he made her laugh by whistling "Don't Worry, Be Happy." He'd decided the next time she came for a refilled spreader he would say, "Hey, how about if we go to Bing's for some fries or something after work?"

But this time as Lisa was approaching, a voice rang out behind him.

"Schoolgirl!"

Mick glanced around. It was Janice Bledsoe, sitting warm and dry alongside Maurice in a covered golf cart. She said, "Our guy's a whole lot nicer than your mean old Maurice. Our guy told us to clock out, get our checks, and go home."

Lisa smiled gamely. Water streamed down her face and neck.

Janice looked down the street at the other jeeps and said, "Hey, you guys look like a fertilizer-spreader drill team."

Maurice laughed. He seemed slightly different than he had all morning. Happier. More alert to sudden possibilities. He said, "Maybe we'll enter our little fertilizer-spreader drill team in the next Fourth of July parade."

Janice laughed as if there were some wit hidden within the remark that only she recognized. Then she turned again to Lisa. "Anyhow, my mom's here. Want us to wait for you?"

Lisa shook her head. "That's okay. I'll just call home when we're done."

"You sure?"

Lisa nodded. "I'm sure."

"Okay," Janice said and then, turning a playful smile at Maurice, she said, "Home, Jeeves." As they were U-turning, she looked back over her shoulder and yelled one last thing to Lisa: "Good luck tomorrow with tall, dark, and Mormon. Save me all the juicy details!"

After they were gone, Mick said nothing to Lisa as he rolled a refilled spreader toward her. Before he'd felt happy, but now he just felt wary, and Lisa must've sensed it because she began to explain.

"It's just some guy who's coming to dinner tomorrow," she said. Then she said, "He's a missionary, so it's not a date. He brings his own date, really. Another missionary guy."

Mick nodded stiffly.

"Missionaries go two by two, like on Noah's ark."

He nodded again. He didn't know why she was doing all the explaining, but he did know that the idea of asking her to Bing's for fries had been a mirage that disappeared upon approach. "Hey," he said, trying to grin, "tall, dark, and Mormon seems good."

She looked at him. He hoped she would say something that would make him feel different, better, the way he'd felt just a minute or so earlier, but when she said, "My mom invites them every month," he didn't feel better.

Still, even here on this gray day, with her hair wet and stringy, and with a smear of dirt across her cheek, her eyes were a brown so deep and dark they seemed to pull him into them. "Well," she said, "let's make the green pastures greener," and then she turned away and pushed her spreader up the street toward the next lawn.

At 12:30, when every member of the northeast crew of jeeps was uniformly cold, wet, and hungry, Maurice Gritz said, "There's other work we ought to do, but let's save some of the fun for next time. So let's just clean up the truck, store the tools, and call it a day."

He passed out their paychecks—he'd clocked them out at one, "an extra half hour for working wet," he said—then began to walk away. "Oh," he said, stopping and turning back, "and when you're done, I need Traylor and Doyle to stop by my place for a minute." He pointed to the tin-roofed cottage beyond a small gully and next to the maintenance shed. "Just give a knock on the green door."

The crew put away their tools and swept out the truck. Nobody spoke, and when the other jeeps began to move toward the locker rooms, Mick began moving, too. Lisa said something to Traylor and went off to the girls' side to change.

At his locker, Mick put on a dry shirt and his dry leather jacket, but his Levi's were still wet and his boots were spongy. He was the first one out of the locker room, and when he saw no one around, he climbed on his bicycle.

"Mick!"

Lisa's voice.

She smiled when he turned. She must have brought a complete change of clothes because she was totally dry from the neck down. Only her hair was still wet. She looked pretty great. "I'm waiting for Traylor," she said, and nodded toward the locker room. "He still in there?"

Mick had seen Traylor leaning close to the mirror fussing with his hair. "Yeah, he's in there. He's doing some remedial work with the hair gel."

Lisa laughed. A silence followed, and then she said, "When Maurice is done firing me, I'm going to catch a ride home with my mom. There's room in the trunk for your bike if you want a ride, too."

Mick wanted to say yes, he wanted to a lot, but he had the feeling she was just being polite. And why should she be anything more than just polite? If what she wanted was tall, dark, and Mormon, he was none of the above.

"Naw," he said, "it's okay. It's not that far."

She shrugged and smiled. "All right. Just thought I'd ask."

Which made Mick think he'd been right. She *was* just being polite.

Traylor emerged from the locker room, blinking. His gelled hair went way beyond the normal weirdness.

"Over here, Traylor," Lisa called.

"See ya," Mick said, and stood in the pedals, but as he set off he circled back and, slowing slightly, said, "Just so you know, I think Maurice'd be crazy to fire you."

Lisa grinned and as Mick pulled away, she said, "I'll tell him you said so."

CHAPTER ELEVEN

These Minutes with Maurice

"So whattaya think this is all about, anyhow?" Sean Traylor said to Lisa as they walked across a wet mulch of leaves and pine needles toward Maurice Gritz's cottage.

Lisa didn't like toadies, so she didn't like Traylor. "I'd guess you're going to get some of the brownie points you've been after, and I'm not," she said.

Tall, skinny Traylor threw up his hands in a gesture of mock horror. "*Whoa!* That's kinda harsh."

If this had been someone else, Lisa might've been disarmed, but this was Traylor, who'd laughed at Maurice's Gomez line. "Yeah, I guess it was," she said matter-of-factly, and that ended their conversation.

Rain dripped from the corrugated roof of Maurice's cottage. Gray smoke steamed from its metal chimney. A wooden footbridge spanned the small gully, and the front door was enameled forest green. Traylor stepped forward to knock.

A few seconds passed and Traylor was about to knock again when the door suddenly swung open and there was Maurice, grinning and toweling his head dry. He was wearing only cutoff sweatpants—no shirt, no shoes—and Lisa thought he looked like one of those weird, too-buff, too-smooth guys you saw in muscle magazines. He draped the towel around his neck and motioned them inside.

"C'mon in where it's warm and dry."

Traylor stepped in first. Lisa followed but hovered near the door. Everything was neat—the bed was made, the floor was clean—and almost cozy. Rain tapped on the tin roof. At one end of the room the embers inside a wood-burning stove glowed a brilliant orange.

So, Lisa thought, our manly crew chief has been tending his cozy little fire while his campesinos work in the rain.

Behind Maurice, from the kitchen alcove, a kettle began to whistle. Maurice said, "You guys want some hot chocolate or instant coffee?"

Lisa and Traylor both shook their heads.

Maurice nodded. The whistle continued, but he ignored it. He said, "Look, Traylor, I just wanted you to know you did good work today. When jeeps do bad, I tell 'em. But when they do good, I tell 'em that, too, and you did good work today."

Traylor simultaneously nodded, blushed, and grinned.

From the kitchen the whistling grew shriller and more insistent. Maurice kept his smile fixed on Traylor. "You need a ride home, Traylor?"

Traylor said no, he had somebody waiting for him.

Maurice's tone turned politely dismissive. "Okay, Traylor, good work, and we'll see you next week."

Traylor nodded and set the door closed behind him when he left.

Maurice glanced for just a moment at Lisa, then turned and disappeared into the kitchen alcove. The whistling quieted and a minute later he came back out holding two cups of hot chocolate.

When he presented one to Lisa, she didn't know what to do except take it. She was still standing just inside the door, the doorknob within easy reach.

"You look like you're still freezing," Maurice said in a voice that seemed almost friendly. "Stand over by the stove." He gave an encouraging smile. "It'll warm you up."

Lisa didn't want to leave her place by the door, but she knew it would seem rude if she didn't. She moved over to the stove.

"There," he said, and Lisa had to admit the fierce heat from the stove *did* feel good, but the hot chocolate was stuff from a packet.

Maurice was regarding her. "You want something to eat? I make a pretty stellar omelette."

"No, thanks."

Maurice nodded. He sat down on a weight bench positioned between the bed and the wood-burning stove. He looked at her for a second and said, "Can we talk off the record for a minute here?"

Lisa said, "What does that mean?"

Maurice drank all of his hot chocolate in two or three gulps, then reached for the plastic tub of Bazookas on the bed stand. While unwrapping one, he said, "It means talking honestly and"—he grinned—"not for attribution."

"Sure. Okay."

"Well, for starters," Maurice said, "I think I owe you an apology."

Lisa waited.

"I get the feeling you think the way I've treated Uribe"—he pronounced it *you-rib-bee* again—"isn't quite kosher."

The woodstove made a steady ticking sound.

Lisa said, "You get that from Janice or figure it out for yourself?"

Maurice smiled and shrugged. "Little of both."

Lisa thought about it for a second or two, then took a deep breath. "Okay, first of all, it's *oo-ree-bay*, not *you-rib-bee*, and, yeah, I think you hold her to a much tougher standard than the rest of us, and, finally, it's not me you should be apologizing to, it's her."

To her surprise, Maurice's expression was serious, and he was nodding slightly. "Yeah, I was thinking maybe I ought to do that, too." He looked down at his bare feet for a few seconds, then he raised his eyes to her again. "So how do you like this job, Doyle?"

"Off the record, this isn't the best day to ask."

Again Maurice nodded thoughtfully. Then—and to Lisa this seemed like weirdness on top of weirdness—he lay back on the weight bench, grabbed the massively weighted chrome bar resting on its cradle above him, bowed his back, and began gruntingly working through a set of bench presses.

So that's how Ken-doll does it, Lisa thought. Only Ken-doll didn't appear to be wearing anything beneath his cutoff sweatpants. Lisa looked away.

As soon as Maurice sat up from his bench presses, Lisa set down her empty cup and said, "I've got to go now."

To her relief, Maurice simply nodded, went to the door, and held it open for her. "I'm glad we had this little talk," he said.

"Me, too," Lisa said, though she wasn't sure she was. She stepped into the rain.

"Doyle."

Lisa turned.

Maurice let his eyes settle on Lisa. "Off the record, Doyle, you have the most beautiful goddamn hair."

Lisa had always been taught to thank people for compliments, but if this was a compliment at all, it came covered with slime, so it was to her own surprise and dismay that she heard herself say, "Thank you."

As she turned and walked away, Lisa felt his eyes on her, and she had to fight the impulse to run, actually run for the footbridge.

CHAPTER TWELVE

Soldier on a Roll

The house was dark when Mick got home that Saturday afternoon. He hung his jacket over a chair and pushed the chair next to the radiator, then he went upstairs and took a long hot shower. After that, he checked messages—one from his father saying it was snowing hard at Tug Hill and he and Nora had decided to stay the night, and he'd call later to make sure Mick was okay, and one from Reece saying the weekend with his cousins in Connecticut was something that shouldn't happen to any species above crustacean. Mick smirked at this and went back to thinking about his father. He was glad they were staying over at Tug Hill. As long as his father was with Nora, Alexander Selkirk couldn't be.

In the kitchen, Mick fried onion rings and sliced sausages that he washed down with orange juice he drank straight from the carton. He tried to let Foolish out into the backyard, but the dog took one look at the rain and skulked back inside.

When Mick went upstairs and flipped on the computer, Foolish wedged into the knee well of the desk and curled across Mick's feet. Mick had meant to spend a little time trying to get into Nora's e-mail, but was stopped short when he found e-mail of his own.

I'm in my dorm room. If you get this by 7:00 P.M., call me. 555-5768. Myra.

Mick wondered if this was some kind of hoax Reece had dreamed up, but he called the number anyway. A girl answered.

"Myra?"

"Who?" the girl said. She was almost yelling. There was loud music in the background.

"Myra!" Mick yelled. "I'm calling for Myra!"

He heard the receiver bang down on a hard surface. The bass of the music kept thumping away, and there were girls yelling and laughing. Someone close to the receiver said, "You are so ballsy, Winifred." At least that's what Mick thought the voice said. He looked at the clock. Two minutes had passed. He'd just decided to give it one more minute when a voice said, "Hello?"

"Myra?"

"Yep, this is Myra."

"It's me, Mick."

"Nick?"

"Mick. Em. As in mittens."

"Oh! Hello, Mick as in mittens. I was hoping you'd call. Are you doing anything?"

Mick said he wasn't.

"Well, the commons doesn't serve on Saturdays and I'm starving. Want to get something to eat?"

It took a long moment for the question to penetrate, and another long moment to make himself say, "Sure."

"How soon can you get to Bing's?"

Mick made a rough computation. "Twenty minutes."

"Okay, then," she said, "twenty minutes at Bing's."

Myra Vidal was in a window booth with what looked like a college guy. She looked bored, but her face brightened when she spotted Mick. She waved him over and by the time he got to the booth the other guy was simultaneously sliding out and giving Mick a sidelong inspection.

"Thanks," Myra said to Mick as he sat down. "Frat Boy was making me crazy." She grinned. "I told him you were my study date."

"I guess he might've wondered where my books were," Mick said.

She smiled and looked at him with friendly eyes. After a second or so she said, "You know what's nice? You're even cuter than I remembered."

Mick felt color rising in his cheeks and she laughed. "But just as embarrassable." Another second passed, and already Mick felt himself settling into a comfort zone. "You hungry?" she said. "Do you like cheeseburgers? I love cheeseburgers, but can't eat them. But I'd like to watch you eat one."

"Why can't you eat them?"

"Twelve thousand fat grams," Myra said.

A waitress materialized, and when Mick glanced up, he had to look again. "Mrs. MacKenzie?"

The woman stared at him.

"I'm Mick Nichols. From Cub Scouts. You were my den mother."

Mrs. MacKenzie grinned. "Mick Nichols. You're a whole new you! Good thing you told me who you are." Then she whispered behind a cupped hand, "Former Cubs get extra fries."

After she went away with their order, Myra said, "I'll bet you were the cubbiest little Cub Scout."

Mick grinned and said, "I'd rather not talk about it."

Myra sipped from her coffee. "It was nice of you to show up on such short notice."

Mick waited.

"It's just that the dorm's crazy on Saturday nights, and Pam thinks it's her social responsibility to party on Saturday night." Myra's face clouded—it was as if she'd just had some kind of unpleasant thought—and then she gave her head a little shake. "Anyhow, I just wanted to stay out of trouble with somebody, and I thought of you."

Mick said, "Okay, is this a dis or not?"

"Not." She smiled.

"Good," Mick said, and it was good. Everything about this was good. He was warm and dry and sitting across the table from the kind of girl your average guy would kill for.

The waitress slid their food onto the table—a Caesar salad, no croutons, for Myra, and a cheeseburger for Mick. After a couple of bites, she said, "I've got a boyfriend, is why the whole partying thing doesn't really work for me. Boyfriend's in Berkeley."

Myra took another bite of salad and opened her wallet to a photograph of one of those rugged and casually handsome guys you hardly ever see except in suit ads. His name, she told Mick, was Ethan. Ethan wanted to be an environmental engineer. He'd gotten a full scholarship to Berkeley, is why he went so far off.

Mick nodded and flipped to the next picture—another guy, this one in cap and gown. "That's my brother," Myra said between bites. There were two other photographs, one of Pam and Myra laughing with their arms draped over each other's shoulder, the other of just Pam looking up from a book.

"Nice shot of Pam, no?"

Mick nodded.

"She's photogenic cubed. You will never see a bad picture of Pam Crozier."

110

Mick pushed the wallet back across the table and Myra took another look at the last photograph of Pam before folding the wallet up. "She knows about Ethan, and she knows that's why I don't like to party, but, you know, a guy calls, and she's off like a shot."

Mick said, "I guess a guy called tonight, huh?"

"Yeah. We were going to go to the library and a movie, keep ourselves out of trouble."

Mick had never understood the weird little snarls between girlfriends, and he didn't understand this one. They ate a few minutes in silence, and then Mick turned his head in surprise.

"You just see a ghost, or what?" Myra said.

Mick pried his eyes away. The two people who'd just walked into the diner were Maurice Gritz and Janice Bledsoe. Mick discreetly pointed, and Myra glanced back. "I kind of know those two," Mick said. "The guy's my supervisor at work and the girl's a friend of a friend."

Myra's eyes were wide with merriment. "You work for Maurice Gritz? Sonny, you've got my sympathy."

"You know him?"

"More than I care to. He escorted me to homecoming a few years ago." She smiled. "I had no choice. He was king and I was queen."

"And?"

"Let's just say I hope your friend of a friend is really, really good on defense." She grinned at Mick. "Is she?"

Mick made a little shrug. "I don't really know her, and the friend is really just kind of a friend." He looked down at his French fries. "In fact, today was the first time I ever talked to her."

Myra broke out a friendly laugh. "My smoke detector's picking up something here." He blushed, and Myra said, "I knew it!" Then, "I don't know what I'm doing in comp lit. I should be a psych major." She smiled at Mick. "So what's the new friend's name?"

"Lisa. Lisa Doyle."

"And she was friendly to you today?"

Mick lowered his eyes. "Kind of, but . . ."

"But what?"

Mick told her about the day, and how he was going to ask her to do something after work, but her friend, Janice Bledsoe, had mentioned tall, dark, and Mormon and that had kind of let the air out of the balloon.

Myra waved her hand dismissively. "I wouldn't read too much into it. Besides, what Janice was doing was a classic girl move. She sees you're getting friendly and she plays dumb and throws a wrench into the works."

"You think? I mean, why would a girl care if her girlfriend was talking to a guy?"

A light laugh from Myra. "Trust me on this. The female persuasion is unmatched for complicatedness."

Mick was chasing behind that thought when Myra said, "Describe Lisa Doyle."

He did, as best he could, and Myra, smiling, said, "My my my."

"What?"

"You seem to have all the details down pat."

Mrs. MacKenzie stopped to pour Myra another cup of coffee. When she departed, Myra said, "I guess you'd like it if I changed the subject from Lisa Doyle."

Mick nodded, and as Myra reached across the table to steal one of his French fries, her top loosened at the collar. Mick glimpsed swelling cleavage above a lace-trimmed bra and below the table his important part jumped to attention. Mick sat staring blandly at Myra and tried to think deflating thoughts—a squashed potato bug, his grandmother passing broccoli gas, a dog hit on the highway—but none of it worked, probably because he was still staring at someone as dazzling as Myra Vidal.

Myra licked a smudge of ketchup from a finger and said, "So did you tell that guy I don't know him from Adam?"

Mick didn't understand. "What guy?"

"Alexander somebody."

Color rose again in Mick's cheeks. "Oh, him. No, I haven't seen him." Myra's question had done what a squashed potato bug could not—his important part was again laying low.

Myra was both nodding and chewing. "Well, when you do see him, tell him . . . tell him he should be ashamed of himself."

Mick thought about it. "I will," he said.

He touched his inside pocket, where the green floppy disk was hidden, then he turned and looked out the window.

It was raining again in Jemison.

Myra offered to drive Mick home on her way to the library. She drove an ancient Honda Civic, rusty at the wheel wells and piled with books, but it had a pleasant smell to it, not the damp musty smell Mick had learned to expect from most old cars in Jemison. As she drove, Myra fumbled through a canvas sack of tapes at her feet, glanced at one, then handed it to Mick. "What does that say?"

It said Najma Akhtar, which Mick tried a syllable at a time. "Nadge-mah Ak-tar."

"Close enough," Myra said, and shoved it into the deck. Almost at once a quick rhythmic mix of drum, sitar, and female singing filled the car. "Wow," Mick said.

"Yeah. It knocked me out the very first time I heard it. Pam likes it, too, but only after smoking the demon weed." Myra smiled. "Whereas I don't need any alteration whatsoever to get lost in it." She shot Mick a glance. "It's Pakistani," she said, of the music.

Mick nodded. He'd never heard Pakistani music before.

"Try putting the seat all the way back and closing your eyes."

Mick did, and the pulsing music seemed to wrap around him and lift him up.

"Whattaya see?"

The truth was, he saw dancing women wearing not many clothes. "Dancing women," he said.

Myra laughed. "Yeah, sometimes I see them, too."

Mick kept his eyes closed, listening to the music, until Myra lowered the volume and said, "Okay, which way now?"

Mick popped his seat upright and got his bearings. They'd overshot his street and had to turn around, which Myra didn't seem to mind.

"There," he said as they approached his house. "Just past the old Chevy."

When they pulled up, Myra stared at the house. "Looks dark," she said.

"Yeah, my dad and stepmom got snowed in at Tug Hill, so it's just the dog and me. Except that's a predicate nominative so it should be 'the dog and I.' " He laughed and Myra laughed, too.

It was dark in the car except for the greenish illumination of the dashboard. The Pakistani music was still playing, but low. The windshield wipers went *thip thip thip*. Myra stared straight ahead, as if she were ready to get going. Mick reached for the door latch. "Well, thanks," he said.

"I could study here," she said, still staring forward, but then she turned toward Mick. In the faint greenish dashboard light she seemed to be smiling. "I mean, if you didn't mind."

While Mick turned on lights in the living room, Myra gave scratches to Foolish, then gravitated to the photographs on the fireplace mantel. She picked up one of Mick in his blue Scout uniform. "You *were* the cubbiest little Cub Scout," she said, and then scanned the other pictures. "Who's the dish?" she said.

Mick turned to see which picture she was referring to. It was Nora in swimsuit. "My stepmom. On their honeymoon in Mexico."

"She nice?"

Mick almost said, "I used to think so." Instead he said, "She's okay, I guess."

Myra turned. "Any particular reason she does no better than okay?"

"Not really." There was a sudden stillness Mick didn't like. "Anyhow," he said, "isn't that the deal? Aren't kids supposed to hate the stepparent?"

"You hate her?"

"No," Mick said quickly, and then, slower, "No. In fact, I like her." Then, "I just don't like everything she does."

"Like what?"

"I don't know. Just things."

"Just things like what?"

"I don't know!" He turned away.

He could feel Myra coming close to him, and then she had her hands on his shoulders, slowly massaging them. It felt wonderful. In a gentle voice she said, "You can tell me if I'm shooting in the dark here, but I have the feeling that something about your

115

stepmom has kind of stuck in your craw and one of these days you're going to have to cough it up."

She kept kneading his shoulders. He tried to make a sentence to begin, but couldn't. He just couldn't.

A half minute passed and Myra said, "Well, if you ever want to talk about it, I'd be happy to listen." She stopped massaging his shoulders and wrapped her arms around him so that Mick felt her breasts press against his back. She brought her lips close to his ear and said in a whisper, "Know what I like about this house? It looks like the kind of place that would have popcorn in it." She gave him a friendly kiss on the neck before breaking away.

Mick microwaved popcorn, which Myra absently ate one piece at a time while reading stretched out on the sofa. Mick laid a fire, but kept sneaking sidelong glances at Myra as she read. When he got out his geometry book, he found he had to sit with his back to her in order to concentrate. He was memorizing postulates when the phone rang. Myra didn't even look up as he passed by to the kitchen.

"Hello?"

"Hi. Is this Mick?"

It was a girl's voice. "Yep, it is."

"This is Lisa Doyle."

Without thinking Mick said, "It is?"

Lisa's laugh was nervous. "Yeah. Anyhow, I know it's kind of late, but I just wanted to tell you that Maurice didn't fire me." A pause. "And also how much better you made an otherwise horrible day."

Mick felt himself melting into the phone. "Yeah, you made it better for me, too."

Lisa made a soft murmuring laugh. "So are you going to go back next Saturday?"

"I guess so, yeah. Are you?"

"Yeah. My theory is Maurice was just trying to scare us off and I don't like the idea of being scared off."

Mick said he hadn't thought of it that way, but it sounded as good as anything else to explain Maurice's weirdness.

Lisa laughed. She told him how Traylor got his brownie points, and how Maurice claimed he was going to treat Lizette Uribe better, but that she'd believe it when she saw it.

"And that was it?"

"Yeah." Another pause, as if she was deciding whether to say something else. What she said was, "Except he had a nice cozy fire going while we were out getting soaked."

There was silence then and Mick felt desperate to say something, but he didn't know what. He said, "Where do you live anyhow?"

"On Nottingham Road, 1331. My father says it's a numerical palindrome because it's the same backward and forward. Where do you live?"

He told her: 2469 State Street.

"Too bad it isn't two-four-six-eight State Street," Lisa said. "Then it would be a house with its own cheer."

Mick said, "Maybe I should talk to my dad about moving." He hoped she would laugh, and she did, so he said, "I'll tell him this house is cheerless," and she laughed again. Talking to Lisa Doyle was quite a bit of fun. Also, to his surprise, easy.

"So why'd you ask about my address?" she asked in a playful voice.

Mick to his surprise said, "I looked up 'Doyle' in the phone book. There are eighteen of you."

"There are?" she said, and then, "Why were you looking up Doyles in the phone book?"

He figured she knew the answer—it was because he was interested in her—but what was he going to say, that every time he saw her at school he started to drool? He said, "Just killing time, I guess."

She laughed. "I'll save you some trouble. Want my phone number?"

"Yeah. Yeah, I do."

He had just written it down when she said, "Oh, flip."

"What?"

"Somebody's at the door. Can I call you back in a minute?"

"Sure."

After they hung up, Mick walked back into the living room. He didn't think Myra was paying any attention, but as he was trying to find his place in his geometry book, she said, "Lisa Doyle."

"What?"

"Lisa Doyle just called."

Mick shook his head and said, "You're actually kind of scary."

Myra smiled. "Heard you say Doyle. That helped." She kept smiling. "So what did Doyle have to say?"

"She said she liked talking to me at work today."

"Ha! Soldier, you're on a roll. What else did she say? Gimme gimme."

"Nothing. Or not much. Someone came to her door."

"Still," Myra said, thinking it over. "This is good. This is very good."

For the next thirty minutes Mick stared blankly at his geometry book and waited for the phone to ring again. It didn't. Finally he went into the kitchen to make sure the line wasn't dead. It wasn't. When he came back to the living room, Myra said, "Something wrong?"

Mick told her that Lisa had said she would call right back.

"And for some perfectly good reason she wasn't able to," Myra said. "The fact is she called you. The fact is she was thinking about you and picked up the phone and called you. Things are definitely in motion."

Mick munched a handful of popcorn and began to feel better. He liked the idea of things being in motion. He went back to staring at his geometry. About a half hour later he turned to glance at Myra and was surprised to find she was no longer reading her textbook, but looking into the fire. "You built a spectacular fire," she said. "You learn that in Cub Scouts?"

"Naw, my dad taught me. He loves a fire, everything about it. Every September we go cut the wood, rent a splitter, the whole nine yards."

"Sounds like a pretty good ol' dad."

"Yeah," Mick said quietly.

Myra was looking at Mick now, studying him. "How old are you?"

"Almost sixteen."

"Really? When's your birthday?"

Mick told her. June 2.

"So what do you want for your birthday other than smooching with Lisa Doyle?"

Mick laughed, then shrugged. What he wanted was to feel normal about Nora again, and about his father, and about his life. "Nothing, I guess."

"Oh, we all want something," Myra said. She smiled at him, but it seemed like a sad smile. "Some of us just don't own up to it."

She went back to staring into the fire. A long pleasant silence stretched out, and then Myra said, "I heard a line from a show tune the other day. I don't usually like show tunes, but the line was, 'I want you to see me, to see the face behind the face behind the face.'" She turned to Mick. "Isn't that a good way of putting it?"

For once Mick thought he understood. "Kind of like when Reece and I saw you and Pam in the Jemison parade and thought of you one way, and then that day when we talked to you I remember how surprised I was that you were not only, you know, really really good looking, but also really really nice."

Myra laughed quietly. "The face behind the face." She gave him a strange smile. "You only have one more to go."

Then she was staring again into the fire.

By eleven o'clock, Mick was fighting yawns and Myra was going through the video cabinet. "*On the Waterfront!*" she said suddenly, pulling the video from its case. "I've wanted to see this forever."

"So do you ever sleep?" Mick asked with a grin.

Myra laughed. "Never before two. That wasn't decaf our waitress was pouring me." She pushed the video in, turned off the lights, and settled into the sofa. A minute or so later she said, "God, just look at Marlon Brando. No wonder Tennessee Williams was slobbering all over him."

"Who's Tennessee Williams?" Mick said, not that he cared. He was too tired to care about anything. It seemed like this day had started about fifty hours ago.

"He wrote *Streetcar Named Desire* and Brando was in that, too."

"Oh."

Myra glanced at Mick, and his tiredness must've showed. "Here," she said. "Put your head in my lap and watch till you can't."

Mick lay down uncertainly, but in a few seconds he'd snuggled his head into her lap and she'd covered him with the throw blanket from the back of the sofa. She lowered the volume on the TV and began slowly rubbing his neck. This should've made him sleepy, but it didn't. Just the opposite. He had his right arm beneath him, but the other lay on top of Myra's pant leg, just above the knee. Slowly, timidly, in this dark room with only the flickering bluish light from an old black-and-white movie on TV, Mick let his hand creep up and with every tiny increment of movement he became less sleepy. When his hand reached Myra's thigh, she took hold of it and returned it to the knee. "If I wanted to be manhandled," she said gently, "I would've stuck with a frat boy."

Mick felt stricken with a confused shame. It wasn't just that he'd done something wrong, it seemed like it was something more. Like he'd betrayed her. Or somehow fallen short. Either way, it felt pretty bad, but a second later Myra had gone back to rubbing his neck.

And that was how Nora and Mick's father found them when they unlocked the front door and turned on the lights.

Nora and Mick's father stood in stunned silence.

Mick sat up abruptly and said the first thing that came into his head. "I thought you were at Tug Hill."

His father didn't speak, but Nora did. She looked at Myra and said, "Who're you, the baby-sitter?"

Myra's voice was the slightest bit unsteady. "Actually, I'm Mick's study date."

Mick stared up at Nora and his father. They stared back—his

father looking confused, Nora looking annoyed. Mick didn't understand either one. He said, "This is Myra Vidal."

Myra stood, but nobody spoke until Myra said, "You must be Mick's folks."

They still didn't speak.

Myra said, "We were studying—geometry for him and Gide for me—and then we decided to watch a movie." When Nora and Mick's father met this, too, with silence, Myra turned to Mick. "Maybe I'll catch the end next time." She turned to the adults. "Nice to meet you," she said, and then, after calmly gathering her books, she was gone.

A few seconds passed in silence and then Nora said, "How old is she anyway?"

A sourness flooded into Mick. "Guess I forgot to ask."

Nora glared back. "Where'd you find her, in the Yellow Pages under 'Escorts'?"

"Hey, c'mon, Nora," Mick's father said, and Nora turned her glare on him, but it suddenly dissipated. "Maybe I'm just too tired for this," she said. "I'm going to bed."

After she'd gone, Mick's father said, "We couldn't find a room. Well, we did find one, but it was three hundred bucks, a suite with a hot tub. I would've sprung, but Nora said, 'Three hundred bucks for a place to sleep? I don't think so.'" Mick's father smiled at Mick. "So she sleeps in the car while I drive home."

Mick waited a few seconds. "Nothing went on here, Dad. All we did was study and then we were just watching the movie. And Myra's really nice. I mean, I know she's got looks, but she's been really nice to me."

"Hey," his father said, "maybe she just has an eye for quality." Then, in his joking voice, "Besides, I always knew the Mickman

122

would come home with a knockout one of these days." He looked at Mick. "It was just a day or two earlier than I expected." A pause. "I guess to a parent everything seems a day or two early."

And then he was stepping away. "Okay," he said, "let's kill the lights and hit the hay. I think I can sleep for about three days."

Mick followed tiredly behind. He thought he could, too.

But that night, a little after two o'clock, Mick suddenly awakened in his bed. A faint clicking sound seemed to be coming from the hallway. He went to the door and pushed it open.

It was Nora, in her robe, sitting at the computer.

A look of surprise crossed her face, and then was gone. "Oh, hi, Mick," she said in a loud whisper. "I'm working on lesson plans."

Mick knew that she expected him to nod and go back to bed, but he didn't. He began to walk around the desk. "Which class?" he said, and watched her hand move to the escape key.

"That sheep-to-sweater enrichment class," she said, "but I'm done now."

When Mick's eyes reached the screen, it was dark.

CHAPTER THIRTEEN

The Community of
True Inspiration

It was like stepping into the House of Brisket when Lisa Doyle
and her mother opened the front door after church. Lisa's mother
gave her two-note, I'm-home whistle and slipped out of her black
leather pumps. "You here, Elliot?"

Lisa removed her shoes, too, and padded into the kitchen, but
her father wasn't there. He must have put the brisket on the grill
and then started messing with the greenhouse he was building. It
was cold out, but gorgeous. Ordinarily, sun plus brisket equaled
total Sunday happiness, but Lisa still felt weird about not calling
Mick back and about whatever was going on between Janice and
him who was psychotic Maurice.

It had been strange enough to see Janice loafing around with
Maurice in a golf cart, but then, last night, right after she got the
nerve to call Mick Nichols, there Janice was again, on the porch,
wearing a tight low-cut shirt while Maurice's gangmobile with
tinted windows waited at the curb.

"Want to drive around with me and Maurice?" Janice had
asked, almost breathless, really, as though she were inviting Lisa
to join her and Prince William.

"Um, no, thanks," Lisa said. "I've got that paper to finish."

"The Community of Truly Weird Inspiration?" All sophomores had to write a paper on state history, and Lisa was doing hers on the Ebenezers, who had founded a place they called the Community of True Inspiration.

"Yep," Lisa said. "They knit, they cook, they pray."

"They have no fun whatsoever," Janice said.

Lisa looked at Janice's neck and wondered if those were hickeys.

"C'mon, Leeze. It's Sat-ur-day night."

Over Janice's shoulder Lisa could see the tinted window on the driver's side of the Honda descending, revealing Maurice's face and shoulders. Lisa said, "Did you mention to him how much he creeped us out when we were jogging?"

Janice laughed. "He didn't even know that was us. He said that because we looked so cute and smoochable in our sweatsuits he just felt obliged to introduce himself."

Lisa glanced again over Janice's shoulder, which Maurice seemed to notice. He snapped a quick bubble and said, "*Buenos noches*, Doyle. Coming?"

"Can't!" Lisa called. Then, softer, she told Janice, "I don't think my dad would like it."

"Sometimes you are *so* tame," Janice said.

Lisa became again aware of the internal pilot light that had been burning more or less constantly since Mick smiled at her. Now, before Janice could turn and go, she said, "I called Mick Nichols tonight. In fact, I was talking to him when you knocked."

A laugh burst from Janice. "Well, aren't you the spunky monkey!" Then, as if something just occurred to her, she said, "You were talking to him at home?"

Lisa said she'd called him at home, so, yeah, he was at home. "Why?"

125

"Well, earlier tonight he was at Bing's and you'll never guess who with."

A strange wariness stole over Lisa. "So then I guess you'll just have to tell me."

"Former Miss Jemison. Myra Vidal."

"Myra Vidal?"

From the car, Maurice called, "Yo, Janissimo. Let's get mo-bile."

Lisa gave Janice a look. "Janissimo?" she said.

Janice shrugged, grinned, and turned to go. "Call me later, okay?"

After Janice had raced back through the rain to Maurice's car, Lisa knew she should call Mick back. She'd said she would. But now she didn't feel like it. The pilot light had gone out. She went upstairs, where she read that the Ebenezer men and boys sat separately from the Ebenezer women and girls at the Fourteen Holy Helpers Church. "Good thinking, Holy Helpers," Lisa had said in a soft voice to herself, and had gone to bed without calling anyone.

From the upstairs bedroom, where Lisa had gone to change out of her church dress, she could look down into the greenhouse in progress. A toolbox lay on the yellow, snow-bitten grass, and inside the unroofed framework, her father's bald spot gleamed. He was measuring and making pencil marks. His radio was beside him, and she could hear the droning play-by-play of a ballgame.

Her dad had never been Mormon. He was a history professor, a man who relied on checkable facts and primary sources. "A man says an angel told him to look in the ground," her father said. "He says he dug up gold records, *The Book of Mormon*. He says he translated it, showed the gold tablets to twelve people, then the angel took the tablets back. Took them back! If a history professor tried that, he'd be a laughingstock. A farm boy does it and he's a prophet." So her father came to church only on daddy-daughter nights and bowed his head politely when her mother blessed the food.

Lisa cranked open the window. "Who's winning?" she called.

"Mets," her father said, "but give them an inning or two and that'll change. Want to come listen with me?"

She shook her head. "History paper."

"Ah, the Ebenezers!" he said. "The crazy old knitters. If you need some help, just yell and I'll make myself scarce." Her father's idea of a joke. In fact, both he and her mother would help Lisa with her homework for as long as she could stand it, which wasn't very long.

Lisa left the window open and sat down, but she hadn't been reading long before she heard the compressed sound of car doors. "Missionaries at the threshold!" her mother called.

Lisa checked her teeth and her face in the mirror, and wondered if she felt more of a stomach buzz when she thought of Elder Keesler or when she thought of Mick Nichols. She experimented as she walked down the stairs. *Mick Nichols. Elder Keesler. Mick Nichols. Elder Keesler.* Hard to tell. And probably a sin to think of an elder that way. The doorbell rang, and her whole nervous system seemed to vibrate slightly.

When she opened the door, Elder Pfingst smiled and extended a rough, callused, pinkish hand. Polyester trousers, poly-cotton blend white shirt, but at least his pilled tie wasn't of the clip-on variety. And Elder Keesler was indeed wearing the cool retro tie. He extended a smooth, large hand, and touching it made her stomach do some sort of a flip. Fortunately, before she had to say more than "Hi," her sawdust-sprinkled, Heineken-scented father tramped in the back door and said, "Welcome, Holy Helpers. How goes the work of the Lord?"

Elder Pfingst and Elder Keesler looked confused.

"Um, it's a joke," Lisa said. "The Holy Helpers founded some towns near Buffalo, and I'm writing a paper about it for History."

"Let them come in, Elliot," her mother called from the kitchen. "Ask them into the living room while I get this food into a serving dish."

Her father nodded toward the pile of shoes on the entry floor. "Check your guns and shoes at the door," he said, and they slipped off their shoes. Elder Pfingst's socks were white; Elder Keesler's, an expensive-looking gray.

"So where're you boys from?" her father asked, rubbing his elbows conversationally.

"Clinton, Utah," Elder Pfingst said in a cheerful voice while Palooka, her father's spotted mutt, rammed his nose into Elder Pfingst's privates. "Whoa," the elder said, rubbing Palooka's head. "You're a good old dog, aren't ya? A good old dog."

Lisa's father shifted his gaze to Elder Keesler, who said, "Boston," and got the next crotch-poke from the Palookster.

"Down!" Lisa said, blushing at the way all of their attention was now focused between Elder Keesler's legs.

"Watch the Holy Helpers, Palooka," her father said blandly, and Lisa pulled the dog into the kitchen.

The kitchen, luckily or unluckily, was close enough to the living room so that Lisa could hear her father saying, "Can I get you fellas a beer?"—his standard opening line to Mormon missionaries. "Just kidding," he said, and the sofas whumped a little bit, meaning the sitting down had now occurred. Lisa yearned fervently for an Ebenezer meal, men at one table, women at another, and all conversation banned. Then she wished briefly that her father were not the Howard A. Ballangast Professor of History and self-appointed Mormon-griller.

"So what made you go on a mission, Elder Keesler?" her father asked.

Lisa dropped ice cubes into a pitcher and realized she was nervous for Elder Keesler, who was clearing his throat.

"Well," he said, "if you believe you know a truth, and you think it can make people happy, I think you should share it." He paused, and no one said anything. Then he added, "That, and the chance to ride a bicycle in suit pants."

Her father laughed, a good sign, and Lisa began to breathe easier. Style points to Elder K., she thought.

"What about you?" her father asked Elder Pfingst.

"Same thing," he answered. "I wanted to share my testimony."

This standard-issue pronouncement was met with silence. No style points for Helper Pfff, Lisa thought.

"Okay, people, let's eat," her mother said, and once they were each seated in front of a rose china plate and a white napkin fan, Lisa was free to notice that Elder Keesler's hair was black, but his eyes were gray-blue. That he wore a ring with a flat blue stone in it. That he held his fork hump-up in his left hand while cutting carrots with his right, thereby allowing a quick and graceful biteful the moment cutting was complete. It looked refined and she made a note to try it herself. She was noticing that he hadn't drunk a single drop of milk when her father asked his favorite question: why the Mormons hadn't given the priesthood to blacks until 1978.

"Don't worry," Lisa said quickly. "Dad always asks the missionaries that. It's the price you pay for his brisket."

129

"Oh," Elder Keesler said, running his finger around the rim of his full milk glass. "Did you want to try that one, Elder Pfingst?"

Elder Pfingst shook his head and smiled broadly. "I think the eldest elder should lead the way in all things," he said.

"Well," Elder Keesler said slowly, "you can see it as a sign that the prophet is listening to God, or that he's listening to social pressure."

"Which way do you see it?" her father asked.

"I guess I'd lean toward the former," Elder Keesler said.

"Well, let's see then. Either God once said that blacks didn't deserve the priesthood, and then he waffled and said they do, which even in the most generous light would mean that God used to be racist and now isn't," Mr. Doyle said. "Or the church, run exclusively by white American men, used to be racist and now isn't—or doesn't want to seem so."

"Well," Elder Keesler said, nodding and casting a rueful look at Lisa. "I see your point." Then he looked back at Mr. Doyle. "But I guess I'd argue that it's a little ungenerous to criticize the Church for correcting course in a country that's still correcting course in regard to those whose lives began in a slavery that was not only barbaric but constitutionally sanctioned."

Lisa felt a strange thrill sweep through her, the thrill of hearing someone find the right words and tone to defend the Church to her father. Her mother usually resorted to things like, "Well, Elliot, God's ways are not our ways," and when she herself was cornered the best she could do was, "I just like the way it makes me feel, Dad."

After staring at Brother Keesler for a long second, her father broke into a grin.

"I could quibble over the belatedness of what you call the

Church's course correction, Mr. Keesler, but I'd rather not. In any case, your defense was as cogent as it was spirited." His smile seemed to be one of genuine pleasure. "When you leave your missionary work behind, you might look into politics or the law."

Elder Keesler lowered his eyes.

"So how many notches do you have on your belt?" Lisa's father said.

Elder Keesler looked up in confusion. "Sir?"

"How many converts?"

"Oh." For once, Elder Keesler seemed at a loss for words.

"Slews," Elder Pfingst piped up. "Brother Keesler just has a way of bringing people into his words, letting his testimony wrap around them, and making them feel safe and happy for maybe the first time in their lives." He grinned pinkly. "It's something to see."

Lisa had to keep herself from staring at Elder Keesler. She bet it *was* something to see, and to feel. In fact, she almost wished she hadn't been born into the Church so she could've been converted by Elder Keesler.

Everyone ate in polite silence for a few seconds, and then Elder Pfingst said, "Where did this milk come from?"

"Cows are the usual suspects," Lisa's father said with a smile.

"A local dairy," her mother said, and she smiled, too, at Elder Pinkest, as Lisa now thought of him, because his nose, forehead, and fingertips shone like the curves of a pink piggy bank. "Why?"

"I know good milk," he said. "I come from a dairy farm."

This led to a theology-free discussion of the Pinkest family farm, which led to the Ebenezers, who, Lisa said as she served slices of banana cake, lived communally and were assigned their trades—blacksmith, dairy farmer, butcher, carpenter.

"They surrendered a lot of autonomy, but there were sensible aspects to it, too," her father said, and took another big bite of cake. "For example, if the Church Elders gave permission to couples who wanted to marry, the man had to go away for a year. Sort of a maximum-security waiting period—no communication whatsoever for three hundred and sixty-five days. Then, if the man came back and still loved the woman, and she still loved him, they got married."

"Sort of like missionaries," Elder Keesler said. After he'd finished his cake, he'd taken his full glass of milk and, in six or seven slow swallows, drained it completely. It was what he'd been waiting for, but Lisa wondered how he could have known there would be a milk-worthy dessert. And then she didn't wonder, because it suddenly seemed to her that Elder Keesler might just know everything.

"Do you have a girl waiting for you at home, then?" her mother asked.

"No," he said, "but Holy Helper Pfingst does. Her name is Marie and to help Brother Pfingst remember her, she regularly sends him cookies." Elder Keesler smiled his soft, gray-eyed smile. "Of which I am the happy collateral recipient."

"Oh, how nice," her mother said.

Yes, Lisa thought, relieved that Elder Keesler wasn't taken. How nice.

Elder Pfingst continued beaming over his girlfriend's gifts. "Oatmeal gumdrop are my personal faves," he said. "Those and snickerdoodles."

Lisa turned her eyes on Elder Keesler. Her heart pounded wildly. She could hardly believe herself. She stared brazenly into his eyes. "How about you, Brother Keesler? What're your personal favorites?"

It was as if his gray-blue gaze narrowed somehow and found a way to slip inside her and look around. "I'll tell you the truth," he said, smiling. "I never met a cookie I didn't like."

Before taking up other conversation, he kept his eyes on her for just an extra half second, but it was an important half second, during which Lisa felt a strange tingling in every single part of her body.

CHAPTER FOURTEEN

Mary, Mary, Quite Contrary

Mick and his father had spent Sunday morning digging up a garden plot for Nora. They folded in chicken manure followed by a worm-rich batch of kitchen compost. Then they began rebuilding the wood-and-chicken-wire frame that was supposed to keep the red squirrels out, but never did.

The garden was Nora's summer pastime. Every year Mick's father said he'd do the preplanting grunt work, but after that his only job was to consume the fruits of her labor. Mick wasn't so cavalier. Past summers he'd enjoyed working with Nora in the garden, especially when it was hot and she would work in shorts and a halter top. On those days he'd liked working right along with her. But that seemed now like somebody else's former life, and he was glad Nora wasn't here today.

But then she was.

"Guess who just called?" she said as she arrived with two cold Cokes in hand.

Mick's father wiped sweat from his forehead with the back of his hand. "Well, if it was Kim Basinger, I hope you told her to stop pestering me."

Nora chuckled politely. "It was Clyde D.," she said.

Clyde D. Duzinski was an old high-school friend of Mick's

father's, and in addition to running an auto body shop, he ran a small car lot on the side that specialized in custom muscle cars. The problem was, Clyde D. couldn't fix engines and didn't know anyone who could, except Mick's father.

Mick's father smiled. "Clyde D. got problems?"

"All over the place. He's supposed to deliver a classic B.T.O. to somebody tonight who's willing to pay very big bucks for the classic B.T.O., only the classic B.T.O. won't go."

"G.T.O.," his father said mildly. "It stands for Gran Turismo Omologato."

Nora shrugged. "Anyhow, I took pity on him and you, and said you'd be over there as fast as your cute little legs would carry you."

This surprised Mick—Nora usually hated seeing his father go off to Clyde D.'s because it meant he'd be there at least four or five hours. It must've surprised his father, too, because he said, "Really?"

Nora smiled and shrugged. "You can finish the squirrel frame next weekend. No big deal."

Everyone dispersed. Nora went back into the house, Mick started putting the tools away, and his father drove off to Clyde D.'s. When Mick went back into the house, the shower was running upstairs. So, he thought. The stepmom's stepping out.

A plan took shape in Mick's mind. He'd thought of it before, but only in the abstract. Now he was going to do it. He changed clothes, grabbed his jacket and book bag, then yelled through the bathroom door to Nora, "I'm going to the library!"

He waited for her to yell back, but suddenly the door opened and she was yelling, "What?" and then, seeing him, said, "Oh."

Nora was naked. Also embarrassed.

So was Mick.

She quickly stepped back and peered modestly around the door. "Thought you were downstairs yelling up," she said.

Mick wasn't exactly sure what he'd just seen or what he'd just felt. He did know he was still blushing. "I just said I was going to the library."

She nodded.

Although she'd stepped back, the rich smell of her perfume still hung in the air. He'd seen the perfume in her medicine cabinet. It came in a red box and was called Ambush. "Where're you going?" he said, even though he was pretty sure he knew where she was going.

This time he could read her expression. It turned purposefully vague. "To the mall," she said, "and then I have a spinning lesson."

"A spinning lesson?"

"On a real-life colonial spinning wheel. For that enrichment class. There's a woman in Mattydale who teaches spinning."

Mick nodded and started to leave, but turned back. "Sorry about—" He pointed to the doorway, where her naked body had been.

Nora's face eased. "Don't be. It was my fault, not yours." She smiled. "Worse things have happened. What do you say we just forget about it?"

Mick nodded again, but the one thing in the whole wide world he was pretty sure he wouldn't do was forget about seeing Nora naked.

Mick took his books and left by the front door as if leaving for the library, but then he circled back into the garage by the side door. The garage was pitch black inside. He felt his way to Nora's 320i and didn't hesitate. He opened the back door, slid in, and hid himself under a blanket behind her seat.

*   *   *

Ten minutes later, the garage light suddenly went on. Nora's heels clicked on the garage floor. Mick's heart pounded wildly. He felt like he couldn't breathe. He wanted to leap from the car, say, "Oh, excuse me," and beat it out of there. But he clamped shut his eyes and lay perfectly still.

Nora got in and the car filled with her perfume. She started the engine, remoted open the garage door, and began backing out. He knew how she backed out. She always used her sideview mirrors. She never turned around.

Once on the street, it was as if she were breaking free. The windows went down, the oldies station went on loud, and the rpm's climbed to a whine before she shifted gears. On the corners, Mick had to brace himself to keep from sliding from his little space behind her seat. The floor of the car wasn't clean and Mick suddenly had the feeling he'd just inhaled sheep wool. He felt a faint pre-sneeze tingle in his nose. Once he actually did begin to sneeze, but swallowed it back down just as Billy Joel blasted into "Piano Man" with Nora singing along.

On one smooth straightaway Nora suddenly made a gasping sound and, braking hard, the wheels locked, rubber squealed, and the rear of the car slid slightly sideways. There was something else, too—a quick *thipping* sound followed by the tinkle of glass. Mick waited for more damage, but none came. Still, he wouldn't have been able to fight the impulse to jump up and see what was going on if Nora hadn't said in an exhaling voice, "Okay, pal, you are one lucky pooch." Then she said, "But your doggy life just cost Beelzebub his horn."

So a dog had run in front of her, and she'd missed it, but her devil had smacked against the windshield? That, anyhow, was what Mick guessed. Whatever it was, it seemed to change Nora's mood slightly. She lowered the radio and stopped singing along. She also began driving slower, and at one point she stopped at a light so long that someone behind her tapped his horn to get her going again.

Finally the BMW came to a stop, but Mick had no idea where. It was covered parking, he could tell that, and there were sounds. A car door slamming. An engine starting. People's voices. Nora was quietly doing something up front, maybe putting on lipstick. Then the familiar rattle of a Tic Tac tapped from its plastic case. The windows powered up, her door slammed, the other doors auto-locked, and the clicking of her heels dimmed as she walked away.

Mick slowly raised his head. He was in the mall parking lot, all right, and the red devil on the dashboard, less the tip of one horn, stared back at him with black, curious eyes. Mick turned and, there, perhaps a hundred yards away, was Nora, in a lemon yellow sweater heading toward Kauffman's, and then pausing a full second or two before passing through the automatic doors that spread open before her.

Mick jumped from the car, ran through the parking lot, and entered Kauffman's carefully, scanning the aisles of mens' and boys' wares before working his way through not just that floor but the two floors above. Nora wasn't there. He moved down the promenade toward the food court, looking for lemon yellow sweaters. There were none. He nodded at a couple of kids from school, but kept moving, steadily scanning the sea of faces. With a small and sudden shock of recognition, he spotted Mr. Cruso, his ever-friendly history teacher and just about the last person Mick wanted to talk to, so he sidestepped into Borders until Mr. Cruso passed by. Then he checked the food court, all the women's stores, and went back to the parking lot. Nora's car was still there, but Nora wasn't.

On the dashboard, the red ceramic devil peered back.

He'd lost her.

Mick sighed, pulled the bus guide from his book bag, and twenty minutes later took a bus that dropped him at the steps of the downtown library, where for the next three hours he did his geometry and history homework and read all of *The Metamorphosis* for world lit, even though only ten pages had been assigned. It was about a man named Gregor Samsa who went to bed as a human and woke up as a cockroach.

When Mick closed the book, it was almost five, but he didn't feel like going home yet. In his notebook, he began idly to draw a cockroach. The thought of Gregor Samsa, helpless on his back, left behind in his own house, made him think of his father. Someone had left a dictionary on the library table. Mick opened it to "helpless." "Destitute of help or strength." But that didn't really fit his father. What fit his father was "clueless." Maybe what his father needed was information, and maybe he, Mick, needed to provide it. He tried to imagine it. "Dad, there's this guy named Alexander Selkirk." First his father wouldn't believe it, and then, when he did, it would just turn him quiet and miserable, like when his mother left, and what good would that do?

Mick remembered his father's joking about Nora's ulterior motives, and now he idly flipped the pages until he found "ulterior." "Situated beyond or on the farther side." Well, that's where Nora was all right. Situated beyond. The question—the real question—was how to get her back.

CHAPTER FIFTEEN

Dough

Sunday, 3:25. Elders Keesler and Pfingst had climbed into their hatchback and driven away. For the next hour or so, while her mother minutely cleaned the kitchen, Lisa sat nearby addressing invitations to a Doyle family reunion at Green Lakes in June. "Hope they don't come," Lisa said under her breath after almost every address, until finally her mother said, "God frowns on murmurings and so do I."

When the kitchen work was done, her parents went upstairs to nap. At this time on Sunday afternoons, Lisa usually took a nap herself, but she was too keyed up today. She waited until her parents were settled upstairs and then called Janice.

"Didja kiss the Keesler?" Janice asked.

Lisa laughed. "Oh, yeah, right there in front of his companion, my dad, and the Lord."

"The Lord came?"

Lisa laughed again but started to worry that they were taking God's name in vain. "Wanna make cookies?" she asked. "I feel like taking a bike ride, and I could bring chocolate chips."

"You'd have to bring butter, too. The Momster's boycotting butter right now on the principle that it comes from incarcerated cows."

"Are you a vegan now?"

"Me? No. Mom? Yes."

"Does that mean I have to bring my own eggs?"

"Lemme check." There was a door-opening sound and a pause. "No. We still have some pre-vegan eggs in here. Wow. There's even some bacon."

"Okay. Save the eggs till I get there," Lisa said, and went to put on her shorts, wondering about the moral distinction between mailing cookies to an elder and delivering them in person. Either way, they were just cookies, no?

Lisa's calf muscles were tight from pumping uphill, but before she carried her bicycle up the steps of Janice's building, she cruised along the street to check for Elder Keesler's hatchback. There were eighteen cinderblock buildings in Home Park Gardens, which, as Janice's mom liked to point out, contained no homes, no parks, and no gardens. Just three rows of putty-colored buildings, three strips of patchy grass, and three smooth interlocking streets. Lisa noted that Elder Keesler's back window looked out on a spidery jungle gym, an empty clothesline, and a fire escape. The curtains of Elder Keesler's second-story apartment were open, revealing nothing but the back of a couch and a hanging light fixture. Elder Keesler's car was nowhere to be seen. A little girl was swinging, and she watched Lisa without expression. She stopped swinging and watched Lisa get off her bicycle. Perhaps she was still staring as Lisa climbed three flights of stairs with her bicycle.

"Janice?" Lisa called. She was breathing heavily. "Can I bring in the dairy product?"

Janice came to the door and said the vegan-mother was out.

"She's off interviewing a Buddha or something for the spirituality article," Janice said.

Lisa took a deep breath and said, "That would be Buddhist, I'm guessing." She propped her bike against the outside wall and lay down on the worn Persian rug that covered the living room floor. "Very far," she said. "Your dwelling is very far."

They melted butter, poured sugar, cracked eggs, splashed vanilla, dumped the chips in, and began eating the dough, just like always. But while Janice was sampling a big hunk from the end of a wooden spoon, two quick knocks came on the door. Lisa thought, illogically, of Elder Keesler (whose status she'd been checking on repeatedly via the living room window, whereupon Janice would say, "He's not home yet, Agent Doyle").

Another two raps, softer now, and Janice's eyes widened. "Sounds Maurician," she said, and grinned.

She was right. Maurician shorts, T-shirt, and muscles were suddenly in the room. Maurice smiled and removed his sunglasses. "Hello, Ms. Doyle," he said. "Hello, Janissimo." His eyes were drawn then to the wooden spoon. "Batter?" His tone made it seem distasteful.

"We call it dough," Janice said. "Yummy, yummy dough. Want some?"

Maurice seemed actually to recoil from the thought. "Uncooked eggs? You ladies ever heard of salmonella?"

Janice rolled her eyes and picked up another small hunk of dough with her fingers, which she applied to the end of her spoon and consumed. "Yum," she said again, but with less enthusiasm than before.

Maurice crossed his arms and looked out the window. "You

going to bake those now, or do you want to enjoy the afternoon in *mi carro?*"

"Where're we going?" Janice asked, grinning and dropping her spoon into the sink. She looked happy, Lisa noticed. Very happy.

"Driving," Maurice said. "Out and about. Maybe to Green Lakes."

"We can put the dough in the refrigerator," Janice said, looking hopefully at Lisa. When she saw the look on Lisa's face, Janice said, "Or you can stay here, Leeze, and bake them. My mom won't care."

Which is what she did, uncomfortably. Janice brushed her hair, applied honey-apricot lip gloss, and hopped down the steps behind Maurice. The two of them got into his car and Janice, before shutting the door, waved cheerfully. Watching them go made Lisa feel like Janice's mother. She had to resist yelling, "Be careful!"

Lisa put the cookies in the oven, still feeling motherish. She sat down on the sofa and tucked her toes between the cushions. Her Rockets' Red Glare nail polish was chipped. She nibbled an index cuticle and looked out the window at the meaningful apartment. The sun was getting that gold look, and the trees, filling out now with feathery leaves, were almost transparent in the horizontal light. The motherish feeling dissipated and she sat very still, inhaling the hot cookie smells, aware that she was expecting something and that expectancy was almost as delicious as eating. Soon a car containing two missionaries, two leather-bound Bibles, a street map of Jemison, and the possibility of sin would roll up and park in full sight of the Bledsoes' window.

Then suddenly she wasn't just waiting. The car appeared as it had appeared in her mind: the crimped hood, the white shirts, the twin bodies in their seat belts. She heard the dim kachunk-ing of a car door and Elder Keesler unfolded his long body from the tiny car. Lisa's heartbeat sped wildly. Maybe you shouldn't go over there, she thought, but even as she was thinking this, she was back in the kitchen, sliding warm cookies onto a paper plate that said, HAPPY HALLOWEEN!

It was Elder Keesler who answered the door. "Hi," he said, sur-prised and happy, Lisa thought, to see her there. Then something else crossed his face. Confusion, maybe. He didn't step back to let her in.

"Um, Elder Pfingst was beat," he said, opening the door a bit wider, but still not stepping back. She noticed his stockinged feet. "He's lying down right now." He nodded toward a bedroom door. Closed. Which meant that if she came in, technically they would be alone. Technically, unchaperoned. Lisa realized her palms were sweating.

"Oh!" she said. "Well, I was just going to drop these off, really."

"Chocolate chip?" Elder Keesler asked, leaning over to lift up the foil and peek in.

His forehead was white and peaceful against the darkness of his cropped black hair. "Yep," she said stupidly. "Chocolate . . . chip." She wasn't normally so awkward, but being with him made her stammer. "So why don't I just leave them?" she said. "That way when Elder Pfingst feels better, you can reciprocate. Like with his girlfriend's cookies. Not that this is the same." She was crimson now, and so was his forehead.

"No, I get it," he said.

"Well, okay," Lisa said. She held the plate out, and he took them.

"And it is kind of the same, isn't it?" he asked.

She looked up again, and met his eyes, which were lit up, somehow, by the goldness in the street.

"Yes," she said, no longer feeling stupid, flushed now with a happier, riverlike sensation.

"Okay, then," he said. "I'll see you next Sunday, right?"

"Yes," she said. "Right." She was backing away now. "At church."

She turned around, waved, and crossed the gold, long-shadowed street. The little girl on the swings, Lisa noticed, was no longer there.

CHAPTER SIXTEEN

Sunday Drive

When Maurice and Janice pulled away from Home Park Gardens, Janice did what she always did when she was nervous. She fingered the smooth blunt ends of her long hair, separating the strands and rolling them slightly between her fingertips. Then she pressed the edges against her lips. Finally Maurice said, "So does Doyle live with you, or what?"

Janice made an awkward laugh. "Sometimes it seems like it."

Maurice didn't say anything, which made Janice feel as if she had to. "There's a Mormonoid missionary who lives across the street from me. Brother Keester, I call him. Brother Keester kayoed Lisa with his smoldering eyes and keen Bible knowledge." She hoped Maurice might smile at this. He didn't. "Anyway, that's why we were baking chocolate chip cookies. I guess cookies are for Mormons what making out is for normal people."

Another silence stretched out, and then Janice heard something strange. A cat, she was pretty sure of it—the gravelly stretched-out *yowww* of a cat. She turned to a cardboard box on the backseat. "That a cat?"

Maurice smiled. "Definitely sounded like one."

"Whose is it?"

"Belongs to a lady I know."

Janice had the feeling this was a signal to stop asking questions, but she couldn't help herself. "What are you doing with it?"

Maurice's smile turned mysterious. "You'll see."

Janice glanced again at the box. "What's its name?"

"Harriet."

Who would name a cat Harriet? Janice thought, and then she said it.

Maurice paused. "A lady named Lillian Kinderman," he said. Then, "She used to live in Village Greens."

So when he'd said lady, he meant old lady. Janice felt a strange slackening of apprehension and stared out at the passing street. It was almost four o'clock, the late and laziest part of a spring Sunday afternoon so beautiful it made the people on stoops and bicycles look richer, happier, younger, almost. On the wider streets, Maurice kept the Honda in the right-hand lane, moving along at a crawl. He sat back in his seat with exaggerated relaxation, one arm stretched over the back of her seat without touching her. Janice thought to say, "I like your car."

Maurice nodded with evident pleasure, and words began to flow. "Yeah, well, first thing I did was slam it, then the limo tint—I wanted to do it all around but the cops are on that like flies on shitowski—and then the sixteen-inch rims."

"What's slamming it mean?"

"Lowering it." Maurice grinned. "What planet you been living on?"

Janice would've said *Planet Earth, and that's confirmed whereas with you the jury's out*, but she hadn't figured out Maurice's sense of humor yet. Maybe he didn't have one. She said, "What's that yellow stuff on the side?"

"Body kit. Whattaya think of the offset color?"

She wasn't sure which was the offset color, but she said, "I like it a lot." Maurice seemed pleased. "Then I replaced the taillights with clear corners and put on the loud exhaust. That's a seven-inch tip."

Janice nodded. She had no idea what he was talking about. She'd heard guys talk about trunk woofers, so she said, "How big are the trunk woofers?"

"Twelve inch," Maurice said proudly. "Wanna hear 'em?"

"You know what? I don't even like that loud stuff. It's like it's all bass." She watched his expression and realized she was scared what he would think.

But he shrugged. "Yeah, me neither."

Janice was surprised at her own relief. Her smile brightened. "It's like some weird advertisement for yourself."

Maurice considered it. "I don't know about that. To me, it's just distracting. I like, you know, to *feel* the car."

They both fell silent, and a few minutes later he made a couple of turns and said, "Mind if I make a stop?"

She didn't need to answer. He was already pulling into the parking lot of a place whose sign said COTTAGEWOOD and then in smaller letters, FLEXIBLE ASSISTED LIVING. "This a rest home or something?" she said.

Maurice looked at her. "Actually, it's more of a big tomb where the not-quite-dead get to not-quite-live for a while before they die and make it official." He grinned. "Wanna come in and see?"

She said she'd just wait in the car, thank you, but after she watched Maurice take the cardboard box from the car and set it into one of the tiny low-walled patios, then head for the main entrance, she grew curious and caught up with him at the check-in desk. He was there to visit Lillian Kinderman, he told the woman at the desk.

Janice signed in, too, and a few minutes later they were knocking on a door at the end of a wide, carpeted corridor.

"I'm decent," a voice said from within, and once they were inside, a petite, white-haired woman looked on Maurice—and then Janice—with what seemed like genuine pleasure. "I *knew* you'd be coming today. I felt it in my old bones."

The apartment was tiny but complete—bed, kitchenette, bathroom, and sitting area, where Mrs. Kinderman had been watching an old black-and-white movie, which she now remoted off, and made a motion as if to rise from her chair. "Can I make you tea?"

"Naw," Maurice said. "We're good." He turned. "This is Janice. I found her this afternoon eating raw cookie dough."

Mrs. Kinderman smiled at her. "She looks pretty healthy all the same," she said, and held out her hand, which Janice took, but Mrs. Kinderman didn't shake it, she just held it tightly for a few seconds.

Maurice had slipped out the patio door and returned now with the cardboard box. When he opened it, a black cat popped out and without any hesitation at all crossed the room and jumped into the lap of Mrs. Kinderman, whose hands began running along the cat's back in long calm strokes. "Oh, Harry," she said.

The cat was purring now, a thick throaty purr that made Mrs. Kinderman laugh. "She's not very ladylike, is she?"

A minute or so later, the cat rose and began kneading Mrs. Kinderman's stomach with her paws.

Maurice said, "I can get her to purr, but I can't get her to do that."

Mrs. Kinderman said, "Harriet knows you're a good boy, but she also knows you aren't me." She went on to tell them about Ginny, the woman who cleaned her apartment every other day. "She comes in here and within the minute she's sneezing and leaking and wheezing and *very* suspicious of why. 'There a cat in here, Lillian?' she says, and doesn't even wait for me to deny it. 'What's this black hair here? What's that from? You know there's no cats allowed here.' I say that I certainly do know that cats aren't allowed, and what is she accusing me of?" Mrs. Kinderman smiled at Janice. "I give her a good weekly tip. She's not going to tattle."

When thirty minutes had passed, Maurice rose. "Better go," he said.

Mrs. Kinderman whispered something in the cat's ear, then slid it back into its box. She took Maurice's hand and when he leaned down, she kissed his forehead. "Such a good boy," she said in a murmuring voice, and then held out her hand to Janice, who took it and then—she didn't know what else to do—leaned down and felt the old woman's soft kiss on her forehead, too. "And such a good girl," she said.

Back outside, Maurice reached over the patio wall and retrieved the boxed cat. Mrs. Kinderman, watching from the patio door, waved one last time.

"Okay, then," Maurice said when they were back in the car.

"She's nice," Janice said, and she meant it.

"Yeah." He glanced at her patio window as they pulled away. "She thinks she's coming back to Village Greens, but I don't think so. You wouldn't know it, but she's had a couple of strokes, so her daughters stashed her here where there are doctors and stuff."

Janice asked how he'd met her, and Maurice explained. When he was done, almost as an afterthought, he said, "You should taste her pot roast." Then, "Which reminds me, I'm hungry. You hungry?"

She laughed. "Pretty much all the time."

At a drive-through window a girl handed a bag of hamburgers

and fries to Maurice, who handed them to Janice and said, "How 'bout we go to Green Lakes and eat them there?"

Janice thought that sounded good and said so. Green Lakes was a huge sprawl of a park where people went as much for privacy as recreation. As they swung out onto the highway, Janice peered into the bag and was pulling out a fry when Maurice said, "Ho, girly, not in the car."

Janice grinned unsurely. "You're joking, right?"

Maurice smiled. "Nope. Actual rule."

Janice thought of trying to talk her way into just one harmless teeny-tiny fry to ward off serious deep-fat deprivation but decided against it. She said, "You should see my mom's car. You could survive in there for a week just on the scraps."

Maurice nodded and said, "There you go." They drove into the hushed chamber of the park. It was like driving into a green cocoon. Picnickers' cars lined the parking lot, and Maurice's tricked-out Honda was picking up stares from other cars, stares Janice liked.

Maurice said, "The food rule was my father's rule, too. That, anyhow, was what my mother told me. She said he picked it up in Japan. She said the Nipponese never ate in their cars, and their cars were perfect."

Janice nodded and wondered whether Nipponese was a real word and if it wasn't, whether it was racist. Then she decided the only thing she didn't like about Maurice's Honda was the window tint. It kept people from seeing her riding around in this cool car.

Maurice said, "My father died never having a new car. I plan to have one by my twenty-first birthday."

"Sounds like money to me," Janice said, because she couldn't help but wonder where it would come from.

Maurice must've sensed this. He smiled and said, "Yeah, well, I've got a few irons in the fire."

A second or two passed before Janice said, "My mother couldn't give a shit about cars." Janice almost never said shit, but it felt good saying it now—it made her feel somehow older and freer. "But both my dads gave a shit about cars."

Maurice tossed her a quick amused look. "Dads?"

"Dad One and Dad Two. They came and they went. Usually in brand-new cars." She remembered something. "My mother always tells people that on the highway of life her ex-husbands ran a lot of people off the road."

Maurice grinningly nodded. "Well, sometimes you gotta free up the lanes for the serious drivers."

Janice wasn't sure she understood this, but laughed as if she did. She push-buttoned down her window.

"Pass a little gas?" Maurice said, but she could see he was joking. So at least he had some sense of humor.

"It's just such a nice day, I wanted to let the outside in." She also wanted to let the outside eyes in. Deeper in the park, when they got near the water, Maurice had to stop behind a Suburban that was being loaded with trikes. While Maurice waited impatiently, tapping the wheel with his ring, she spotted the Jeep Cherokee of Brad Pembrook. Brad himself gave her a long look, and she almost had to laugh. This was fun. She scooched down a little in her seat and sat on her hands, which she knew would make her breasts stand out a little, and until Maurice could squeal around the Suburban, Brad Pembrook looked down from his Jeep, checking her out.

Maurice, on the other hand, seemed weirdly indifferent to her, which she wasn't really used to. And the fact that he wasn't checking her out made her want him to check her out. But Maurice was quiet and stayed quiet, letting the slow scan of his eyes pick up everything about other cars, other drivers, other kids on the streets, everything, in fact, but her. It made for a strange stillness within the car, and when Maurice's pager suddenly chirped, Janice almost jumped.

Maurice glanced at the number, then flipped open the center console and pulled a cell phone from its holster. It was the same kind of phone Janice's mother had, and she noticed Maurice hit speed dial 3.

"Yeah?" Maurice said, low, and then for a long time he just listened. Then he said, "Okay," and hung up.

Janice had the feeling it was a girl. Maybe, for all she knew, his girlfriend. "That your mother?" she said, going for a joke.

Maurice didn't smile. "Might as well be," he said, and turned around, leaving the park more quickly than he'd entered it. "Small detour," he said. Janice was annoyed, disappointed, and hungry, watching the leafy greenness and the picnic tables pass away.

The small detour turned out to be driving all the way to some decrepit street downtown. She was starving, absolutely starving. The cookie dough was going to her head, making her feel faint. What was it? Six o'clock? Six-thirty? Maurice pulled up in front of an unmarked store. "Be right back," he said. "And keep the doors locked. This ain't the best neighborhood."

He went to a door that had about twelve locks on it. He pushed a button and said something brief into a speaker. A few seconds later the door opened—she couldn't see who opened it—and Maurice went inside.

Janice reached into the brown bag and ate, very carefully, three French fries. She started to eat a fourth, but something

153

stopped her. She put it back and carefully refolded the top of the bag. She glanced at the door into which Maurice had disappeared. Nothing. She wiped the grease off her fingers, popped open the console, glanced again at the door, then quickly pulled out Maurice's phone and speed dialed 3. She was pretty sure a girl would answer, but she was wrong. On the first ring, a firm male voice said, "Jocko's Unsurpassed Security, is this an emergency and if not how can I direct your call?"

Janice hung up at once, then quickly returned the phone to the console. She pulled the cardboard box forward and let out the cat, who sniffed around, then settled pleasantly into Janice's lap. After a few strokes the cat began to purr and kept purring. Janice glanced at the storefront door—still closed—then looked around the street. Maurice was right. It wasn't the nicest neighborhood. What had looked like two plastic bags of trash on the opposite sidewalk was, she suddenly realized, somebody who'd passed out on the pavement and was now slowly coming to life. He was wearing a Hefty bag over his clothes as some kind of a coat. Once he was standing, he turned to face the wall. Peeing, Janice suddenly realized, and she turned quickly away.

On this side of the street, an old woman was moving haltingly in Janice's direction. When Maurice emerged from the storefront, the woman followed him toward the car. As Maurice approached, Janice reached over to flip the lock, but the old woman arrived just as he was opening the door. Her cheeks and nose were red and veiny, and her face seemed loosely gathered around her tiny mouth. "Two dollars soup money's all I need, friend," she said to Maurice. "Just two bucks." When she smiled there was nothing but gums.

Maurice got in and slammed the door. The cat stiffened for a second, then relaxed again. The old woman steadied herself on the car and tried to peer through the tinting. Maurice made a heavy sigh of annoyance, then pulled a five-dollar bill from his wallet and handed it to the woman, who looked like she might weep with surprise and gratitude. Maurice slowly eased the car away from the curb.

"That was nice," Janice said.

"Not really," Maurice said, his voice stony. "I just wanted her grimy hands off my car." But after he glanced down at the cat in her lap, his voice softened slightly. "Looks like Harriet's found another lap to call her own."

They drove to Thornden Park, close by but depressingly urban after Green Lakes. Maurice found them a table where they sat eating their cheeseburgers and fries. Harriet was in her harness, tethered by a slim leather leash, but after some ritual exploration with tail held vertical, she'd curled in Janice's lap. The food was cold now, and the sun was ebbing fast. Maurice had finished his cheeseburger and was eating his fries slowly, dipping each bite in mustard, then ketchup, when he said, "So Doyle's your girl chum, right?"

Janice nodded. "We're friends, yeah."

Maurice ate two more fries. "She a real redhead?"

The question alarmed Janice. "What do you mean, real?"

Maurice grinned. "You know what I mean. You've seen her in the shower room, haven't you?"

Janice knew what Maurice meant and she had of course seen Lisa in the shower room, but the very fact that she could tell Maurice wanted to hear that Lisa was a true redhead kept her from saying it. A new feeling had taken hold of Janice. She began some tight scratches of the cat's ears and said, "The thing is, I promised Lisa I would never tell."

Maurice smiled a loose, easy smile. "Promised to never tell what?"

A lie composed itself in Janice's mind. She knew she shouldn't say it, but she wanted to say it, and she did. "That she's a Lady Clairol redhead."

Maurice's eyes seemed to dilate for a moment as if in surprise, and then he was slowly shaking his head. "Well, that's a real fooler," he said.

Janice pretended to stick up for her friend. "I don't see why it should make any difference one way or the other. She's still really cute."

Maurice poked a fry into his mouth. "The thing is, it does make a difference," he said in a serious voice. "Sham redheads are a dime a dozen."

"Well, it's not like she's on the market anyway," Janice said, and smoothed her hand over the cat's back. "She's got two guys on the line—the Mormon and another one—and she's having a hard time deciding which."

Maurice crumpled his empty fry bag. "They can have her," he said. There was something hard in his voice now, as if something had been irreversibly decided.

For a moment—but only a moment—Janice wondered why she didn't feel worse about what she'd just done.

Maurice had gone to the trunk of the Honda and brought out a soft rag and begun to wipe clean his car, which, to Janice, already seemed perfectly clean. As he worked, he carefully folded and refolded the rag to keep a clean side out. Then he began applying wax.

156

"Want me to help?" Janice said.

He didn't even look up. "Naw. I have my own way of doing it."

As he worked, he was humming. It was an infectious tune, and Janice found herself wanting to hear it better, but she didn't move or say anything. A few minutes later, Maurice stopped and pulled off his T-shirt, which he brought over to the table and folded neatly. His upper body was so white and smooth and tightly muscular in the twilight it reminded Janice of the marble Olympians in the art museum sculpture garden. While she was thinking this, Maurice caught her looking at him, and she began to blush. But he did something surprising. He leaned forward and gave her a gentle nip on the ear. Everything about this—his touch, his closeness, his smell—affected her. He was still humming. When he leaned away, she had to fight the impulse to pull him back.

"What's that song?" she asked.

"Something my mom used to sing all the time."

> Rosy apple, yellow pear,
> Bunch of roses in your hair.
> Gold and silver by your side,
> I know who will be your bride.

He stopped singing and smiled. "Weird, huh?"

What was weird was how well Maurice could sing. It was like he was some bare-chested medieval troubadour. It was quite possibly the sexiest thing a man had done in her presence, and she wanted him to sing it again, but closer.

"Know what you can do for me?" he asked.

Janice wondered what, if anything, she would say no to. "What?"

Maurice fixed her with a set smile. "You can tell me why you called Jocko's Unsurpassed Security on my cell phone while you were sitting in my car."

Janice felt the color draining from her face. "What do you mean?"

His smile seemed actually to relax slightly, as if a small pleasure had just been presented to him. "Jocko himself answered the phone. I was sitting next to him at the time. On hang-ups he routinely checks the caller ID." Maurice's smile widened. "After he checked, Jocko turned to me and said, 'Your phone just called me.'" Maurice paused. "Since my phone was in the car and the only person in the car was you, it wasn't that hard to figure out."

Janice lowered her eyes. "I just wondered who'd called you," she said in a small voice. "I thought it might be a girl. I know I had no right to be jealous, but I think I was."

Maurice took this in. "How'd you know what number to call?"

"Watched you speed dial. It's just like my mom's phone."

"Smart girl," he said.

She looked up. She wasn't sure whether he was about to be mad or about to be friendly. She had the feeling he wasn't sure himself. Finally he went to the back of the Honda and lifted the hatch cover to reveal a small cooler filled with ice. He pulled out two bottles of cold beer, opened them at the table, and clicked them lightly together. "Here's to the smart girl," he said.

He handed Janice the bottle of beer.

She took it. It tasted bitter, but she drank it.

He drank his off quickly, in six or seven gulps, and leaned forward to give Janice another little nip on her ear. This one was slightly less gentle than the first one, but it affected her the same as before, only more so. She felt dreamy. The cat purred in her lap. Maurice was smiling at her, a relaxed I-own-you smile, and she felt as if with his merest touch all of her clothes might loosen and slide free.

But he stepped back, and then, in the fading daylight of a Sunday afternoon in an out-of-the-way corner of Thornden Park, she watched him go back to the careful waxing of his car.

CHAPTER SEVENTEEN

How Does Your Garden Grow?

The house was dark when Mick got home. It was nearly eight o'clock, but he was the first to arrive. In the pantry the answering machine was blinking and the message readout said 2. Mick hit play.

"Greetings from Reeceville and let me tell you, Mr. Mickster, thanks to the uncle Arnold, the woe in Connecticut has turned golden and then some. Details at eleven. You will definitely want to stay tuned."

Mick was interested, but also mildly disappointed. He'd hoped the message might be from Lisa, and the second message wasn't from her, either. It was from his father: "Nora? You there? If you're there, pick up." A pause. "Okay, I'm still at Clyde D.'s but I'll be home no later than eight-thirty." Another pause. "I thought you'd be home now." Pause. "Okay. See you later."

In school Mick had learned that the temperature at which a flammable gas bursts into flame is called the flash point, and, later, he would realize that listening to this message had brought him to something similar. His eyes squeezed shut. *"God!"* he said aloud through clenched teeth. It was too much. That was all. It was just too much. He felt overmatched, overwhelmed, over-everything. He took the disk from his pocket and threw it hard against the kitchen wall. It clicked and fell. He looked at it lying on the linoleum and thought, Good. Let somebody else find it. Let somebody else carry it around.

Foolish came warily forward, sniffed the disk on the floor, and walked away.

So did Mick.

Upstairs, he found an e-mail waiting for him from Myra. *Hi, Mick as in mittens. I left so fast last night I didn't get to tell you how much I enjoyed your company. You probably didn't know it, but you were a comfort to me, a little weird I know, but there it is. We should do it again some time, yes?*

Being a comfort didn't seem great exactly, but it didn't seem so bad, either. He composed three or four different responses to Myra, but didn't like any of them. Finally he just wrote *Yes. Definitely yes.*

Then Mick went to his room, lay down on his bed, leafed through a car magazine for a few minutes, and fell asleep.

He awakened a while later to a gentle tapping sound—his father's knuckles on the doorjamb. "You already eat?"

The room was dim and Mick was trying to get his bearings. He looked at the clock. Eight-forty. "No, I didn't," he said in a thick voice. "Guess I wasn't hungry." The truth was, he'd just forgotten to eat.

"You drop this?" His father was holding a computer disk. *The* computer disk.

Mick, who'd been groggy, was suddenly totally focused, but he had no idea what to say next.

"It was on the kitchen floor," his father said.

Mick didn't know what to say, but he had to say something. He said, "Is it green?"

His father looked. "Yep."

A second or two passed and Mick heard himself say, "It's mine, then."

His father nodded. "What's on it?"

Another pause. "A paper for history," Mick said. "It's on the muckrakers."

His father was nodding. "Ida Tarbell and Upton Sinclair," he said.

Mick, surprised, said, "Yeah. Those guys."

His father, grinning, came fully into the room. "I wasn't one of the whiz kids," he said, "but those teachers pounded a few things into me." He laid the disk down on Mick's bedside table. "Better put that someplace safe," he said.

Mick stared at it lying there.

His father turned to go. "Nora's not here yet, so how about if us guys grub up something to eat?"

Mick nodded. "Sure, Dad."

After his father left the room, Mick sat up and swung to the edge of the bed. He opened his mouth, breathed in, breathed out. Then he picked up the green disk and zipped it back into the interior pocket of his jacket.

By the time Mick got downstairs, his father already had bread in the toaster, peas in the microwave, and chipped beef in a Ziploc bag and was mixing up a white sauce at the stove. Creamed chipped beef and peas over toast was his standard bachelor meal, which was fine by Mick. It wasn't bad.

As his father stirred the sauce over a low flame, he was whistling something Mick didn't recognize, neither too fast nor too slow, but he abruptly stopped whistling to ask Mick if Nora had said where she was going.

"The mall. And then to some spinning lesson in Mattydale, she said."

His father nodded and glanced at the clock. Mick knew what his father was going to say next even before he said it: "I hope she's okay."

He resumed his whistling.

"What's that song?" Mick said.

His father stopped and cocked his head as if listening for the song he'd just been whistling. "Not sure," he said. But as he was mixing the chipped beef with the white sauce it suddenly came to him. " 'Moonlight Becomes You,' " he said. He moved his voice to a lower register and mock-crooned, "Moonlight becomes you, it goes with your hair. You certainly know the right things to wear."

Mick said, "Kind of sorry I asked."

They ate their dinner in front of the TV. Time seemed to thicken and slow down. When they were done eating, Mick lay on the sofa and his father stretched out in his recliner, but his father couldn't sit still. He kept checking the clock, and he fidgeted through the movie they'd settled on. Once or twice he got up and peered out the front window.

Finally, at 9:45, Mick heard the downshifting whine of Nora's 320i and then the dull grinding of the garage door. His father jumped up and went to greet her. Mick couldn't hear what his father was saying, but he heard Nora say, "Oh, you're so sweet, but I would've called if anything had been wrong."

They came together into the front room. "Hiya, Mick," Nora said with a breeziness Mick threw right into the bogus pile. "What're we watching?"

The movie had gone to commercials and his father hit the mute button. *"One False Move,"* he said. "Kind of a guy movie." Then, "You hungry? There's more chipped beef."

Nora declined. "I'm not quite that desperate," she said, and Mick's father laughed and said, "Hey, what doesn't kill you makes you stronger."

This geniality annoyed Mick, and he said, "So how was the spinning lesson?"

Without the slightest hitch Nora smiled and said, "Frightening! The yarn kept breaking and the woman kept saying I'd get the hang of it."

Mick's father laughed and said, "Well, she's right. You will."

Nora kissed him on the cheek and looked around at the dishes with their hardening white sauce. "Guess I'd better clean up after your little bachelor party." She began gathering plates and glasses.

His father helped.

Mick just sat.

The next day after school, alone in the house, Mick looked in Nora's knitting basket. Balls of yarn, ropes of wool, eighteen inches of what Mick supposed was the front of a cabled sweater, a half-eaten box of Junior Mints, and a business card with a small drawing of a spinning wheel in the corner. The address said Mattydale. Mick called the number and a woman answered, "Dyed in the Wool. Can I help you?"

"Is this the Alberta Scott who gives spinning lessons?" he asked, feeling both foolish and determined.

"Yes," Alberta Scott said cheerfully. "What can I do you for?"

"This is Mick Nichols," he said quickly, so it sounded like migniggles, and then he purposefully slowed himself down. "My

164

stepmother left her wallet somewhere, and I'm helping her retrace her steps. Did she leave it at your house last night?"

"Last night?" Alberta Scott repeated.

"At her spinning lesson."

"I think you must be mistaken. I didn't give any lessons last night. Who did you say your stepmother was?"

"What was that?" Mick said, calling over his shoulder into the empty house. "Never mind," he said into the mouthpiece. "She found it. It was in her other purse all the time."

He thanked the woman, hung up, and rubbed a rough-looking blob of wool between his fingers. It had a strange smell to it— thick and rancid—that quickly transferred to his fingers. He remembered Nora's phrase for freshly sheared wool. "In the grease." Mick wiped the sheep oil on his pants, and then he just sat there, staring into the picture of Nora in her swimming suit, staring at her wide smile and bright eyes, wondering just what the face behind the face behind the face might look like, if he ever got to see it.

CHAPTER EIGHTEEN

Trunky

There was a word for how missionaries felt at the end of their two years. Trunky, they called it, like they had their trunks packed and waiting by the door. But trunky was how Lisa Doyle felt, too—like she was waiting for transport to another place entirely. Some place where only Elder Keesler lived. Or maybe where Mick Nichols lived, and Myra Vidal didn't.

Meanwhile, she helped her mother cut up potatoes for the ward dinner. She folded her father's ribbed black socks, her mother's pastel sweatshirts, and limp stacks of Jemison High Field Hockey T-shirts. She wrote a two-page paper about suffragettes, filled out Cruso's worksheet at the Erie Canal museum, had quick, say-nothing conversations with Mick when they passed in the halls, and ran mindless laps with the rest of the field hockey team. But before and after these things she was trunky.

For what, beyond the notice of Elder Keesler, she didn't allow herself to say. She used a large portion of her first Village Greens paycheck to get her hair cut at a chic new salon in Armory Square, and added her baby-sitting money to the rest of it for a cream-and-lavender dress that Janice—lounging on a chair in the dressing room and holding up various outrageous negligees—

166

called "certifiable Keester bait." On the following Sunday, wearing the cream-and-lavender dress, wearing the salon haircut and the salon hair gel, she'd gotten to church early enough to reapply lip pencil in the women's room. She and her mother had then seated themselves in the usual pew—off to the left side, where widows, divorcées, and people with nonmember dads always sat—and she'd pretended not to be waiting for the elders to come in.

Lisa knew the rules about elders and the girls who were waiting for them back home. No phone calls and no visits, not even from relatives, but elders could and did receive letters, foil-wrapped loaves of banana bread, snickerdoodles, shirts, ties, slippers, photographs, and candygrams. They did not, as far as Lisa knew, ever fall in love with girls in the wards where they happened to serve.

But that afternoon, while Lisa was washing an encrusted lasagna pan, the phone rang. "Lisa," the voice said. "It's Elder Keesler."

"Hi," Lisa said, stopping instantly. Her mother was at the counter, and she turned.

"I just wanted to make sure you knew about the fireside tonight."

"The fireside?"

Of course she knew which fireside. It had been announced from the pulpit and in the ward bulletin and in the program she'd read during the boring parts of sacrament meeting. A fireside was an extra hour of testimony on top of the three hours you'd spent in church already, but you didn't mind because the guest speaker was a professional athlete or a burn victim with an inspirational message. Or so Lisa had thought in her crankier moments.

"This African American woman I met in Buffalo, Mary Louise Jenkins, is going to sing a spiritual at the end. As a favor to me. She's spectacular. I thought maybe your father would enjoy it."

"I'll ask him," Lisa said, knowing her father wouldn't come to a fireside if the speaker were the Dalai Lama. "That sounds great."

"Okay, well, see you there?"

"Sure," Lisa said.

"Who was that?" her mother asked when Lisa hung up, and her look turned even more dubious when Lisa explained that Elder Keesler was calling to invite her father to the fireside.

"Really," her mother said. "Has he called you before?"

"No," Lisa said, stung at the suggestion. Then, sliding the lasagna pan a little too forcefully into the cupboard, she asked, "Why do you hate him?"

"I don't hate him." A pause. "I've just seen his type."

"I thought you wanted me to date Mormons."

"I do. But he's a missionary, Lisa. He's not supposed to date *anyone*."

"This isn't a *date*, Mom," Lisa said in a tight voice. "It's a *fireside*. At *church*."

So that night she sat trying not to stare at Elder Keesler while listening to a weirdly uninspirational story about a near-death experience and waiting for the stout black woman who sat near Elder Keesler to sing. When at last the woman stood, she cleared her voice and seemed about to open her mouth, but didn't. She closed her eyes and left them closed and only after a complete calm came into her face did she begin to sing. As the woman's voice took over the room, Lisa sat transfixed.

When you listened to a woman sing "His Eye Is on the Sparrow" without accompaniment or human assistance, and the woman made the song swell so far beyond normal human limits that she seemed to leave the chapel entirely, looking out and beyond you to some other place, and when you felt all the time that the other place was the place you wanted to be with Elder Keesler, what was that? It wasn't a date. But it was a communion of some kind, and surely he felt it, too.

For Lisa, the following week slid numbly by. Spectacular weather, spectacular greenness and goldness and blooms. She ran, she wrote, she read, and she stared out the windows of buses and cars at blue Toyota hatchbacks in hopes one would contain Elder Keesler, but none did.

Then, on Saturday, the window she stared out of was Janice's, and what she saw were the straight iron rails of Elder Keesler's fire escape, which reminded her of a Mormon hymn. "Hold to the rod, the i-i-i-ron rod," it went. It was about holding on to the rail so you wouldn't fall into temptation. Lisa looked back at her history book, which was open to a page about the Iroquois. She tried to focus on the confederacy of the Five Nations.

All the windows of the Bledsoe apartment were open to catch a breeze, but the day was unbelievably hot and stuffy. Everything, including the air, hung still in the grainy, thick afternoon light.

"Want a burrito?" Janice asked. She had her history book open, too, but Lisa noticed that what Janice was really doing was doodling with a blue gel pen, and in the midst of some loopy flowers, she had written, in cursive, the name MAURICE.

"Sure," Lisa said, trying to memorize the names of the five original nations by writing them over and over again in her notebook. Mohawk, Oneida, Onondaga, Cayuga, Seneca. "Moocs," she said.

"Mooks?"

"It's a mnemonic acronym for the Five Nations. M-O-O-C-S. Want me to teach it to you?"

"No," Janice said. "But if you can get a cute Mohawk to take my test for me, I'd be grateful." Janice stood up, stretched a little, then yelped. "Holy Helpers, Batman! Red phone to the White House! They're doing their laundry!"

And they were. What Lisa had been pretending not to wait for had finally occurred. Outside on the fresh green grass of Home Park Gardens, Elder Keesler and Elder Pfingst, both in T-shirts and knee-length shorts, were draping white shirts over the community clothesline.

"It must be p-day," Lisa said.

Janice gave her a look. "P as in pea pod or P as in men's room?"

"P," Lisa said, "as in preparation. It's their day off."

"Oh," Janice said, directing her gaze back outdoors. Then, without any hesitation whatever, she stuck her head out the unscreened window and said, "Hey, kids. How's the P going?"

Both elders turned.

"P as in preparation," Janice said.

The elders still said nothing.

"Need some clothespins?"

After a pause, Elder Keesler said, "Sure. We're actually running short."

Janice snatched a cotton bag of clothespins and, checking her hair in the mirror, said, "Ask not what you can do for your girlfriend."

The concrete steps felt smooth and cold under Lisa's bare feet. After the concrete came sharp gravel, then hot asphalt, then the cool tongues of grass. When Elder Keesler smiled at her, Lisa dropped her eyes, and her stomach wadded together like gum.

170

She reached down into the basket and lifted up a wet, white, clumped-up shirt. Without saying anything, she shook it, held it upside down, and pinned it precisely in four places.

"Well, that looks tidy," Elder Keesler said. "After we're done, we'll have a quiz to see who pinned what." He picked up the next shirt, extracted some clothespins from the cotton bag, and hung it exactly as Lisa had done hers. They continued until the basket was done, and Janice, who had been introducing herself to Elder Pfingst, asked where the underwear was.

Elder Pfingst blushed. "Indoors," he said. "It's kind of sacred."

Janice raised her eyebrows at Lisa, and Lisa said, "You know. Like your Miracle Bra." She could just imagine what Janice would later have to say about sacred underwear. For now, though, everyone laughed, and Janice climbed the rungs of the metal spider, where she perched and asked Elder Pfingst what he and Elder Keesler had done for fun last night. Elder Keesler had read a book but Elder Pfingst had watched *The Wizard of Oz*. "We're not supposed to watch videos," he said a little sheepishly, "but someone had left it in the apartment and it's rated G."

Janice said, "It shouldn't be. I mean, it's a girl and three men on an overnight, right?"

Elder Pfingst laughed and said it wasn't actually overnight, or actually anything since it was technically all a dream.

"Seriously, that green witch gave me nightmares," Janice said. "And I still can't watch that monkey part." She climbed a little higher and said, "I liked the I-wish-I-had-a-brain song, though."

Lisa and Elder Keesler sat on the swings and talked about their favorite books (his was something about bushmen in Africa, which he called a "postcolonial masterpiece"), the weather, his aunt in California, and how his mother had taught him to iron.

171

"My mom says that a shirt dried outdoors looks nicer when it's ironed," Lisa said. "It's like the sun starches it."

They were quiet a few seconds, then Elder Keesler said, "When we started hanging the clothes I was hoping you'd see us and come out."

Lisa didn't know what to say. "Oh," she said, trying to ignore the whirling in her stomach. "Really?"

"It's been really distracting, knowing you," he said. "I can't keep my mind on my work now."

This was easily the most wonderful thing anyone had ever said to Lisa.

"I've been distracted, too," she said, staring at his dry, bony, surprisingly delicate hands. She didn't know what else to say. Distracted seemed like a safe word, not sinful or bad.

"I'm going home next week," he said. "President Atkins, our good-old-boy Southern mission president, doesn't like us to talk about departure dates. He says, 'Brethren, there are but two answers to the question, "How long have you been out?": "Just ova a year" and "Just unda a year."' " Elder Keesler was grinning, and then he wasn't. In fact, he turned almost somber. "I didn't want to just vanish on you."

"No," Lisa said.

Elder Pfingst looked at his watch, climbed down from the spider, and walked their way. "Ready to go? We've still got the marketing to do."

"Yep." Elder Keesler stood up and offered Lisa his hand. She took it and stood up, aware of his warm palm, his smooth hard ring, and the stupefying heat that was either her own response to his touch or the general stickiness. "See you at church, okay?" he said.

Lisa nodded. The forest across the street was dense and still, full of leaves as soft as rose blossoms. She could feel the watchful deer in it, even though she couldn't, from where she was sitting, see them.

"Toodle-oo," Janice called. "Can I see the miracle briefs next time?"

"No," Elder Keesler said good-naturedly, and when he waved for the last time, he looked directly, sweetly, unswervingly into Lisa's eyes.

PART THREE

The maid was in the garden,
Hanging out the clothes,
Along came a blackbird,
And nipped off her nose.

CHAPTER NINETEEN

Alarm Systems

Mick lay awake in the middle of the night. His bedside digital clock said 4:08 and then, as he stared at it, 4:09. He tried to think what day it was. Saturday night, now Sunday morning. At least he could sleep in.

This had been happening lately. At night he'd fall asleep at ten or eleven and then he'd awaken five or six hours later, still tired, but not tired enough to empty his mind and go back to sleep. He scooched to the edge of the bed and reached a hand down to Foolish, who raised his head for a quick scratch, then resumed his tight-tuck sleeping position. Mick got up, found his flashlight, went to the window, and shined its beam toward the gap in the chimney brick where the nest had been wedged. The light caught the blinking eyes of an adult phoebe. Maybe it was the male, waiting for the female to come back. Or maybe it was the female, back from wherever she'd been to lay her small white eggs. Hang in there, pal, Mick thought, and then wondered who he was privately talking to.

Almost three weeks had passed since Nora had come home late from the fake spinning lesson. The green disk was still in Mick's jacket pocket. School had that itchy, get-it-over-with feeling: fifteen endless-seeming days to go.

The house had turned quieter. Everyone acted more or less normal, talking about fixing the garage roof (they hadn't), planting the garden (they had), and the first sheep-to-sweater class (a big turnout), but it seemed to Mick they were all merely impersonating their former selves—it was as if the real versions of himself and his father and Nora had withdrawn to their own corners in a strangely adult game of wait and see. Mick's father hadn't started whistling the slow songs again, but he'd taken the happy songs and slowed them down so it was hard to tell what they were anymore. The couple of times Mick had seen Nora around Melville, she'd seemed cheery as ever. One day he'd seen her bustling into the art wing, talking and laughing with Wes Eaton, a student teacher who, Mick noticed, was carrying Nora's bag of carded wool for her. Another time he'd seen her standing in the Melville parking lot with Mr. Duckworth, a youngish widower, Nora waving her arms and talking while Mr. Duckworth rolled out his deep thunderous laughter.

But then, in the last week or so, something odd had occurred. Nora had turned quiet, a strange, deep-down, un-Noralike quiet. It was as if her mind was someplace else, and if anyone spoke to her, she would start slightly and say "What?" And a few days ago Mick had seen her outside his history room at the high school looking almost lost. It was just after the final bell and he was filing out of the room with the other kids when he spotted her standing still, a rock in the stream of passing students.

Mick was going to duck his head and slip by, but he thought she'd already seen him. He said, "What're you doing over here?" and it was as if it took her a second to remember. "Delivering something to a Mrs."—and here she looked at the name on the manila envelope she was carrying—"Eckstein." Mick turned and pointed. "You're close. She's two doors down." Nora nodded, but didn't move. Mick raised the paper in his hand. "Got an A from Cruso on my muckraker paper. A-minus actually. The minus was for being late." Nora said that was great, really great, but she was glancing beyond him, as if she was waiting for him to go. "I better keep moving," she said, and they'd parted. When Mick glanced back from the head of the stairs, Nora had disappeared, into Mrs. Eckstein's room, he presumed.

Lisa Doyle was talking to Mick at work, joking mostly, and every now and then they would talk on the phone, but he could tell she was intent on keeping a certain distance between them. If Mick talked about how it was fun to ride bikes to Green Lakes this time of year, or if he said he didn't usually go to dances but the band at this year's underclass prom was supposed to be really good, Lisa would fall silent for a second or two and then steer the subject somewhere else, to Maurice Gritz, say, who was such an idiot, or to her friend Janice, who she couldn't believe was hanging out with such an idiot, and pretty soon Mick and Lisa would be back in the safe zone, talking and chuckling. Mick thought of it as exercycle talk—it was easy, and gave the appearance of movement while going absolutely nowhere.

On May 2 Mick had received a birthday card from his mother in San Francisco. It included a note saying *Sorry I haven't called in a while—things so frantic here—think of you often—much love, Mom.* The card included a computer-generated check for five hundred dollars made out to Michael C. Nichols. His mother's signature was a hasty scrawl. He'd watched her sign her personal checks once during a visit. She had a service who went through all her bills, and they would write the checks and present them to his mother for her signature. The time Mick was there, she'd kept

178

talking on a conference call while she hurriedly signed each one after the barest glance, and then pushed them aside (the service sealed, stamped, and mailed them). He supposed that she'd registered his birthday and the amount of money to be paid with the company, but either his mother or the service had gotten the month wrong, because every year he got the card and check exactly one month before his real birthday. He had never forgotten his father telling the attorney that day in the courthouse that he and Mick didn't need any of his mother's money, not one penny, and this year, as with prior years, Mick folded the check back into the birthday card and slid the card into its envelope and put the card into his old plastic-covered Fisher-Price record player, where the others lay. There were eight of them now.

Reece's big news from Connecticut was automotive. His uncle Arnold had restored an old VW bug and gotten tired of it. If Reece got straight As on his spring report card, his uncle said he'd register the VW in Reece's name on his sixteenth birthday in July, free of charge, a proposition that had turned Reece into a studying fool as the term neared its end. "The bug is black," Reece reported, "and with the right rims and sound system, it'll be the perfect vehicle for touring the many-splendored streets of Reeceville." When Mick asked him about the copy of *Moll Flanders* he was carrying around, Reece said, "World Lit. Extra credit." Mick had widened his eyes in mock surprise and Reece said, "Dude, for a free car, the Reeceman'd read *War and Peace* in Latvian."

The big news at Village Greens was the recent run of houses that had been broken into, a fact that for some homeowners was made more alarming by sketchy evidence that the housebreakers were black. Someone thought they'd seen two black men in stocking caps, and twice the burglars had spray painted the same message on living room carpets: *World been white way too long.* Another time they left a note in Marks-A-Lot on a kitchen cabinet that said *You got too much good stuff. We be back for rest.* A number of the Village Greens seniors had put up FOR SALE signs, and the homeowners' emergency meetings at the community room had turned tumultuous. Etta Hooten, the chairwoman of the homeowners' association, appealed for calm. She cautioned against letting the discussion rely on racial stereotypes or, worse, turn racist. The color of the intruders, she correctly noted, was incidental; what mattered was that there *were* intruders. She noted that the thieves were thought to enter the property on foot since they took only such items as jewelry and cash, which could easily be hidden on one's person. On this basis, Etta Hooten said, the board had authorized expenditure for the installation of motion-activated lights on all perimeter fencing, as well as the provisional hiring of Vigilance Patrol Service, "who come highly recommended."

This temporarily satisfied the senior homeowners, but the burglaries increased dramatically during Vigilance Patrol's first two weeks of operation, and the night after the motion-detecting lights were installed, five different homes were broken into. More FOR SALE signs went up, but there were suddenly no buyers. At the next association meeting, a woman stood up to say that she was eighty-eight years old and for the first time in her life she was spending her nights in fear. A salesman from Jocko's Unsurpassed Security signed up more than seventy residents for installation of state-of-the-art alarm systems, and another thirty for installation of security bars for doors and windows. All but a few paid an extra hundred dollars for expedited installation. Mick knew all this

180

because he'd heard it from Lisa who'd heard it from Janice who'd heard it from Maurice, who attended the meetings.

Saturday work was okay. Mick had begun to learn his way around, and Maurice, who had seemed intent on keeping Mick away from Lisa, no longer bothered. He was also nicer to Lizette Uribe, calling her by her real last name and even pronouncing it more or less right. One day Mick had overheard Maurice ask her if she was interested in some fast-cash catering work and when she'd nodded, he'd said, "Okay, then. Stop by my place after work and I'll go over the details with you." None of this seemed to improve Lizette's attitude toward Maurice, though—she kept her eyes down when he was around, and when he would turn to go, her eyes would follow him with a kind of sullen, smothered hatred. And she wasn't that friendly with any of the other guys, either. Once when Mick was working near her pulling oak seedlings from the clubhouse ground cover, he'd noticed she was moving like a zombie and said, "You okay, Lizette?" and she'd glanced at him for a second and said in a low flat voice, "I'm fine," and then she'd turned and begun to work with her back to him. The only one she would talk to at all was Lisa, which made sense to Mick. Who *couldn't* get along with Lisa? Getting along with Lisa Doyle was easy—getting close to her was the problem.

The one improved element in Mick's life was Myra Vidal. He'd hung out with her two of the last three Saturday nights, and each time he was around her, he felt a little more normal about it. He'd gotten used to the way a lot of guys would stop in their tracks to stare at her, and how most of the rest would slide glances her way when they thought she couldn't see. He'd also gotten used to the looks *he* got—it was clear they couldn't see the attraction, and the truth was, there wasn't any, at least none that Mick picked up on.

181

He was like her little brother, and for some reason he couldn't grasp, hanging out with a little-brother type was comforting to her. Both Saturday nights they'd gone to the library, and then around ten o'clock, they just rode around in her Honda Civic, listening to Pakistani music and talking. Myra hardly ever talked about her boyfriend in California, but she liked to talk about Pam (in a serious voice), and school (semiserious), and her weird, drooling professors (amused). Mick had asked if Myra had a history professor named Doyle. Myra said no, but she'd heard you had to camp out in the history wing the night before in order to sign up for his classes, which gave Mick something to tell Lisa the next time they raked leaves from the lawns of Village Greens.

The exercycle conversations always interested Myra. Once when Mick told Myra how Lisa would fall silent whenever he even hinted about doing something together, Myra said, "Whatever happened to tall, dark, and Mormon?" and Mick said he didn't know. The truth was, it was the one question he was afraid to ask Lisa. Myra said, "Okay, you just have to accept her keeping her distance for a while. Probably it means that either she's got her eye on someone else or her mother is trying to keep her away from non-Mormons, which is you." This sounded right to Mick, but it didn't make him feel any better.

Sometime during the evening, usually when things seemed most comfortable, Myra would slip in a question about Nora, and Mick would feel something within him clamp tightly closed and he'd just stare out the window. This past Saturday night Myra had waited while this silence collected, and then said, "Okay, let's look at her from a different angle. What was it about her that you'd always liked until whatever it was you didn't like happened?" This was easier for Mick. He said, "I don't know, I just always liked being with her, you know? Whether it was in her classroom, or in our kitchen or out in the garden, I just liked being around her." Myra waited a second and in the quietness of the car said, "Kind of like how you like being around me?" Mick was surprised by the directness of this, but he nodded. "Yeah, I guess so." He'd expected Myra to say something more, but she didn't. She'd seemed satisfied to stop right there, as if his answers had led her to something she could see, but he could not.

CHAPTER TWENTY

Joe Keesler

Sunday evening, Lisa Doyle sat at the table with her parents, moving her carrots slightly to the left.

"What's made you so mawkish all of a sudden, cupcake?" her father asked. "You stare out the windows all the time, like you're watching for somebody, and then you sigh."

"Nothing," Lisa said.

"It's that missionary," her mother said.

Lisa glared at her mother.

"Young Goodman Brown?" her father asked. "I thought missionaries were undateable."

"You can still have a crush on one," her mother said. "And missionaries can still cultivate crushes, whether they're supposed to or not."

Lisa picked up her plate and said, "Well, if everyone has that all worked out, I think I'm going to go study for my World Literature final."

It's not a crush, she thought as she set her plate by the kitchen sink. And he's not "cultivating crushes." Though as she climbed the stairs to her bedroom, she was once again glad her mother had not been in the church foyer this morning to see Elder

Keesler hand her a book and say, "Sorry it's so tattered, but it's my only copy. I wanted to give it to you before I leave."

His only copy. *His* copy.

She'd thought he was going to shake her hand then, but the foyer was nearly empty. Elder Pfingst was writing something in his daybook. Somewhere a baby screeched. Far away, at the opposite end of the church hall, a door closed. Quickly, Elder Keesler leaned forward, and to Lisa's surprise, put both arms around her. The hug had been brief, but she was pretty sure he'd kissed her hair. "My address is in there," he'd said. "You can write and tell me what you thought of it."

Lisa sat down on the edge of her bed and opened the book so she could see his name again. "Joe Keesler." Joe Keesler. Reading the name in his own cramped, scribbly handwriting was like seeing him without a shirt on. And holding the book—his book— even if it was some kind of African travel book called *The Heart of the Hunter: A Journey into the Mind and the Spirit of the Bushman*, was feeling herself once again pressed gently against his collarbone. She started reading the parts he'd underlined: "There is a dream dreaming us" and "It is position in the spirit that matters, not magnitude." Then she read the first chapter, hoping it would give her something intelligent to say in the letter that he had said—definitely said—she could write to him.

Dear Elder Keesler, Lisa wrote.

I guess I should call you Joe now but it feels a little forward. Thank you for giving me the Bushman book. I read the first chapter and it just amazed me. I especially liked the description of the desert.

"O-kay," Lisa said to herself. "That was incisive. Now what?" Nothing came to her. She lay down on the bed with the book over her stomach. Still nothing came to her. Maybe she should try the dippy writing exercises they did in English. It was called clustering. You wrote a topic in the center.

Elder Keesler.

Then all around it, like flies, you put words the topic suggested. *Smart. Funny. Handsome. Likes aboriginal people.*

"Then write anything that comes to mind," her teacher had said, and told the class about a famous Hollywood choreographer who when stumped about what to do next told his dancers, "Well, do *something,* and then we can change it!"

Lisa wrote, *The bushman seems really sweet. Innocent, I mean.*

This was worse than writing an essay for the annual high school history competition. She touched the book again and wondered if Elder Joe Keesler would write long letters to her from Boston. Would she go visit him, perhaps by train? Would he wait for her to graduate from high school? Maybe she could go to college in Boston, and then they would emigrate to Kenya. Maybe they would sleep together under mosquito netting and he would wash her hair in a stream, like Robert Redford did in *Out of Africa.*

She flipped through the book again, reading lines from it, wondering what to say, when she found the line that seemed perfect. She wrote it out. *What am I to do without you, to know the things I think before I know them myself?* Then she signed the note *Love, Lisa,* and folded it in two.

CHAPTER TWENTY-ONE

Propensities

Wednesday night Janice was at Maurice's, sitting on the floor near the wood-burning stove, eating fat-free popcorn while Maurice helped her prep for her Thursday vocabulary quiz. He'd opened a bottle of beer for her—she held it in one hand and took the occasional sip.

"Propensity," Maurice said.

Janice spelled it, defined it, and used it in a sentence. "Maurice has a serious propensity for Bazooka gum."

Maurice grinned, snapped a quick bubble, and went on to "promulgate." When she'd finished the list without a hitch, Maurice said, "Well, ain't you a brainy thing."

Janice got up, smiling. "Brainy thing gotta pee."

It was the beer. She hadn't drunk that much, but it turned her into a sieve. It also gave her the teeniest headache. In the bathroom she opened the medicine cabinet, found some generic aspirin, and was tapping out three when she noticed an old photograph wedged under the mirror brackets inside the medicine cabinet door. Actually it was half a photograph, of a girl, a pretty girl, but someone who'd been standing next to her had been cut off. All that was left was a disembodied arm wrapped around the girl's shoulders. Janice slipped the photograph out.

"Who's this?" she said when she came out of the bathroom. She held up the picture for him to see.

Maurice shrugged. "My mother."

Janice looked at it again. "She's pretty."

Maurice was quiet.

"Whose arm is wrapped around her shoulders?"

"Some boyfriend's. It was before she married my dad, but she liked the picture of herself, so she cut the boyfriend out. She was pretty good at cutting people out."

Janice was staring at the photo when something suddenly struck her. "She's a redhead."

"Fake redhead," Maurice said. "Almost everything about her was fake."

Was, Janice thought. "But your mom's alive, right?"

Another shrug. "Far as I know."

"How about your dad?"

"He died when I was, like, three. I'm not even sure I remember him. I think I just remember pictures of him."

Janice waited a second or two. "You don't know what he was like?"

Maurice took a last long drink from his bottle of beer. "Well, he did one heroic thing. He was in Vietnam, in the Air Force, a PJ—a parajumper—on one of the Sikorsky helicopters that would go down into the jungle under fire to rescue downed bomber pilots."

Maurice had been standing, but now he sat down on the edge of the bed. "This particular day, one of the other PJs got hit trying to pick up a wounded pilot, and this PJ was my father's buddy. He was hit bad and the Vietcong were moving in for the kill and he was radioing for help. My father's name was Gordon and his buddy was saying, 'Gordy, can you read me—for God's sake, can you read me, Gordy?' "

Maurice had begun peeling bits of paper label from the beer bottle and dropping them inside. "Anyhow, the fighter planes that protected the Sikorskys were called Sandys, and they were out of ordnance, and my father's helicopter was almost out of fuel, but my father talked the pilot into going back down for his buddy." Maurice kept staring at the bottle in his hands. "This is where it gets interesting. The story I was told was that my dad went down on this cabled penetrator thing to lift his buddy out, and he had him in his arms a few feet into the air when the Cong shot them both."

Janice said, "That's horrible."

Maurice nodded. "Horrible but heroic. So at least I grew up knowing my dad had been this pretty great guy. And then one day when I was sixteen and having about the millionth big daylong argument with my mother, I said I wished she had died and not my dad. She opened her mouth to yell something back, but then she just stopped. I knew right then she had a card up her sleeve, a real good card. Sure enough, she went into her room and came out with this newspaper story."

Maurice opened his wallet and unfolded a yellowed clipping and handed it to Janice. The headline said

MAN FLEEING POLICE
DIES OF HYPOTHERMIA

The story was about a man who had died after wading into an icy river to escape police who wanted to question him about a series of purse snatchings and home burglaries. The police officers' names were Eleazar Mendoza and Gilberto Silva. The dead man's name was Gordon L. Gritz.

Janice looked up. "This was your dad?"

"Not so heroic, huh?" Maurice smiled bitterly. "You know what pisses me off most of all, though? Those low-rider cops driving my dad into the icy water, and then *they* stand around waiting for firemen in wet suits and shit to get him out. I call that just a little bit gutless."

Maurice kept peeling strips off the label. "Anyhow, when I ask my mother why she made up the hero stuff, she says, 'First of all, your father *did* go back down after his buddy, and his buddy got shot as they were being lifted out.' While she's talking, she has this weird faraway look in her eyes. She says, 'I told you he was killed that day because I always believed that was the day he'd really been meant to die.' She says, 'Besides, it was the right version for you. You were little. You needed a role model.' Then after staring off a while, she turns to me and her face turns harder and she says, 'You're not little anymore. It's time you knew the truth.' "

Maurice looked at the bottle in his hands. "The next day she tells me she thinks it's about time I move out on my own, and so what was I going to do?" A pause. "I took my clothes and stuff and left, but I forgot my clock, so a few days later I went back for it and, I couldn't believe it, my own house key didn't work anymore. She'd changed the locks on the doors. It was the weirdest feeling, and, I don't know, something just snapped. I'm pounding on the door and even though she's inside, she won't open up, which makes me even madder. I start yelling. From inside my mother tells me to go away and I yell louder. This is a real scene now. Our neighbor Mr. Farnsworth comes out and says, 'Come back when you're calmer, son,' and I drill him with all the good words I've been saving up for him for about ten years.

"My mother's crying and yelling, 'Go away, just go away.' And then she says, 'Go away or I'll call the police.' I say, 'What?' And she says she'll call the police, yells it really, and then Mr. Farnsworth yells he already has. I'm thinking, What? They're calling the cops on *me* who's trying to get into his own house? And I walk over toward Farnsworth, who beats it back into his house, as well he should. I go back to my mother's front door and knock lightly this time because, it's funny, I really want in, I want to get my radio but I also want to hear about my dad, what he was really like and stuff, and"—here Maurice tried to smile, but it looked more like a sad facial distortion—"also just to talk to my mom and, you know, be with her like normal, but she wouldn't open up and pretty soon I hear sirens and I don't know what to do. I wanted to say, 'I'm not going away. You can ask me to leave and you can change the locks, but it's not that easy because I'm not going away.' " Maurice took in and released a deep breath. "But I was only sixteen and the sirens were wailing and what can I say? I just beat it out of there." He slowly closed and opened his eyes, and seemed more like himself again. "Anyhow, that's the last conversation I had with her. If you can call it that."

Janice was quiet a second or two before a question occurred to her. "How'd you get the clock?"

Again the bitter smile. "Went back a couple nights later when my mother was gone, broke a window, and took it." He paused. "Two days later I get notice that she's got a restraining order against me, which was kind of a slap in the face. I whited out the names and wrote over them in reverse so it was like a restraining order against *her* and I mailed it to her, but it came back addressee moved, no forwarding address." Maurice peeled the last strip from the label. His voice was quiet—it was almost as if he was talking to himself now. "It bothered me at the time, but who knows? Maybe it was all for the best. You know, my wrestling coach found me a good place to stay and I really got into the wrestling." He made a little smile. "For a couple of years there, I was a regular wrestling fool."

He turned away and Janice drew close from behind and began massaging his shoulders and neck with both hands. His neck seemed to loosen, and then his shoulders. She let her hands slide under his T-shirt and up his back, and then she wrapped them around his smooth chest. She could feel him giving in to her. She'd just begun moving her hands down his stomach when the phone rang and his body again turned wooden.

Don't answer it, she thought.

He answered it. After listening for a few seconds, he said, "Where?" and then he listened some more until finally he said, "Okay, no problem. I'm on it."

He turned to Janice. "There's a pump problem at the long pond." He smiled. "Can you stand thirty minutes without me?"

Janice shrugged, and Maurice went out in black galoshes that made her think fleetingly of Paddington Bear.

After he was gone, the room felt suddenly quiet. She finished the popcorn. She got up to feed a couple of logs into the fire. She walked over to Maurice's dresser, picked up the clock, and turned it in her hands. There was an inscription on the back. It said *To Maurice on his third birthday from his everlovin' Dad.*

Janice's eyes lifted to the dresser mirror, and with a sudden shock of recognition she saw reflected there the smaller Janice she once was, the girl who over the years had received and saved dozens of gifts from absent fathers—strange dolls and empty jewelry boxes and even a horrible tiara. In the mirror her face looked as miserable as Maurice's had when he was talking about the clock. That's who she and Maurice were—the left behind. Except now they weren't. Now they had each other.

The sudden sharp ring of the telephone gave her a turn. She wondered if it might be Maurice but knew she shouldn't answer. After four rings, the answering machine connected, but the volume was turned down so Janice couldn't hear anything. She glanced at the door through which Maurice would at any moment return, and then she slid the volume control up.

A man's voice was saying, "The board of directors are ninety-nine percent ready to sign, absolutely primed, and this contract is fat, Maurissimo, but they just need the teeniest push, if you read me."

Click.

Janice slid the volume control back down. The voice was familiar—she'd heard it before, she was positive of that, but she didn't know where.

And then all at once she did.

It was the same man who'd answered at Jocko's Whatever-it-was Security. But whose board of directors was ninety-nine percent primed to sign what? And what kind of push was he talking about?

Janice idly pulled open a couple of Maurice's dresser drawers. The T-shirts were neatly folded and stacked. All the socks were paired and rolled. His briefs—all black Calvin Kleins—were tightly folded with waistbands up. Only when Janice lifted the stack of T-shirts to peek beneath did she realize that she was unconsciously looking for something. What, she had no idea.

Thirsty. She was thirsty. She went to the refrigerator, supplied as always with fat-free cottage cheese, high-energy smoothies, and Rolling Rock beer. Toward the back was a half-gallon orange juice carton. Janice pushed the bottles aside and pulled the carton out, but something was funny. As she tilted it slightly, its weight didn't shift. Whatever was in the carton wasn't liquid.

Janice folded back the pour spout and tipped it toward a glass. Nothing came out. She peered inside. It was nearly full of something black and rubbery looking. It was creepy, and she didn't know if she wanted to see inside or not. And there was something else: The pour spout had been opened on both sides, so she could pull back both flaps and reach inside.

She reached inside.

What she felt was rubbery and tightly balled up. She took hold and pulled. When it popped free of the carton, the rubbery substance seemed to expand, and come to life. Janice suddenly saw two great white eyes, a nose, a face.

It was a rubber pullover mask of a bald African-American male, a mask, only a mask, but still, it was creepy. Why would Maurice have it? And why would he hide it in an orange juice carton in his refrigerator?

A shadow passed the kitchen window.

Quickly Janice stuffed the mask back into the carton, slid the carton back in the refrigerator, and was replacing the bottles in their position in front of it when the front door opened. She grabbed a beer, closed the refrigerator, and began opening kitchen drawers.

"Hey." Maurice's voice, behind her, calm and low.

"Oh," Janice said, turning. "You're back. Now you can tell me where the bottle opener is."

Maurice glanced at the beer she was holding, then fixed her with an even stare. "It's a twist-off."

Janice's face, already flushed, flushed further. "Oh."

"And you haven't finished your first beer yet."

"It got warm," Janice said. "And kind of flat."

194

Maurice went to a window, pulled back the shade, and stood staring out. Janice's heart was pounding wildly, whether from excitement or fear, she couldn't tell. She walked over to him and stood quietly for a few seconds. He'd seen her through the window with the mask. She was almost certain he had. She took an actual deep breath. Then she said, "So what is that thing, anyway?"

Without surprise Maurice said, "What thing would that be?"

"The mask hidden in the juice carton."

She was watching his face. A faint smile appeared. "It's a Shaq mask. Shaquille O'Neal. I wear it Halloweens."

Janice just stared at him.

"It's more fun than you'd think. I say things like, 'Dayam, Shaq be superhumanic!' " He made a little grin. "You just don't get that many chances to say that."

Janice nodded uncertainly. "So why do you need to keep it in a juice carton in the fridge?"

Maurice seemed slightly annoyed. "Look. I used to have it hanging on my closet door in more or less plain sight as kind of a joke, but then with all these break-ins by black guys, it suddenly didn't seem so funny. I was going to throw it away, but I didn't really want to, so I just stashed it."

He waited a few seconds, staring forward, then turned slowly to Janice. His face had changed. The annoyance was gone. He was serious now. In a low voice he said, "I wouldn't care if someone else believed me or not, but I care whether you do. It's important to me that you believe me."

Janice looked at him. His eyes were different. They seemed suddenly soft, almost gentle, and vulnerable. She leaned forward and kissed him on the mouth. Then in a whisper she said, "I believe you."

Because she did.

CHAPTER TWENTY-TWO

Retrieval

Early Thursday evening, Mick was home staring out at the nest when the phone rang. The phone was on his desk, and without taking his eyes from the nest, he picked it up. It was Reece.

"Mister, you've been on the phone."

Mick had been exercycle talking to Lisa Doyle. "There a new rule about talking on the phone?" he said.

"There should be. Especially when I've got breaking news."

Mick was still watching the nest. The female was sitting. She'd laid four eggs so far. "What news would that be?"

"I figured out where you got Alexander Selkirk."

These words sent a shock wave slamming through Mick. "What do you mean, where I got him?"

"I'm doing a report on *Moll Flanders,* so I was reading about the author, Daniel Defoe, who also wrote *Robinson Crusoe.*" Reece waited expectantly.

Mick said, "Okay, I'm lost so far."

"You are? Swear?"

"Swear."

"Well, it turns out Robinson Crusoe was based on an actual guy, and his name was—" Again the expectant pause.

"No idea."

"Alexander Selkirk!"

Mick couldn't quite believe what he was hearing. Alexander Selkirk. "But how—" His voice tailed off.

"So you really didn't know that?"

Mick said he hadn't.

Reece worked up a quick theory. "Maybe you'd read the name and thought you'd forgotten it, but actually filed it away. Supposedly we file everything away—it's the retrieval that's tricky. I guess something clicked and you retrieved it without knowing it."

"Maybe," Mick said, and fell silent. He was chasing behind all this. If Alexander Selkirk was the real name of somebody dead, then why was Nora calling her e-boyfriend that? Or could it just be coincidental? Maybe there were two Alexander Selkirks. Or this one was some distant relation to the dead one.

"You there, Mickman?"

"I am," Mick said, "but you know what? I gotta go. Thanks for the revelation, though."

He punched the off button and sat staring at the nest. He stared a long time, so long it was as if his mind went empty. And then with a sudden, calm, certain clarity it came to him.

If Robinson Crusoe was based on Alexander Selkirk, then Alexander Selkirk was based on Mr. Cruso.

The happy bachelor.

Who'd been in the mall the day Mick had lost Nora.

Whose room Nora had been hovering near that day in the hall.

Who drove a fancy emerald green Porsche.

So it was Mr. Cruso, and some new raw emotion within Mick clamped hard on this fact and would not let go.

He went to the backyard shed and found an empty gas can. He

filled it with the silica sand his father had used when mortaring their brick patio.

Mick hated Mr. Cruso, he hated his fancy emerald green Porsche, and he had a plan.

CHAPTER TWENTY-THREE

Home Park Gardens

Twenty blocks away, at 1331 Nottingham, Lisa was hatching her own little scheme. She was going to drop off a farewell present for Elder Keesler. He'd given her a book, so surely it was okay to give him one. She'd decided that *A Farewell to Arms*, which was her actual favorite book, was no good because it was clearly a love story, but *Out of Africa*, which she'd read after seeing the movie six times, would be fine. It was African, for one thing, and even though the movie was chock-full of men loving Isak Dinesen and men leaving Isak Dinesen, the book itself made no mention of affairs or kissing under mosquito nets. So she strapped her copy on the back of her bike and rode to Home Park Gardens. She was going to leave it by the door and go away.

In some apartments, yellow lights were on. The air was heavy and greenish and made everything glow supernaturally.

There was no light in the missionary apartment. No bikes out back, either, and no Corolla. A bird was singing urgently, a long complicated tune. She looked up and saw that it was a cardinal, who took note of her, stayed put, and sang some more. She wheeled her bicycle warily toward the entrance of Elder Keesler's building. There was his mat, the meaningful mat. She leaned down and placed the book faceup on it. Then she paused before the meaningful door. Should she knock? Maybe she just missed seeing the car. Maybe the bikes were inside. She gave the door three raps, but nothing happened. She knew she should be relieved, but, heart still racing from the thought of seeing him once more, she knew she wasn't relieved.

Slowly, she mounted the bike again and rode under the cardinal, past the mailboxes, to Janice's building, where a third-story light was on.

"Hi," Lisa said, smiling as usual when Genevieve opened the door. From the climb up, Lisa felt glazed with sweat. "Is Janice home?"

Genevieve's expression was quizzical. "I thought she was meeting you at the library."

"Yes!" Lisa lied, throwing her hand up to her mouth. "That's what I meant. I was supposed to meet her, but I was late and by the time I got there she was gone. She might've thought we were meeting at the college library, because we talked about that, too."

As Mrs. Bledsoe stared at her, new sweat seemed to rise from Lisa's every pore.

Finally Mrs. Bledsoe said, "Okay, Lisa. What's going on here?"

"I don't know exactly," Lisa said, and quickly turned away. "Just tell Janice I'm sorry I goofed up and missed her."

Riding home fast, standing up so she could pump harder, feeling the black roads beneath thin whirling tires, Lisa felt a strange confusion of disappointment and anger, disappointment that Joe Keesler wasn't there, that Janice wasn't there, anger that she'd been caught in Janice's lie, and—this was the strange one, the unexplainable one—anger that she hadn't gotten to see Joe Keesler. Why hadn't he been there? Was he already gone, without her knowing? He'd said he was going, of course, but he hadn't said which day.

She stopped for a red light and felt suddenly certain that Elder Keesler was already gone, and that she had just done something ridiculous, something that would make Elder Pfingst and his new companion stare oddly at her on Sunday.

Which made her angrier still.

Lisa pumped harder and, once home, the first thing she did was find the Village Greens business card. There, underlined in red, was Maurice's cell phone number.

Maurice answered. "Village Greens," he said.

"Hi," Lisa said, not even trying to sound polite. "This is Lisa Doyle. Is Janice with you?"

"It's your twin," Lisa heard him say, and then Janice said, "Hi, twin."

"Don't ever tell your mom you're with me when you're not!"

"Just fine, thanks," Janice said. "And you?"

"Did you hear what I said? I went to your apartment, and your mom asked me why I wasn't with you at the library."

"Oh," Janice said. "Whoops."

"Whoops?"

"I'm sorry you got mixed up in it, but, I mean, what can she do? Lock me up?" Then, "Besides, Genevieve isn't my priority anymore. Maurice is."

Lisa took this in. She wondered if Maurice was sitting there, or, worse yet, lying there. He was a predator, a regular Visigoth, but this clearly wasn't the time to point it out. After a long second, she said, very softly, in almost a whisper, "Are you crazy?"

Janice laughed easily. "Maybe. But no more than the next gal."

CHAPTER TWENTY-FOUR

Penal Code

Last period, Friday.

It was Mr. Cruso's class, but Mrs. Stallings had been sitting at his desk when the period began. Mrs. Stallings was all business. She'd noted that Mr. Cruso had been called away on urgent business, written an assignment on the board, and explained that students "should hold any questions, concerns, or feeble ideas about leaving the classroom until Mr. Cruso's return." When Dale Deckert in his most polite voice asked Mrs. Stallings if she "was a distant relation to Joseph Stalin," she'd promptly written him up for Saturday school, and the classroom had thereafter fallen silent.

At 2:30, Mr. Cruso walked in and exchanged places with Mrs. Stallings. But something was different about his manner. There was a strange stiffness to his face. He looked almost mad, but nobody had ever seen him mad before. He stared silently at the students for a few moments, scratching his neatly trimmed beard with what almost seemed like agitation. Then he silently went to the chalkboard and wrote $2,375.00 in large numbers.

He turned around and scanned the room, where everyone sat waiting for whatever was coming next.

Finally Brittany Allen said, "What's that number for, Mr. Cruso?"

"Ah," Mr. Cruso said. "That number represents the large sum

of U.S. dollars I have had to pay to repair my Porsche after running it with sand in the gas tank."

For a less popular teacher, this statement would've drawn smirks and possibly even sneering laughter, but Mr. Cruso was popular, so nobody made a sound and Mr. Cruso continued. "You might wonder why a reasonably intelligent man would run his Porsche with sand in the gas tank."

Mr. Cruso began slowly to prowl the room, letting his intense black eyes fix on one student after another as he went. Mick sat watching him with interest. Mr. Cruso was mad, all right, mad and hungry for revenge. Mick knew he ought to be afraid, but he wasn't. He felt nothing but a strangely giddy pleasure in Mr. Cruso's seething anger. Mick was wearing his leather jacket and began idly to slide the interior zipper back and forth.

Mr. Cruso said, "I ran my Porsche with sand in the gas tank because I didn't *know* there was sand in the gas tank. I didn't know there was sand in the gas tank because some deviant put it there."

He slowed at Dale Deckert's desk, and moved on.

"Someone so slimy, so swampy, so shall we say primordial in intellect that he, and I use the male gender advisedly, might turn to vandalism to vent his diseased spleen over some offense that was itself probably only imagined."

It was a pretty good speech. Mick guessed he must've practiced it on the way in.

Mr. Cruso was at the back of the room now, and as he stalked back down the next aisle he pulled a paper from his pocket. "According to the New York penal code, a person is guilty of criminal mischief in the second degree, when—and I quote—'with intent to damage property of another person, and having no right to do so nor any reasonable ground to believe that he has

203

such right, he damages property of another person in an amount exceeding one thousand five hundred dollars.' End quote."

He stopped and again scanned the room, this time with a strangely unpleasant smile on his lips. "Reasonable ground, children, is not getting a B when you wanted an A, or an F when you wanted to pass."

Mr. Cruso resumed his slow, prowling walk toward the front of the class.

"A Class D felony is punishable in the state penal and correctional complex for not less than one year."

He paused a second or two to let this sink in.

"The good news is that the perpetrator was evidently unaware of the video monitors in the garage where my Porsche was parked. In those videotapes, the male perpetrator can be clearly viewed pouring something into my gas tank from a gas can. There was also an eyewitness who got a good look at the perpetrator, so it's just a matter of time before the vandal is apprehended."

This worried Mick a little, but not much. He'd been wearing a no-logo sweatshirt with the hood up, so how much could a camera pick up? And, besides, this was a vandalism case—it wasn't like they were going to call out the F.B.I. or anything.

Mr. Cruso had again reached the front of the room. He pivoted slowly and let his eyes scan the entire class. This time his voice was softer, more sympathetic, almost caressing. "I'm sure the boy who did this isn't a bad kid." He paused, and for that moment he looked more like the old Mr. Cruso, the Mr. Cruso who liked people and brought out the best in everybody. Even more softly he said, "The detective in charge of the case advises me the charges will be less severe if the boy presents himself voluntarily to me."

He waited. His waiting hung over the room, which felt suddenly small and close. Nobody spoke. Nobody moved. It was almost as if nobody breathed. When Mick slowly ran his pocket zipper open, its low sibilant sound seemed almost loud.

Mr. Cruso turned. "You have something to offer, Mick?" he said.

"Not really," Mick said. "I was just thinking how terrible it would be to have something you really liked get damaged like that."

Mr. Cruso's eyes changed slightly. Hardened. "So?"

"It just seems weird, you know, that somebody would go to that kind of trouble over something as puny as a grade."

Mr. Cruso was taking this in when the bell rang. All at once everyone stood and began quickly filing from the room. If this were a jail, the doors had just swung open.

"If any of you know anything at all about this, contact me privately!" Mr. Cruso shouted after them. "Anything you tell me will be confidential!"

None of the students even glanced back at him; they just kept filing ahead. Mick was himself nearly to the door when Mr. Cruso said, "Mick, can I see you for a moment, please?"

Mick turned and let the others slip around him until the class was completely empty except for him and Mr. Cruso, whose eyes were fixed on Mick. "Sit down, Mick."

Mick sat on a student desk. He reached inside his jacket and began fiddling with the interior zipper. Open, closed, open.

"So what was that question all about, Mick?"

Mick shrugged. "I don't know, it was just interesting to me."

"What was interesting to you?" His voice low and coaxing.

"That somebody would go to all that trouble to do that to your car. I mean, it's awful, but I was just sitting there thinking about it while you were talking. It didn't sound like something casual, you know? I mean, when I lost my muckraker paper, you believed me and gave me an extension. That's what made me wonder why whoever did it, did it. You're pretty fair about grades, so, you know, maybe it's not about grades."

Mild impatience crossed Mr. Cruso's face. "Thus did speech evolve. When we have problems, the customary thing to do is talk about them."

Mick shrugged. "Yeah, well, that's not always so easy."

The teacher raked his fingers through his neat beard and kept his eyes on Mick. "So your theory is that this was the voiceless trying to speak."

Mick imagined a face with a blank space where the mouth should be. "Maybe, yeah. Who knows?"

Mr. Cruso made a thin smile. "Oh, somebody does."

There was a short silence before Mick said, "But you think it's a kid from school, right?"

"Right."

"Well, then," Mick said, "it's just a matter of time, like you said." He ran the zipper open, then closed. "Because whoever it was will blab to somebody, and somebody will blab to somebody else, and pretty soon some nice kid with good moral values will walk through the door and tell you all about it."

Mr. Cruso kept his eyes on Mick. For the next half minute neither of them spoke. There was only the dim sound of the sliding zipper. Open. Closed. Open. Closed. Finally Mr. Cruso said, "How about you, Mick? Would you walk in here and tell me if you heard who did it?"

Mick picked his words. "I guess it would depend on the kid's reasons. But yeah, if his reasons were bogus and I thought you were a good guy, I guess I'd come in and give you some kind of hint about it."

Mr. Cruso slowly took this in. "Ah. So it would depend. It would be conditional." A few seconds passed. "How old are you, Mick?"

"Fifteen. Sixteen in a few days."

"Well, your answer would normally be a good one. Very mature. It recognizes that lots of moral questions aren't as black and white as we'd like." His eyes seemed to narrow slightly. "But the line between right and wrong on this one isn't blurry. It's as straight as can be. Whoever deliberately vandalized my car is a felon, Mick. That much is a fact. He can, however, make things easier on himself. If, for example, he were fifteen when he committed the crime, he'd be treated as a juvenile. His records would be sealed after a probationary period, and there would probably be no actual punishment beyond compensation."

Mr. Cruso kept staring at Mick, who stared back and kept moving the zipper back and forth. Neither of them blinked.

In a soft, sympathetic voice Mr. Cruso said, "Is there anything you want to tell me, Mick?"

Mick's hand on the zipper stilled for a second, then kept moving. Open. Closed. "No," he said. "I already said everything I had to say." He let his eyes drift for a second, then brought them back to Mr. Cruso. "Why? Do you have something you want to tell me?"

A startled look crossed the teacher's face, followed at once by annoyance. "No," he said through tight lips, "I certainly do not."

Mick nodded and let his gaze float. "So can I go now?"

In a brittle voice, Mr. Cruso said, "Yes, you can go now." He turned and began putting papers into his briefcase, but as Mick left the room he felt Mr. Cruso's eyes drilling into his back.

Waiting just opposite the classroom door, smiling in her green plaid skirt, white top, and braided red hair, was Lisa Doyle. "Hey," she said.

"Hey."

They fell in together, walking the corridor toward the stairs. She said, "I heard Cruso went weird last period."

"Jeez," Mick said, "it only happened ten minutes ago."

She grinned. "Weird news travels fast." They kept walking and when Mick said nothing, she said, "So? Did Cruso ballisticize?"

"A little," Mick said. "Somebody trashed his fancy car."

"Yeah, that's what I heard. Which is in itself weird because I thought everybody liked Cruso."

"A few more periods like that one and the tune might change," Mick said, a thought that pleased him. He was beginning to feel good about holding his own with Cruso, and about Cruso's annoyance and frustration. He suddenly chuckled and when Lisa gave him a quizzical look, Mick said, "Cruso said the guy who did it was swampy, sleazy, and primordial."

Lisa didn't laugh as expected. She thought about it and said, "I would've just called him cowardly."

Mick fell silent. Cowardly? He never thought anyone would think of what he'd done as cowardly.

They turned down the stairs together and Lisa said, "So how come he kept you after class?"

"I guess because I asked in class why somebody would want to do that to his car."

"Does Cruso think you know who did it or something?"

Mick made a small laugh. "Actually, I think he might think it was me."

Lisa pulled up short. "What?"

Mick shrugged. "He didn't say so straight out, but, yeah, that was my impression."

They walked on a few steps in silence, then Lisa stopped again and looked Mick in the eye. "I guess I'm sorry for Cruso and his car, but I think it's horrible he'd think it might've been you because if I know anything at all, I know you'd never do anything like that."

She stood looking into him from eyes that expected to see nothing but virtue, and Mick felt a strange compulsion to tell her the truth. They were in the foyer, and from the steps someone called out, "Hey, Doyle, we're waiting on you!"

She reached forward and squeezed his hand. "Bye-ya," she said, and as she left, she called over her shoulder, "Call me!"

CHAPTER TWENTY-FIVE

Mail

When Lisa Doyle opened her mailbox that afternoon, she found a catalogue for fireplace tools, a dry-cleaning coupon, a gas bill, and an envelope that made her skin prickle. The scribbly handwriting was Joe Keesler's, and it was postmarked Cambridge. She sat down on the grass, still prickling and almost giddy with the feel of an actual letter from Him, and ripped open the envelope:

Wednesday, May 23

Dear Lisa,

I feel very confused and sorry, but the long and short of it is that when I came back home, my old girlfriend from Duke had driven all the way from North Carolina (she called my mom and my mom told her when I'd be released) and even though she broke up with me when I decided to go on a mission (she's agnostic), she said she wanted to be with me again and I have to say that when I saw her, I felt the same way. I really wasn't leading you on. I really, really care for you. I cared for you more than I should have, given the situation. But I have to see where things are going with Kara.

Please forgive me for any hurt this has caused you.

Joe

Lisa crumpled the letter in her fist, then smoothed it out, reread it, and crumpled it again. She let it drop to the ground. Wednesday. He wrote the letter on Wednesday. Which meant he'd left on Monday, long before she set the book on his doormat. Was the book sitting there still? Or did Elder Pfingst have it on a shelf somewhere in the apartment, wondering what to do with a used book by Isak Dinesen and a note from a girl signed Love?

She looked at the balled letter. She picked it up, unwadded it, and then with the flat of her hand tried to iron the letter smooth again.

CHAPTER TWENTY-SIX

Perambulation

That same afternoon, Mick headed for the library, then changed his mind and started toward his father's shop, then changed course again and wound up at Reece's. He called in through the back door and heard Reece yell, "Down here!"

Reece was in the basement lying on the sofa reading *Moll Flanders* by Daniel Defoe.

"How is it?" Mick said, nodding at the book.

Reece made a mock grimace. "Every time Moll does any of the stuff she's famous for—you know, the good wanton stuff—she pays the price, and then some."

"Kind of takes the fun out of the fun stuff, huh?" Mick said. The problem was, he thought, sometimes you don't know what price you're going to pay. Getting caught by Cruso—if he did get caught—didn't bother him. Whereas Lisa Doyle indirectly calling him a coward did.

The phone rang. Reece waited for the third ring, then picked it up and said, "Reeceville."

Mick saw his eyes brighten and heard his voice deepen. "This is Mr. Reece speaking."

Mick knew at once it was a telemarketer. Reece loved asking

telemarketers increasingly weird questions until finally the tele-marketer would hang up on him, which was the object. Today Reece began, "You know, I *haven't* been very happy with our long-distance service. I've been calling the Cayman Islands a lot lately—what kind of rates do your people have to the Caymans?"

Mick went over to the piano and played "Invention 13," twice. When he finished, Reece was still on the phone, smiling and talking in his husky adultoid voice.

Mick closed the key cover. As he headed for the stairs, Reece covered the phone and said, "Who gave you permission to leave?"

Mick smiled, waved, and kept walking.

The house was empty when Mick arrived home ten minutes later. He took Foolish to the park, threw him Frisbee after Frisbee, shot him a stream of water from the fountain, then went over to the spot where he'd first met Myra and Pam. He sat on the ground and scratched Foolish's stomach until the dog stretched out and went limp with sleep.

Mick lay back and closed his eyes, but he didn't feel like sleeping. He didn't feel like anything. In fact, things seemed pretty grim. He'd thought making Mr. Cruso feel bad would make him feel better, but it didn't. It made him feel worse, especially after hearing Lisa's ideas on the subject. And two thousand, three hundred and seventy-five dollars. He had no idea that a little sand in a gas tank could rack up that kind of money.

"That you, Mick?"

Mick's eyes shot open. Myra smiled down at him. He said, "What're you doing here?"

Myra fingered the sleeves of her jogging gear. "Running. Getting stuff out of my system." She smiled. "How about you?"

Mick nodded at Foolish. "Giving the hound a little quality Frisbee time."

Myra gave him one of her big, easy smiles and sat down close enough to Foolish that she could stroke his stomach. They were quiet for a while, then Mick said, "My history teacher was freaking out last period because somebody vandalized his car."

Myra asked who his history teacher was, and when Mick said, "Cruso," she kept smoothing her hand back and forth over Foolish's stomach. Finally she said, "I wouldn't feel too sorry for Mr. Cruso."

This surprised Mick. "Why's that?"

In a quiet voice Myra said, "He's got a slimy underside."

"What does that mean?"

"It means he makes passes at female students."

Another surprise. "I didn't think teachers did that."

Myra laughed. "Yeah, well, in a perfect world they don't." A few seconds passed. "Here, for example, is what Cruso said to me. It was after a practice for *Anne Frank,* and he gave me a ride home in his little roadster, and before I got out he said, 'You know, Myra, you are strangely vivifying. You breathe life into things. You should give me a call sometime late at night, after you turn eighteen.'"

"Cruso said, 'You are strangely vivifying'?"

Myra smiled unhappily. "Direct quote."

"What did you say?"

She kept scratching Foolish. "Well, in this weird way, I was flattered. I mean, *vivifying.* Nobody ever called me vivifying before." She smiled. "But afterward I thought it was creepy. Lining up girls for future, you know, plucking."

Mick nodded. Myra was the local version of a rock star. He'd never imagined feeling sorry for her, but he felt a little sorry for her now, or at least for the younger Myra that Cruso had been hitting on. "Not so easy being a girl, huh?" he said.

Myra shrugged and smiled. "Not so easy being anybody," she said. They were quiet a few seconds, and Myra said, "Okay, this is fun, but it ain't aerobic." As she bent to stand, her strapped top loosened and drew Mick's attention to the smooth whiteness that swelled there. She gave him a knowing look, then set something on her watch. As she turned to go she said, "Check your e-mail when you get home."

Mick watched her start into long loping strides. She had her hair in a ponytail and when she got far enough away that he could no longer tell the color of her hair, she reminded him of someone else.

He leashed Foolish and started walking. He thought he was going home, but when he got there, the house was still dark and he kept walking, just walking, block after block, first in one direction, then another. He walked past houses, Duz Bro, and the First Presbyterian Church. He checked his pants pockets, found $3.75, and stopped at McDonald's for four eighty-nine-cent hamburgers and a cup of water. He sat at one of the outside tables, ate two of the burgers, and gave two to Foolish. They kept walking. When the sun set and it turned cool, he zipped up his jacket. He turned east into a snug-looking neighborhood, glanced into the lighted homes and saw people eating dinner, watching TV, reading newspapers. He walked block after block, heading generally toward the high school but in a totally new way that made him feel he was a tourist in his own town. He crossed streets named after birds and governors and forgotten officials, then followed one that led to a series of English names. Cumberland, Westmoreland, Nottingham.

Lisa Doyle's street.

Mick followed the numbers down the street until he stood in front of 1331, the numerical palindrome.

A Dutch-style house on a hill. The front room was lighted, but nobody was in it. To the right was another room, also lighted, but the interior was made indistinct by sheer curtains. Mick glanced around, then looped Foolish's leash over a fence picket and walked over to the window and glanced in.

It looked like the breakfast room. Lisa Doyle was still in her green skirt and white blouse, lying on the window seat with a letter in her hand.

He tapped lightly, then a little harder until Lisa looked up, startled. She came over and cranked open the window. She looked a lot different than she had after school this afternoon, a lot worse. Her face looked puffy and wet. "Hi," she said.

"Hi," Mick said. "What's the matter? Is something the matter?"

She lowered her eyes. "Not really." Then, looking up, "How'd you get here?"

Mick saw the envelope on the window seat. "I don't know." Pause. "I was just out walking the dog."

Lisa raised her eyebrows. She sniffed a little. "Kind of a long walk." Then, touching her nose with a wadded tissue, she seemed to be thinking about something. When she met his eyes again, she asked, "Want to walk a couple more blocks with me?"

This seemed like a good way to find out what was going on. "Sure. If you want to."

As they headed away from her house, Lisa crossed her arms and said, "It's nice out."

Mick nodded and didn't say anything. It was nice, especially now that Lisa was there. There was the clicking of Foolish's nails on the pavement and the gentle stirrings of light wind moving through the street trees.

She said, "Were you out walking because of that Cruso thing?"

"I guess so," Mick said. He couldn't tell her he'd watched Myra Vidal running and her swishing ponytail had reminded him of her, which, he realized now, was exactly what Myra's ponytail had reminded him of. He stopped so Foolish could do a little bush marking. Lisa stopped, but she didn't say anything.

Mick thought of the wrinkled letter on the window seat looking like it'd been wadded up, then smoothed out. "Was that letter something bad?" Mick asked.

She looked like she was about to say no, not really, or some version of it, but then her shoulders dropped and she said, "Kind of, yeah."

"Yeah?"

She gave him a long, wondering look. "You really want to hear this?"

Mick put up a little laugh. "No, I mean, yeah, I do want to hear."

Lisa seemed to be collecting her thoughts. "Okay. Remember a while back how I told you about the missionaries coming to dinner?"

Mick took a deep breath. "You mean tall, dark, and Mormon?"

Lisa nodded. "Well, tall, dark, and Mormon came to dinner. Tall, dark, and Mormon sort of said that he liked me. Tall, dark, and Mormon went back to Boston, where he immediately wrote me a letter informing me that his girlfriend from Duke, who he'd never mentioned, had decided to take him back."

The "who" should've been "whom," but Mick wasn't about to say so.

"Her name is *Kara*," Lisa said. "The petty part of me thinks, how could he go for somebody named *Kara?*"

They walked half a block in silence, and Mick said, "So you liked him, I guess."

"Yeah."

For Mick, this made everything seem a little less nice. "Well," he said.

Lisa didn't say anything for a while, and neither did Mick. The streets were dark now, and a big, squashed moon was rising. "What're you thinking about?" Lisa asked.

Mick looked at the squashed moon, then down at Lisa. "Oh, I guess I was thinking about how, before I got to your place, the houses I was passing seemed to be full of all these happy-seeming people doing happy-seeming things."

Lisa looked down at the sidewalk. "And now they don't?"

"Now they seem to be full of disappointed people."

"Like me?"

"Yeah," Mick said. "Only I think it was probably my disappointment I was feeling right then."

She didn't say anything.

They walked past a man practicing his golf swing in a dark front yard. The club head made a quick *shush* as it swept past the grass. Foolish turned to see what had caused the sound, but seemed confused.

Mick looked at the dog and said, "That's why we call him Foolish."

Lisa's small laugh was delicate, and, to Mick's ear, almost musical.

After a minute or so, he said, "Once this college girl told me her favorite time ever was eighth grade because she and her boyfriend would just walk around everywhere together. Walk and talk."

They crossed a street and Lisa said, "So would this college girl be Myra Vidal?"

Mick was surprised she knew this. "Yeah."

Lisa asked how he met her, and Mick told her about the bet with Reece.

"And sometimes you see her?"

Mick remembered sitting with Myra in Bing's when Janice Bledsoe and Maurice walked in. "Guess your friend Janice reported that, huh?"

Lisa laughed. "The night has a thousand eyes."

The sighting at Bing's had happened weeks ago. Mick was wondering why Lisa had waited until now to mention it when she said, "I guess you still see her sometimes?"

"Not very often, but sometimes she calls me when her best friend is occupied. She's got a boyfriend in California and tries to stay out of trouble. I guess I'm one of her ways of staying out of trouble."

Lisa seemed to be thinking about something. Finally she said, "Do you think a relationship with somebody older is always bound to be kind of, you know, uneven?"

Mick said he guessed it depended on the people, "but, yeah, with Myra, it's kind of like she's this really cool older sister."

Lisa didn't say anything. They kept walking and then all of a sudden Mick felt Lisa's hand take his, and his hand at once clasped hers, tightly, almost hungrily.

They walked three more blocks in a state of silence that Mick didn't want to end. Only when they got back to her house did she let go of his hand. They stood awkwardly for a second or two, and then Mick said, "Thanks."

Lisa's face wasn't quite so puffy anymore. "For what?"

"I'm not sure. I guess just everything."

Lisa Doyle smiled at Mick Nichols and then she did something surprising. She leaned quickly forward and kissed him on the cheek. "Bye-ya," she said, and was gone.

CHAPTER TWENTY-SEVEN

Suggestions

When Mick got back to the house, the living room was lighted. He crept to the window and peered in. Nora was sitting beside his father, knitting with thin black needles while some commercials flashed on the TV. It looked normal, as normal as anything he'd seen in any window during his walk that night, but he knew it wasn't.

Mick opened the back porch door, hung Foolish's leash, and tried to slide through the kitchen, but his father said, "Well, here comes the Mick."

"Hey," Mick said, and waited to be quizzed on his where-abouts, but his father surprised him. "You eaten?" he said.

"Yeah."

"Well, eat a little more. There's chicken tetrazzini in the oven." He stood up, turned off the TV, and looked at Mick. "You're wasting away, kiddo."

It was true Mick had lost a few pounds. "Sure, okay," he said and followed his father to the kitchen, where Mick found himself devouring the plate of tetrazzini set before him. He was surprised how hungry he was, and how good it all tasted.

His father brought a fresh cup of coffee to the table and said, "Okay, Mick, what happened today at Mary Jemison High?"

A standard question, and Mick gave his standard, nothing-much shrug, but tonight his father pressed him. "Hey, c'mon. Give us a little campus news."

Nora came into the kitchen and started dunking dishes in the sink.

Mick slowed his chewing. "Yeah, okay. My history teacher, Mr. Cruso, kind of freaked out seventh period." Mick was watching Nora. He thought he caught her hands stilling for just an instant at the sink.

"Freaked out over what?" his father said.

"His car. Somebody put sand in the gas tank."

Mick's father grimaced in disgust. "What does he drive?"

"An old Porsche. A '59, I think he said."

"Nice car," his father said, "and sand in the gas tank's big money."

Mick nodded. "They're charging him over two thousand dollars to fix it."

His father let out a low whistle. "You know, I'll bet Essa would let me do it for cost. That'd save him a third, easy." He turned to Nora. "You know this guy, Nora? Could you talk to him?"

When she turned, her face seemed slightly misshapen. "He teaches at the high school. We don't generally run in the same circles."

"Yeah, but still. You must know somebody who knows him." He winked at Mick. "Tell him we'll give him the educator discount."

Nora kept washing dishes.

"Well, anyhow, it's a real shame," his father said. "They know who did it?"

Mick shook his head. "He thinks it's somebody from school, a male, but it could be a girl, I think. I guess Cruso makes a habit of hitting on girls."

Nora shut off the water and turned slowly. "What do you mean, hitting on girls?"

Mick finished his bite of rice, then wiped his lips with a napkin. "I guess he gets them alone and makes, you know, suggestions, or whatever. He told Myra she should call him the minute she turned eighteen." Mick paused. "He told her she was strangely vivifying."

Nora's face went suddenly pale. She turned back to her dishes.

"Jeez," his father said. "Talk about sleazy. A teacher going after students. They ought to can the guy." He turned to Nora. "Couldn't they can him for that?"

In a low voice, without turning, she said, "These things are hard to prove."

His father grinned. "Yeah, okay, but I just retracted the educator discount."

Nora carefully folded her dish towel and turned to Mick's father. Her face had a wooden look. "It's late. I'm going up."

"Sure," his father said, and then, "You okay, Nora?"

"I'm fine," Nora said. She talked evenly, and as she left the room her step was slow and careful, like, Mick thought, a drunk person trying to act sober. Or, he thought later, lying in bed replaying it in his mind, like someone mad trying to act calm.

Mick took his empty bowl to the sink and went upstairs. Nora was in her bedroom with the door closed, and Mick quickly tried a few new passwords to get into her e-mail—Cruso and Defoe and even vivifying, plus five or six others—but nothing worked. He checked his own e-mail and found out why Myra had told him to check it. She'd left him a message. *Hey, Mick as in mittens, how would you feel about letting me cook for your sixteenth birth-day? Filet mignons, plus a little birthday surprise. Saturday night sixish?*

Mick wrote back *yes*, sixteen times.

CHAPTER TWENTY-EIGHT

Resolutions

On Memorial Day, Lisa went with her parents to visit her grand-parents in Homer, which her father liked jokingly to call his ancestral burg. She ate baked beans and her father's red cabbage cole slaw. She spread out an old quilt on her grandmother's back lawn, put her hair in a bun that she secured with a pencil, and, feeling freckly and white in her one-piece bathing suit, wrote a list.

- *Will be cheerier around house.*
- *Will be better friend to Janice.*
- *Will ask Mick to bake cookies Sat. night.*

She put down her pencil and stopped.

- *Will totally and completely stop thinking about Joe Keesler.*

Lisa set down the list and looked up at the clear blue sky. She closed her eyes. She thought about how it felt to hold Mick's hand, about how she didn't have to feel guilty about it, even though he wasn't Mormon. It wasn't like she was going to marry him or anything, she thought, and then immediately her mind drifted in just that direction, trying to imagine what a grown up Mick Nichols would be like. She knew one thing. It would be easy to talk to him—it had always been easy to talk to him.

Lisa opened her eyes, and wondered if there was any more of her grandmother's chocolate meringue pie inside the fridge.

CHAPTER TWENTY-NINE

In Which Janice and Maurice Exchange Gifts

Maurice at this moment was shaving his chest. Janice was lying on the bed, stroking Harriet (who Maurice had brought home to live with him), and watching Maurice's work with real amusement. "Okay, children, we'll title this fable 'How the Maurician Got His Smoothness,' " she said. Then, a few seconds later, "That's just gotta hurt."

Maurice had his chin tucked down, trying to see what he was doing. When he'd finished his left pec, he looked up. "I hear Marky Mark went the electrolysis route." Maurice grinned. "But then Marky Mark has more discretionary income than I do."

Maurice lathered his right pec and got back to work. About halfway through, he said, "Got a present for you in my front pants pocket."

This drew a snorting laugh from Janice. "I'll bet you do."

Maurice worked his razor carefully around his nipple. "Check it out," he said. "Front left."

The cat slid from Janice's lap as she stood. Janice came over and eyed the pocket. The bulge was squarish. She patted it. A small box maybe. She reached in and slid it out.

It *was* a small box, wrapped in gold foil. She held it up. "Should I open it?"

"Only if you want to see what I bought you."

Under the wrapper, inside the small, lidded box, nested into a soft bed of cotton, was a gold-rimmed red stone attached to a gold necklace. Janice let out an actual gasp, it was so beautiful. "Oh, my God," she said. "It's . . ." She didn't know what to say, and then she did. "It's devastating." She looked then from the necklace to Maurice. "You're devastating."

Maurice, toweling bits of lather from his chest, grinned and said, "I could've told you that."

Janice was looking again at the necklace. The stone was a garnet. The tag on the necklace said 18 KARAT. She turned, beaming, to Maurice. "So how'd you afford this thing? Rob a bank or something?"

Maurice seemed pleased. "*How* isn't anything you should worry your pretty head about. Let's just say some of Maurice's investments are paying off."

Janice was hardly listening. She'd clasped the necklace and went to the medicine cabinet mirror to admire it. She loved it. She absolutely loved it.

"There's some yellow cream in a bottle in the cabinet," Maurice said. "Could you grab it?"

She swung open the cabinet and took out some Hecho in Mexico Genuine Turtle Oil. It was yellow and—she gave it a sniff—a little weird smelling. "What's this stuff for?"

"Soothes the razor burn."

Janice was going to hand it to him but suddenly had another idea. She began to do it for him, rubbing the cream in, her flat hand moving in slow circles, as if polishing his smooth chest smoother. The cream smelled faintly metallic, like a washed soup can or something, but she got used to it.

Maurice closed his eyes. "That feels good," he said.

CHAPTER THIRTY

Detour

On Friday, June 1, under a sky patterned with rows of hazy clouds, the field hockey team—minus Janice Bledsoe—ran past Herman Melville Junior High, the Sno-Boat Parfait stand, white fences, red tulips, and the gray-tongued cemetery where, to Lisa Doyle's surprise, Mick Nichols was poised and waiting on his bicycle.

He grinned and lifted a hand.

"Hi!" Lisa called, turning around to run backward. The other ponytailed girls kept jogging.

Mick started pedaling and cruised up beside her.

"I'm not a great backward runner," Lisa puffed, "so I'll just about-face here, okay?"

"Okay," Mick said, standing on his pedals and keeping just to her right.

"So what're you doing in the cemetery?" Lisa asked, trying not to sound out of breath.

"Watching to make sure the field hockey team doesn't get detoured by ice cream outlets."

"Oh, we save that for the end," Lisa said. "That's how we get through the four miles." She jogged and listened to the whirring of his wheels. She felt light and almost giddy, happier than she'd felt since the day she got Elder Keesler's letter.

"Speaking of sweets," she said, jogging around a trash can, "do you want to come over on Saturday night?"

"This Saturday night?"

"Uh-huh."

Mick paused.

"I was just thinking we'd make pfeffernusses, maybe," Lisa said, slowing down a little so that the whole field hockey team wouldn't hear Mick shaft her. "They're a kind of cookie."

"I really, really want to do that," Mick said. "It's just that I already said I'd do something else."

Lisa absorbed this. "With Myra, right?" She felt like sprinting right out of Jemison. She should have known that boys were never just friends with ex–beauty queens.

"Maybe I could change it," Mick said. "Why don't I call her?"

"Nah," Lisa said, beginning to quicken her pace. "It's okay. See you tomorrow on the chain gang, though."

Ten or eleven ponytails and one bob glistened in the sun ahead of her. Speeding up, Lisa ran past Heather Guzman, Dai Malone, Beth Niederhauser, and Jo Craythorne. Then, weaving and accelerating, she passed the rest. She didn't look back until she led them across the street, and by then Mick and his bicycle were gone.

CHAPTER THIRTY-ONE

Pine Needles

Lisa was polite to Mick at work on Saturday. Polite is what she meant to be, and polite is what she was. Besides their regular duties, the northeast crew was pruning roses, and after Maurice gave a quick demonstration, he issued a pair of clippers to each jeep. When the crew fanned out, Lisa waited to see which way Mick went, then went the opposite direction. It was quiet except for the steady *snip snip snip* of the clippers, and Lisa finally said to Lizette, who was working beside her, "So what's the Spanish word for creep?"

Lizette turned sharply. "You thinking of Maurice?"

Lisa was surprised at the vehemence behind Lizette's expression, and tried to dispel it with a laugh. "Nope. Another candidate."

Lizette's face seemed to shut down—it was as if she'd just lost interest. "*Infeliz,*" she said. "Or *dañado.*"

Lisa repeated it—"Dahn-yado?"—and Lizette nodded and said, "Yeah, more or less." When she finished the rose she'd been clipping, Lizette shifted to another row while Lisa finished up the row they'd been on.

The way to prune floribundas, Maurice had said, is to look for the first five-leafed branch below the spent rose, and then cut diagonally just above that branch. It was easy, once you got the hang of it, and pretty soon Lisa's thoughts persistently drifted toward Joe Keesler and Kara Agnostic, and then toward Mick Nichols and Myra Vidal, back and forth, Joe and Kara, Mick and Myra, until pretty soon she began to feel the tightening clamp of a headache. By the time Maurice came to pick up the crew, it was after four o'clock and Lisa never wanted to see another boy or floribunda in her life.

After cleanup, it was nearly 4:30, and it seemed to Lisa that Mick was anxious to leave—twice she'd caught him checking Traylor's watch—but Maurice wasn't quite done with them.

"Good news," he said and scanned the group with an easy grin. "I've recommended everybody on this crew for upgrade from jeep status. So beginning next pay period you'll all be considered normals and"—here he widened his grin—"will get the pay bump that goes with it." He stopped then and, to Lisa's surprise, he seemed actually tongue-tied. He looked down for a second to regain his composure. When he raised his eyes he said, "I want each one of you to know I was proud to recommend you for upgrade. Each one of you has gotten better with every passing day, and I'm betting each one of you will get even better yet."

Lisa suddenly thought, Maybe I was wrong. Maybe he's not so bad after all.

"Okay," Maurice said, back to his old self-sure voice, "everybody's out of here except Traylor and Uribe, who I need to see for just a second."

As they broke up, Lisa felt Mick giving her a look, but she turned without looking back and vanished into the women's locker room, where she took her time changing. She wanted Mick long gone before she came out. What was she going to say to him? Have fun tonight? My regards to the beauty queen?

She didn't think so.

When Lisa finally came out of the locker room, everyone was gone, which was what she'd thought she wanted, but what her real self wanted, she realized with a sudden pang, was for Mick to have waited for her on his bike like he'd done the other day when she was running with the field hockey team. But he hadn't. Well, she thought, that's what you get for being Miss Fridge. He'd tried to make eye contact with her, and when that failed he'd changed and ridden away without a word. Who could blame him?

Lisa sat down on a bench to wait for her mother. From here she could see Maurice's brown-shingled cottage just beyond the gully and footbridge, which made her think of Maurice, which made her think of Janice, who had quit working at Village Greens the week before, citing a "conflict of interest." That plus Janice's total lack of interest in mandatory field hockey training runs meant that Lisa had seen Janice maybe once in two weeks outside of school. It was like Maurice had taken over Janice's life. Lisa rubbed her right temple—her head really was aching now— and wondered if Janice was in the Maurician bungalow right now, Conflicting with her Interest.

But when the bungalow door opened, the person who stepped out was not Janice. It was Lizette Uribe, and she was crying.

"Lizette?" Lisa said when Lizette had crossed the footbridge.

Lizette glanced toward Lisa, gave a quick wave, and started walking in the opposite direction.

Lisa ran and caught up with her. "What's the matter?"

"Nothing," Lizette said.

Lisa kept walking. "Please, if it's Maurice, you have to tell me. I think Janice is in love with him."

"Well, she can have him."

"Has he been dating you, too?"

Lizette shook her head and wiped fresh tears off her face. "Dating me?" she said bitterly. "I wouldn't call it that."

"Then what? What's he doing?"

Lizette took a few more steps and then, suddenly, did something odd. She stopped short and pressed an open hand over each eye, and just stood there, very still, with the rest of her face contorted, like some kind of weird statue of someone pressing tears back inside.

"Oh, Lizette," Lisa said. "Don't do that." She reached for Lizette's wrist. "Here—let's go to that little picnic area. You know, where the pine trees are."

Lizette allowed herself to be led across the street and up a smooth dirt path to a stone table that said IN MEMORY OF JOAN POKOJSKI. They sat down on either side of the table, and Lisa waited while Lizette wiped her cheeks with the back of her hand.

"Okay," Lizette said. "I'm fine now. See you next week, okay?" She stood up.

"Come on, Lizette," Lisa said. She paused. "If you don't want to tell me, okay, I understand, but you should tell somebody."

Lizette didn't say anything, but she didn't leave. She picked up a pine needle and started poking it into Joan Pokojski's plaque. Slowly, she started talking. "He makes me *do things*," she said. "So I can keep this job and get catering work."

"What do you mean, do things?" Lisa asked, looking up to see if an approaching car was her mother's.

Lizette cleaned out an engraved letter and brushed the dirt off the table. "Well, right now he wanted me to clean his kitchen wearing just my underwear, and the worst part is, I started to do it, but then I just couldn't." She turned now to Lisa. "You know what he said as I was leaving? That I could say adios to the cater-ing work."

Lisa felt sick. She asked if there was other stuff, and Lizette just lowered her eyes and nodded.

"We have to tell someone," Lisa said. Another car passed, slowly, like a big barge, but a tiny old woman was at the wheel, trying to keep the barge afloat.

"No," Lizette said emphatically. "What I have to do is quit and get another job." She began again to work dirt from the plaque with the pine needle.

Lisa looked at her and thought about it, but she couldn't stand it. "No," she said. "No, no, no. We can't let him do this to people."

"We?" Lizette looked up. "We?" she repeated and set her face with a bitter look that made Lisa wonder for a moment if she was doing the right thing. Then she pressed on.

"I mean that I'll help you if you want. He shouldn't be able to do this to you. He shouldn't get away with it."

"Well, he will. They always do."

"Not if you tell somebody important. Like the owners. Or maybe you should take him to court. Sue him for harassment. Then he'd be embarrassed in front of everybody."

"No, *I* would be embarrassed in front of everybody. I'm not going to tell a bunch of strangers what I just told you. Besides, they'll say, 'If it was so bad, why didn't you tell us sooner, or why didn't you just quit?' "

Lisa was quiet. It was true, those probably were the kinds of things people would ask.

"Just so you know," Lizette said, "my family needed the money, is why I didn't quit. My dad's been in Mexico for seven months

234

because his mother's real sick, so the only income we have is from my mom's cleaning houses and what I make."

"And I suppose Maurice knew that?"

Lizette smiled bitterly and stared off. "Maurice knows everything."

And he's the one who gets to decide who's a normal and who's not, Lisa thought. Well, she didn't feel normal, and it was plain Lizette didn't, either.

This time, the car that cruised past the pines was her mother's gray-green Camry. "There's my mom," Lisa said. "Please, please let us take you home. I have an idea, okay?"

Lizette stood up, and Lisa dashed through the bushes to wave down her mother's car. "Okay?" she asked, turning back.

Lizette nodded, crunched the pine needle with her hand, and followed Lisa to the car.

CHAPTER THIRTY-TWO

Faces

Five-fifty Saturday night. A twenty-minute bicycle ride had brought Mick to the upper end of Teal Avenue, where he stopped to pull out the directions Myra had e-mailed him. Okay. Left on Rugby, right on Wendell Terrace, then straight to what Myra called the Dickensian mansion.

Mick folded the map back into his jacket pocket. It was funny, a few days ago he'd been really looking forward to this dinner thing, but now—now he just kind of wished he was over at Lisa's making pfeffernoodles, or whatever those things were.

A few minutes later he wheeled up to the address, but there were two separate driveways, and beyond the broad, brilliantly green, and perfectly crosscut front lawn there were two buildings, one big and one small, both brick and Victorian looking. The big one was dark, but the small one glowed with yellow light, so Mick moved in that direction. As he drew closer, he could hear Pakistani music drifting from the open windows.

The door of the little house was rounded at the top, and an iron knocker in the shape of a hand holding an orange was affixed to it. Beneath the knocker was a note that said *If it's your birthday, come on in.*

Beyond the door, Mick slipped into the soft throb of drums,

sitar, and a beautiful voice singing words he couldn't comprehend. He passed through the entry to the front room—leather furniture, expensive area rugs over oak floors—and from there he could see the kitchen, where Myra stood at a counter intently slicing red grapes. She was wearing a short black dress.

"Hi," Mick said.

Her face immediately relaxed into a smile. "You're here!" She glanced at the clock on the oven. "And right on time." She wiped her hands on a dish towel, came over, and gave him a big hug. "Happy birthday, Mister Mick."

When she stood back, Mick, beaming, gave her dress a look and said quietly, "Wow."

Myra laughed. "Yeah, well, Pam gave me this dress, but I don't wear it out in public much. Gives too many characters too many big ideas."

They both stood smiling, and then Myra turned and looked out the window at a rose garden that reminded Mick of trimming roses with Lisa all afternoon. "Nice view, huh?"

Mick gazed out. "Yeah," he said, turning back to Myra. "It really is." Then, scanning the house again, "Whose place is this, anyhow?"

"Pam's rich boyfriend's rich parents. His name's Kelso, and this little guest house is where Kelso lives now that he's a *collegian.*"

"Kelso's his last name?"

"First." Myra smiled and shook her head. "Guess if you're rich enough you can call your kid whatever you want."

Mick laughed. "So where's Kelso now?"

"New York City with Pam. Dining out, going to plays, staying someplace very deluxe." There was a faint sourness in her voice, but then she brightened. "The nice thing is that Kelso offered his place to us for your celebratory dinner! So. Are you feeling celebratory?"

"I guess so," Mick said.

"Good. Because I guess I am, too." She handed him a glass of lemonade. "Okay," she said, "these are your jobs. Shed your coat, go sit on the deck, and drink your lemonade while I finish up in here."

Mick hung his jacket on the back of a chair, then wandered out to the brick patio, where an iron and glass table had been neatly set for two. The lemonade was good—fizzy, with a strangely pleasant tang to it. Nearby, under a gazebolike roof trailing honeysuckle, there were benches and a round sunken tub from which steam rose. Mick walked over. The water gave off the faint smell of chlorine. Mick bent, put his hand in the water, and pulled it quickly out.

Myra, materializing behind him with a cooking platter, laughed.

"Kinda hot," Mick said.

Myra lifted the barbecue cover and forked two steaks onto the grill. "That's why they call it a hot tub." She set a timer, and then, in the most casual voice possible, said, "I thought we might jump in later." She gave him a quick smile. "Would you like that?"

"I guess so," Mick said. He tried to sip more lemonade, but there was nothing left but ice.

Myra poured him some more.

"Lemonade's pretty good," Mick said.

Myra laughed and was about to say something, but the timer beeped and she began to turn the steaks. When she leaned over, Mick, from behind, caught a fleeting glimpse of her underwear. It was black.

Suddenly Mick said, "Lisa asked me to bake some kind of German cookies with her this weekend. Pfeffernougats or something."

At once, Myra turned, beaming. "Really? A cookie date?"

Mick gave a ducking nod.

"This is good, Mister Mick. In fact, this is gooder than good! When?"

Mick glanced down. "Maybe tomorrow."

"You know what this means? It means we have even more to celebrate than your birthday!"

They ate the steaks with asparagus and a salad that had walnuts and grapes in it, and some kind of cheese Mick had never heard of before—something like "Chevrolet," he thought she said—and everything was delicious. It was as if Mick had entered a world where the senses were more alive than in the normal, boring everyday world—and things were moving in a smooth forward momentum that carried him easily along with it.

He opened the present she'd wrapped for him. A Pakistani CD, which she slid into the player for him.

They did the dishes. She washed, he dried, they chatted happily.

She put ice in a silver bucket, and asked him to set it beside the hot tub.

She showed him how to ease the cork from a bottle of champagne.

He stared at the sunlight between the tiny, tiny leaves of the immense backyard hedge. It was a liquid orange.

She filled their glasses and said, "To sweet sixteen."

They drank the first glass fast.

When Mick set the empty glass down, he did it with extreme care. His head was swimming slightly. "Whoa," he said. "That hit kinda fast."

Myra laughed. "That and the hard lemonade you've been gulping."

He quizzed her with a look. "Hard lemonade?"

Another big grin from Myra. "Yeah. The stuff with the teeniest bit of alcohol in it. Of which you liberally partook before dining."

"Oh."

"It's okay," she said. "You're all right. Just go slow with the champagne." She poured herself another glass, and let out a soft laugh. "Besides, that'll leave more for me. Kelso left us the good stuff."

She drank another glass, then said, "Shall we get in the tub?"

Mick wasn't sure what exactly this entailed. What, for example, would he wear when getting in the tub? "Sure, I guess so."

She switched on a pump that began to swirl the water. "I brought a swimming suit or I can just wear my underthings. It's up to you."

"It's up to me?"

Another easy laugh from Myra. "It's your birthday. You get to make all the big decisions"—she kept smiling—"as long as you don't get any big ideas."

No manhandling, in other words, Mick thought. "Whatever's easiest," he said.

Myra reached behind to unclasp the dress closure behind her neck. Then there was a zipping sound and she was stepping out of her dress, which she hung neatly over the chair. Both her briefs and bra were black and nearly sheer.

She turned and, seeing Mick, gave a quick full laugh. "You look stricken," she said.

Mick didn't know what to say. "Yowza," he said. "And I should tell you, I've never said yowza in my entire life up to now."

Myra laughed and slipped into the tub with absolute ease, like, Mick thought, a goddess in a Greek myth except he didn't really know a Greek myth where a goddess gets into a hot tub. Once submerged, Myra gave Mick a grin. "C'mon in. The water's great."

Mick wanted to get in, but he didn't want Myra to see the effect she'd had on him, and he guessed she understood this because she turned away and took her time pouring another glass of champagne. He quickly stripped to his boxer shorts and stepped into the tub opposite her.

"Wow," he said, settling in. "It's really hot."

Myra made a slow blink, took a deep breath, and smiled lazily. "You'll get used to it," she said, and she was right. He did. Pretty soon his whole body felt as lazy as Myra's smile.

After a few minutes, Myra reached behind her and switched off the aerating jets. Everything turned quiet. The Pakistani music no longer played. Crickets chirred. Far away, a truck changed gears. Myra sipped from her champagne. "Nice, huh?"

"Nicer than nice," Mick said and after a minute or so of pleasant silence he said, "Can I ask you a question?"

She sat up slightly and her breasts rose just above the water line. "Shoot."

"How come you're doing this?"

She gave a laugh and slipped back down into the water. "I just thought it would be fun. Not just for you, but for me, too."

Mick closed his eyes. Somewhere a dog was barking.

Myra said, "My last birthday Pam and I were going to drive up to Stowe and just hang out for the whole weekend. We'd planned it for ages, and then at the last second she flaked out. It was just a pretty bad birthday, and then when I heard yours was coming up, I just felt like doing something nice."

Mick opened his eyes. "This is pretty nice, all right."

Myra rose from the tub, went into the house, and came back with another bottle of champagne, which she handed to Mick to open. After he had, he said, "You know you're really really beautiful."

Myra smiled, poured, and sipped. "Okay, tell me what Lisa said today."

Mick did, and when he was done, Myra seemed to consider it for a few seconds. "So when exactly did she want you to bake these pfefferdoodles with her."

"Today."

Myra stared at him. "Today?"

"Tonight actually."

Myra slowly shook her head. "Tonight? My God, Mick, you're killing me here. I go and decide you're a smart guy, and it turns out you haven't heard of prioritizing? We could've rescheduled. We could've done this anytime."

"I didn't want to cancel. And, besides, I know how you hate it when Pam does that at the last minute."

Myra's face clouded slightly. "Pam's different."

Mick was trying to make sense of that when Myra said, "Okay, here's a question for you, Mick. A simple little question. Tell me what it is about Lisa."

Mick closed his eyes and waited for the right answer, but it didn't come. "I don't know," he said finally, "it's just that she gets to me. I mean, really gets to me, like she's pulling my insides out, only in a good way."

Myra made a low, appreciative murmur. "I think you've been smitten." Then, "Or maybe you've been smited." Then, "Or maybe you've just been smit."

Mick laughed and wondered if he'd ever been happier than he was at this moment, sitting in the water with Myra Vidal, talking about Lisa Doyle. Out of politeness he said, "What about Ethan? Is that how you were smit by him?"

Myra, who'd been gazing up at the night sky, raised her head. "Who?"

"Ethan. Your boyfriend in California."

"Oh," Myra said, and she looked vaguely off. "You know what? To be absolutely truthful, I don't think I was ever really smitten by Ethan."

"How come you're waiting for him then?"

Her eyes grazed Mick's for just an instant, then floated off again. "A good question." She turned again to Mick and smiled. "I'll get back to you when I have the answer." She took a sip of champagne and slowly, almost dreamily, closed her eyes.

A silence stretched out then and as Mick stared at the skies, the first reaches of dark clouds started to cover the stars—it was like putting out lights. There was a wind coming up, too, and as it moved through the hedge it made a shivery sound. It was still beautiful, but somehow the giddiness Mick had been feeling began to give way to something more somber. He said, "Is it supposed to rain?"

But Myra didn't answer. She sat very still, the water at her neck, her head tilted back, her eyes still closed. For an instant, Mick wondered if she was asleep or unconscious or even dead, but then—finally, slowly—she lifted her head and looked at Mick. "Remember when I told you there was a face behind the face behind the face?"

"Yeah." He wondered what she was driving at. "In fact, I think about it every now and then."

Myra took one deep breath, and another. Then in a quiet

voice she said, "Can I tell you something I've never told anybody in my life?"

Something about this scared Mick a little. "I guess so," he said.

"And you promise you'll keep it to yourself?"

"Yes," he said, and made his voice firmer. "Yes. I do promise that."

"Close your eyes."

"What?"

"Close your eyes. I don't want you to look at me when I say this."

Mick closed his eyes. For what seemed like a full minute, it was absolutely still, just the sound of shivering leaves and the lapping of water, and then Myra said, "The thing is, I don't think of Pam as just a friend."

Mick opened his eyes.

Myra was staring directly at him. She said, "The face behind the face behind the face is of a girl who likes girls." She said this in an even voice, as if it were something she'd said in her mind many times before, but once she'd finally said it out loud, her face turned rubbery and misshapen, and then she was crying.

Mick didn't know what to do. "It's okay," he said. "It's okay." He moved closer to her, and she kept crying while he kept saying, "It's okay, it doesn't matter, it's okay."

Perhaps five minutes passed in this way and then, at last, Myra began to snuffle and wipe her cheek and catch her breath. "I'm sorry," she said. "I mean, it's kind of mean passing something like this on to someone as nice as you, but, I don't know, I've had it cooped up inside me for so long." She tried to smile. "Anyhow, it's weird, but I feel a little better now." She leaned over and kissed Mick on the ear. "So, thanks."

"What're you going to do now?"

Myra shrugged.

"Tell Pam?"

She tried to laugh, but it came out as more of a snort. "I've got this letter I wrote to her about two weeks ago, and I've been carrying it around in my backpack ever since. I keep thinking I'll give it to her at just the right time, but the right time never seems to come up."

Myra said some other things, but Mick's mind had fastened to an idea. When it was quiet again, he said, "Would it be okay if I tell you something I've never told anybody else?"

Myra released a quick, somber laugh. "About Nora?"

"How'd you know that?"

She made an unhappy smile. "Sometimes people with secrets are good at sniffing out others of their species."

"Okay, then," Mick said. He cleared his throat and when he started to speak, the story about Nora came out in a long gushing stream—the e-mails from Alexander Selkirk, Nora's sneaking around, the link with Cruso, the sand in Cruso's gas tank, all of it.

When he was done, Myra said, "So the e-mails are on that disk you've got zipped up in your jacket pocket?"

"What?"

"You're always fiddling with that zipper. So when you were out on the deck and your jacket was inside, I couldn't help myself. I took a peek."

Mick was a little shocked and his face must've shown it.

"Oh, I know," she said. "Invasion of privacy." Myra made a small smile—her face still didn't look quite normal to Mick yet—and said, "You just have to remember that I'm on your side, pal." Then, "So what do you mean to do with the e-mails?"

Mick shrugged.

Myra waited a second or two. "Okay, let's try a different tack. Why exactly did Nora's behavior make you so angry?"

A familiar sullenness began to gather in Mick, but, suddenly, almost to his own surprise, he heard himself say, "Because it's so wrong! Because she's lying to everybody! Because she's betraying my dad!"

Myra was quiet for a time. The moon glimpsed down between clouds, then was lost again. In a gentle voice Myra said, "Maybe you weren't mad so much because she'd betrayed your dad as because she'd betrayed you."

Part of Mick wanted to dispute this, but it was a small part. The bigger part of him guessed it was more or less true. When he'd left the house tonight, for example, he'd noticed that something must be wrong with Nora because she was wearing grungy jogging gear around the house and her hair was unwashed, but what he'd really noticed was that under her grungy sweatshirt she wasn't wearing a bra. "So what should I do now?"

Myra smiled. "Spend more time with Lisa Doyle. I call it displacement theory. Let Lisa push Nora right out of your wee little mind."

Mick nodded. This sounded possible. But then, "What about my dad?"

Myra shrugged. "Your dad and Nora are big kids. They'll work this out for themselves."

The wind had stiffened and, overhead, the sky was now nothing but black clouds. A sudden gust skidded one of the canvas-backed chairs a few inches forward on the patio. Myra said, "Either we've got ghosts or there's a storm coming."

Watching her get out of the tub and towel dry still affected him. After she slipped back into the dress, he said, "Well, nothing you told me here tonight made you any less yowza-worthy."

"Happy to hear it," she said, and went off to jot a thank-you note to Kelso while Mick got dressed. After they'd locked up and turned off the lights, Mick rolled his bicycle alongside her until they reached her Civic. From the driver's seat she gave him a long look. "Good birthday?"

Mick nodded. "Best yet," he said, and he meant it.

A first fat raindrop splattered on the Civic's windshield, then another.

"Sure you don't want me to drive you?"

There was no room for his bike in the Civic. "Naw," he said. "Besides, it's all downhill from here." Which was literally true.

The figurative sense, however, was another matter.

CHAPTER THIRTY-THREE

Maurice Steps Out

As the first raindrops fell, Maurice Gritz wheeled his Honda into Mrs. Kinderman's garage, quickly fed the two marmalade cats, and went to the pantry closet where he kept the set of dark clothes he used for these occasions. It had been simpler keeping the stuff at home, but Janice was the snoopy type, and besides, she might've done him a favor. This was safer. Nobody was going to get a search warrant for Lillian Kinderman's cottage.

When he was into the dark clothes with the big interior pockets, he added the finishing touches—black vinyl gloves, Shaq mask, black ski cap—and took a look in the mirror. Okay, then. He wasn't sure who he was, but he had to admit it, he liked what he saw. He grinned behind his mask.

He flipped off the lights, and then it came to him.

Shaqman, that's who he was.

Shaqman on a night stroll through Lilliput.

CHAPTER THIRTY-FOUR

Sleepwalking

Janice didn't feel that great. She lay in the dark listening to the watery gush build in the little gully outside Maurice's bungalow, listening to the rain tapping on Maurice's tin roof. "Tintinnabulation" came to mind. A vocabulary word. The tinkling or jingling of bells. A word she'd gotten right, back when she cared about vocabulary words. That was only three weeks before, or maybe four, but it seemed like such a long time ago.

Janice lay on top of the bed fully dressed and rested her feet on a doubled pillow. Harriet slept curled nearby, but Janice couldn't make herself comfortable. She'd been fitfully dozing, and when the chimes of Maurice's mantel clock struck, she awakened, counting.

Ten, eleven, twelve.

He'd said he'd be back by eleven. Eleven-thirty at the latest. So where was he? She knew he'd had lots of girlfriends before—some Isabelle woman was always leaving messages for him, and she was pretty sure that little Latina sexpot from Lisa's crew was scheming after Maurice, too—but Maurice had told Janice he was the one-woman type, and she had wanted to believe him.

Harriet rose, stretched, jumped from the bed, and Janice soon heard the delicate crunching of kibbles. She switched on a light, went to the kitchen nook, and opened the refrigerator. Same old same old: nonfat cottage cheese, high-energy smoothies, Rolling Rock beer. And there in the back, as always, was the orange-juice carton that had held the Shaq mask. She didn't know whether it was still there or not. Janice hadn't touched the carton since. That was because, to her, the carton wasn't a carton. It was a peephole into a part of Maurice's life she never wanted to see.

Tonight, though, she kept staring at the carton, staring at it so long that it seemed to exert a pull and, almost as if hers were the hand of a sleepwalker, it began slowly to move toward the carton with outstretched fingers, pulled by the idea of just lifting it, testing its weight, learning whether the mask was there tonight or not, but then, abruptly, at its first touch, as if suddenly waking, she pulled back and closed the refrigerator tight.

In a cupboard, she found some gingersnaps, and ate seven, nibbling each one like a mouse.

Janice knew she ought to go home. She'd told her mother she was spending the night with Lisa, and how would she explain coming home in the middle of the night? Still, she knew she ought to go, but she also knew she wouldn't. She would wait until Maurice got back. Because she wanted to see him, and be with him.

Janice switched off the lights.

She lay back on the bed, closed her eyes, and fell asleep.

When she would next awaken, it would be to the relentless shrieking of sirens.

CHAPTER THIRTY-FIVE

Illumination

Thunder awakened Mick in the middle of the night. The bedroom was dark. A wind blowing from the south made the window glass tremble. Outside, at a distance, a skittering flash of lightning. Mick counted to six before the thunder cracked—the lightning was just over a mile away. Foolish, who had jumped onto Mick's bed and coiled at his feet, now jumped down and slunk into the closet.

Another deep resonant roll of thunder. As it rumbled past, it was as if the whole house rolled slightly. Mick had gone to sleep thinking about Myra and now, awake, he was thinking of her again, of how happy she'd seemed during dinner, and then, in the steamy water, when she'd said what she'd said, how her face had stretched in that awful taffylike way before she'd begun to cry. And she was so nice. So how was that fair? That someone so nice should be so miserable? Isn't that where a good God would step in and do something?

A flash of lightning brightened the night for an instant, followed three, four, five seconds later by another crackling snap of thunder. It was getting closer. The rainbeat on the roof loudened. From the closet, Foolish made a tight, urgent-sounding whimper.

Mick got up, took his flashlight to the window, and pointed

the light toward the gap in the chimney brick where the nest had been wedged. The nest was still there. The bird was still there. The small dark eyes of the phoebe peered out over the brim of her nest. She looked scared, but she still sat on her nest, keeping her five small white eggs warm and dry.

Mick switched off the beam and stared out through the watery glass. He yawned. He was ready to go back to sleep. But a few seconds later a broad bright flash of lightning illuminated the sky and Mick, looking down, was frozen in dumb wonder at what he saw.

There, standing in her bathrobe on the back lawn, was Nora.

She held an umbrella.

She was barefoot.

And then it was dark again.

Mick, stepping back a foot or two, kept his gaze fixed on the exact spot where Nora had been, but when the lightning next illuminated the yard, no one was there.

Mick listened for sounds of Nora coming into the house, maybe coming back upstairs, or maybe turning on the downstairs TV, but there was nothing but the dense thrum of rain and inter-mittent crashes of thunder. Mick took his flashlight and went downstairs. Nothing. He scanned the flashlight across the front yard, and then the back. Nothing.

The garage came to mind. Could she have driven away without his hearing it?

He ducked his head and dashed across the yard to the garage's side door. He inched it open and peered in. Her 320i was there. Mick stepped fully into the garage and ran the flashlight beam from dark corner to dark corner. Nothing. He heard something—the steady plink of water—and, scanning the beam of light, found not only a puddle on the floor from an overhead leak, but also something chilling. In the middle of the puddle, peering still with curious eyes, lay the head of Nora's little ceramic devil. The rest of the figurine lay in scattered pieces on the concrete floor. Mick flashed his light toward Nora's car. The dashboard was bare, and there was nobody in the front seat, but there, curled up on the backseat, was Nora.

Mick switched off the light. He wavered between going back in the house and going over to the car. He went over to the car. "You okay?" he said, but the windows were up. He opened the front door, which triggered the overhead lamp. He didn't ask if she was okay again. He could see she wasn't. Her eyes were blurry and her face was wet, either from the rain or from crying. She stared straight ahead.

Mick eased into the front seat and pulled the door closed so it was dark again. It was surprisingly quiet in the car—he could barely hear the rainbeat outside. For a few seconds he stared at the dark outlines of his stepmother. Then he said, "What happened to the little devil guy?"

She didn't answer and he said, "What happened to Beelzebub?"

A few seconds passed and in a dull voice she said, "I guess he broke."

Mick stared at her through the darkness. "What's going on, Nora?"

She hesitated, and said, "Oh, it's just the thunderstorm." Words that might've been reassuring if her voice weren't so small and broken.

"Didn't know you didn't like thunderstorms."

Nora gave a snuffly laugh. "Me, either." There was a silence, and a roll of thunder, muffled-seeming now, passed by. Quietly Nora said, "My father wasn't around when I was little, so it was

253

just my mother bringing us up. She was so strong. . . . Nobody intimidated her—not the landlord, not her boss, not the nosy neighbors—nobody."

She waited. "But you know what scared the pants off her? Thunderstorms. Whenever one hit, she'd grab blankets and rush my sister and me out to the garage and put us in this old Lincoln that was parked out there but didn't run, and that's where we slept."

Mick said, "Doesn't sound too comfortable."

"It's funny. We always loved sleeping in the Lincoln. We'd all say the Lord's Prayer together, which was kind of funny in itself, because my mother wasn't religious, and then we'd fall into the snuggest, deepest sleep."

Another silence, then Mick said, "But we've had lots of thunderstorms and you've—"

"—never ridden them out in the garage?"

"Yeah."

"I don't know, Mick." A pause. "It's just that tonight I felt so . . . small."

Mick waited. Then, quietly, "How come?"

Nora's voice was low and seemed to flow from regret. "I think you know how come."

Mick didn't say anything.

In her low, broken voice Nora said one word: "Cruso."

When Mick still didn't say anything, she said, "I think I knew you knew for a long time, but pretended you didn't."

Mick blurted a question he'd been carrying around a long time without really knowing it. "Why did you marry my dad if you were just going to cheat on him?"

A few seconds passed before Nora spoke. "I married your father because he's the kindest, gentlest, handsomest man I've

254

ever known. I married him because he made me feel good, and safe. I married him because I loved him, Mick." A pause and her small voice became smaller. "I still do."

Mick sat silent.

He looked at the empty dashboard where the little hand-me-down devil had been and thought, Cruso gave it to her.

She said, "It's over, you know. Been over. Was nearly over when you told your dad about him and that Myra girl. He'd used that line on me, by the way. *Strangely vivifying.*" Nora shook her head as if in disbelief. "The same line he was using on teenaged girls is the one that worked on me." She turned toward Mick in the darkness and her voice was low and regretful. " 'The heart is the tyrant who spares no one.' "

Mick said, "But I thought adults knew how to . . . you know, resist that kind of stuff. I thought that was what adults are supposed to do."

A few seconds passed and she said, "Adults are like everybody else, Mick. Usually they do what they're supposed to do. Sometimes they don't."

Another silence.

She said, "So how'd you find out?"

"The e-mails. You saved some of them to a regular file and then you threw the file out. Then you didn't properly empty your trash."

Nora made a small, unhappy laugh. " 'She didn't properly empty her trash.' When they write my book, that'll be the epigraph."

"But why'd you save them in the first place?"

Another stony laugh. "I wanted to reread them, I'm embarrassed to say, and it seemed safer to take them off e-mail. But then I wanted to get rid of them, so I put them in the trash and thought that was that. I didn't know I had to empty it, too." A silence stretched out, and she said, "You haven't mentioned the e-mails to your father."

It was more a statement than a question, but Mick said, "No."

"Any plans to?"

Mick felt for the interior pocket of his jacket. He considered unzipping it and handing Nora the green disk, but he didn't. "I don't know," he said.

"But you're still angry."

"I guess so, yeah."

After a little while Nora said, "I would be, too. If it was my dad."

Mick thought about the conversation he'd had with Myra. "It was that, all right," he said. He paused, and then he said, "But it might've also been more than that."

In a gentle voice Nora said, "You'll outgrow those particular feelings."

Another roll of thunder, but from here, in the BMW, it seemed far away, as if it were somebody else's storm. Quietly Nora said, "You know, Mick, it's true that lots of people get stuck in bad patterns, but it's also true that lots of good people outgrow the bad things they've done."

Mick thought about that for a while. He thought it might be true. Anyhow, he wished it was. Finally he said, "I guess I'll go back to bed now." He peered in her direction through the darkness. "You going to stay here?"

"For a little while."

Mick reached for the door handle, but stopped before he triggered the overhead light. He said, "You know, I kept trying to get into your e-mails to see what more was going on. I'm not proud of it, but that's what I did. But I could never figure out the password."

256

He expected her to say he shouldn't've done that, but she didn't. She said, "Those e-mails stopped a long time ago, Mick. But if you want to check it out for yourself, you're more than welcome."

Mick waited.

" 'Foolish,' " Nora said. "The password is 'foolish.' "

The rain had slackened when Mick stepped out of the garage, and from somewhere far away he heard the faint sounds of sirens.

CHAPTER THIRTY-SIX

Night Stroll in Lilliput

It had been a good night, Shaqman thought. A real good night. He'd picked up a few nice trinkets, but that wasn't the red meat of this operation. He'd turned a few more Lilliputians' thoughts to security, which was good for Jocko's big scheme, but that wasn't the red meat, either. The red meat was being somebody else, somebody who slipped in and out of houses and scared the shit out of people. Shaqman didn't just steal people's jewelry. He replaced it with fear.

He strolled the string of trees that fringed the seventh fairway. It was raining, but his gear was up to it. It had been a good night, and he could slide over to the ninth fairway and slip into Mrs. Kinderman's yard without so much as a step on a street or a cart path, then change clothes and go back to sweet little bed-warmed Janissimo, and that was what he'd meant to do, he really did, but there was a snug Lilliputian house right there, with a Lilliputian TV on, and some interior lights, and nothing but a rose hedge between Shaqman and the backyard.

Almost without knowing it, he stepped through the rose hedge.

First he cut the telephone wire and checked for a security system (there was none). Then he found the electric pedestal in the carport, unscrewed the faceplate, and flipped the main breaker.

Click.

The interior lights went dark.

He slipped behind a storage shed and, sure enough, a few seconds later a woman in a robe appeared at the head of the wooden steps that dropped from the house to the carport. She had a flashlight and directed it at the panel of smaller circuit breakers set into the carport wall. He waited until she'd begun flipping the switches before he stepped out and said in a deep voice meant to sound black, "What you lookin' for, Mrs. White?"

All at once the robed woman turned, shone a light into his dark face, and let out what sounded like a squeaky hiss. Then she ran for her door and could be heard locking it fast behind her.

He walked calmly to the door. He knocked politely. In his black voice he said, "Mrs. White, I need in now."

The woman inside said nothing.

"Mrs. White, I need in."

A small voice said something he couldn't understand.

"Whad you say, Mrs. White?"

"I said go away."

He actually laughed. "You think it's that easy? You think you say go away, and I just do?" He lowered his voice. "No, I need in there, Mrs. White. I really do." Then he said something he didn't expect to say. He said, "I just want to talk to you."

In a brittle, high voice the woman inside said, "Go away or I'll do something."

He tried to make his black voice soothing. "You don't need to be afraid."

"Go away!"

He clicked on his light and shone it through the semi-opaque glass of the door. He could see the faint outline of her form standing behind the door. In the dim light he noticed something else and pointed the beam to his other hand. Red blood dripped from a tear in the black rubber gloves. The rose hedge, he thought.

Maurice said, "I'm bleeding here. I need a little first aid."

And then with a shock he realized he'd forgotten himself. He'd used his own voice.

"What?" the woman inside said.

"I need in there," he said, and it was his own voice again.

"Who are you?"

"I need in there," he said. "I need your help."

"Go away!" she shouted. "Go away or I'll do something!"

He was suddenly hot. He loosened his mask, peeled it up over his mouth and nose. "I'm not going away," he heard himself say.

"What?"

"I'm not going away," Maurice said.

From within, nothing.

He tapped at the door.

Still nothing.

He shone the light through the window.

Was she still there? He couldn't tell if she was still there.

He pounded on the door.

Suddenly the woman inside spoke. "I'll do something," she said.

So she was there, but turned sidewise, that's what it looked like.

"Go away!" she screamed.

"I'm not going away," Maurice said.

CHAPTER THIRTY-SEVEN

Three Steps from the Bottom

Sunday morning, something was different at Village Greens. When Lizette and Lisa got to its entrance, a Jemison police car was parked beyond the waterfall and entry gates, and two officers stood near it talking and drinking coffee. A familiar face peered out from the Village Greens security booth, but he didn't say, "Howdy-ho, girls," the way he usually did. Instead, in a somber voice, he said, "What can I do for you?"

Lisa said, "We have a letter to deliver to the head of Village Greens. I think her name is Etta Hooten."

The security guard said, "You can just give it to me and I'll—"

Lisa cut in. "We want to hand deliver it." This didn't make it sound urgent enough, so she added, "It's very important." Which also felt puny, so she said, "It's about the illegal behavior of a Village Greens employee."

This sparked the guard's interest. "What employee?"

Lizette looked at Lisa, who could feel the color draining from her face. Lizette shook her head. Lisa turned back to the guard. "We can't say. But it's in the letter to Mrs. Hooten."

The guard waved one of the officers over—a sturdy, square-jawed woman—and as she approached, Lisa had a strange impulse to run. But she and Lizette stood, frozen, listening to the

261

guard explain to the officer what they'd said. Then the officer turned to them. When she spoke, her lips barely moved, and you couldn't see her teeth. "I'll keep it confidential," she said, "but it would be good if you told me the name of the employee."

Lisa didn't speak. Neither did Lizette.

The officer had piercing black eyes, which she directed first at Lisa, then Lizette. Again her lips barely moved. "Okay, how about if you just nod yes or no to one question. Is your letter about an employee named Maurice Gritz?"

The question gave Lisa a turn. She looked at Lizette, who nodded. Lisa turned to the officer and nodded yes.

"Could I read your letter?" the officer said.

Again Lisa and Lizette exchanged looks, and again Lizette nodded. Lisa handed over the letter.

The officer opened the letter, read it once, and read it again. Then she looked up at the girls. "Kind of a sicko," she said.

They nodded.

"So what do you want to happen to him?"

Lizette snorted. "I don't think what I'd want is legal," she said.

"Okay," said the officer, smiling so slightly her teeth didn't show. "What's your second-favorite scenario?"

Lizette thought for a second. "I guess I was hoping he'd get fired."

Lisa quickly added, "And she should be able to keep working without any kind of . . . you know . . . backlash."

The officer smiled at Lizette. "Go find yourself an attorney and you can probably get a lot more than job security."

Lizette shook her head. "We don't want anything more than what we just said."

The officer said, "Well, you got that, and then some."

The girls waited, but when the officer didn't elaborate, Lisa asked, "What does that mean?"

The officer glanced at the security guard and then fixed her eyes again on the girls. She seemed to be studying them. "Okay," she said finally. "Last night your Maurice Gritz was caught burglarizing the wrong home."

It took a second or two for this to sink in. Then Lisa said, "What do you mean, the wrong home?"

The officer stretched her tight-lipped smile. "Gal who lived in this particular home had a gun and knew how to use it. She shot your Maurice Gritz. Twice. He'll survive, but for the next little while his work days are going to belong to a penal institution."

Lisa stood dumbfounded.

Lizette looked off to the side and said, "Good."

There was a pause, then the officer said, "Justice ain't often quick, but it's nice when it is." She held up the letter. "I'll need to keep this. You got a copy?"

Lisa nodded.

"Well, then, thank you," the officer said. She smiled tightly again, and they could tell she was ending the conversation.

That afternoon, Lisa mounted the stairs to the Bledsoe flat. She rang the bell three times before Janice's mother came to the door, but she hardly looked like Genevieve Bledsoe. Instead of harried and hurried, she looked frowsy and exhausted. Her eyes had sunk into her head and seemed unfocused. There was a grape stain on her top. It seemed to take real effort for her to say, "Hi, Lisa."

"Is everything okay?" Lisa said.

Mrs. Bledsoe nodded.

"Janice, too?"

Mrs. Bledsoe started to nod, but then quickly twisted her face away. "Not really."

There was another long silence, with Mrs. Bledsoe leaning against the doorjamb while Lisa stood on the landing wondering what to do next. Then Mrs. Bledsoe turned to Lisa and said, "Did you know this was going on?"

Lisa felt immediately squeamish. "Know what was going on?"

"Janice and this Maurice character."

Lisa lowered her eyes. "Kind of," she said. She wanted to say that she'd tried every which way to talk Janice out of it, but that wouldn't've been loyal to Janice and, besides, what was the point now?

A cat meowed from somewhere behind Mrs. Bledsoe, who said, "She brought his cat home."

Lisa nodded blankly. It was news to her that Maurice had a cat. He didn't seem like the cat type.

A few seconds passed and Mrs. Bledsoe cast a glance back over her shoulder and said, "Know what Janice is in there doing now?"

Lisa shook her head.

"She's in her room on her knees thanking God that this Maurice character wasn't killed."

All through the conversation, beyond the exhaustion and frowsiness, there had been in Mrs. Bledsoe's expression a look of disappointment, but with these last words she looked suddenly as if she might cry. She tried to smile and in a soft voice she said, "I'm sorry, Lisa, I just need a little time now," and gently closed the door.

Three steps from the bottom of the stairs, Lisa stopped, sat down, and stared across the street at Home Park Gardens. A few weeks before, these apartments had seemed enchanted, bathed in

golden light, but now they had the unhappy aspect of abandon-
ment. Someone had tagged one of the cinderblock buildings with
red spray paint, the wind had pinned trash across the chain-link
fence, and a long broken tree branch lay by the carports. There
was an odd tinkling sound that Lisa couldn't guess the source of.

She stood and rolled her bicycle across the street, through the
pedestrian gate, and stopped. It was the suspension chains of the
swings, moving in the breeze, *tink, tink, tink.* Lisa settled herself
into the seat of the swing, which hung so low she had to stretch
her legs out before her. From here, she suddenly realized, she
could see both Janice's kitchen window and the window that had
been Joe Keesler's.

Joe Keesler.

Everything had been so simple before Joe Keesler.

Lisa tucked back her legs, closed her eyes, and began slowly to
swing. She didn't swing high. She swung slowly, easily, with her eyes
closed, and it made her remember when she and Janice were little,
swinging and laughing, and then, when they were a little older,
swinging and talking or else just swinging and being quiet like this.

Maurice had a cat. Who would've thought that Maurice
would have a cat?

And yet who would've thought he would treat Lizette Uribe
that way?

He was like some weird Jekyll and Hyde.

Lisa stopped pumping and let the swing coast in slowly shortening arcs. When it came to rest, she walked back to her bike.
She stared up at Janice's window—the blinds were closed—then
looked around Home Park Gardens one last time. "Bye," she said
under her breath, and when she stood on the pedals to begin
pumping, she wasn't sure where she was headed next.

CHAPTER THIRTY-EIGHT

The View from Above

Mick was sitting on the roof. The garage leak still hadn't been fixed, which meant the ladder offered ready rooftop access, and it was nice up here, it really was. You could see forever, but it wasn't just that. It was that everything looked better from up here. Cleaner. Problem-free.

And the truth was, to this point, it'd been a pretty good day. He'd been sleeping fitfully this morning when his father knocked on the door. "Up and at 'em, Mick."

Mick had yelled that he didn't have to get up, it was Sunday morning, and then pressed the pillow over his head, but his father kept knocking. "Got something for you," he said, and wouldn't leave until Mick had pulled on sweats and come out.

His father was dressed in his good pants and shirt—definitely not his around-the-house gear—and he led Mick downstairs to the kitchen where Nora was cooking with an apron over her nice clothes. She didn't look in any way like the woman hiding in the car in the middle of the night. She looked fine, good even. Normal.

"Where're you guys going?" Mick said, and then he noticed a package sitting on the breakfast table beautifully wrapped in slick red paper with a broad black ribbon, Nora-style. "What's that?" he said.

Nora smiled. "Open and see."

Mick peeled back the paper to reveal an enormous box of Twinkies.

The truth was, Mick was off Twinkies, but he didn't say so. He grinned and nodded and said, "Thanks, Dad. Thanks, Nora." To Foolish he said, "Look, pal, they got us the megabox."

"There's a card," Mick's father said, pointing.

It was a homemade card with a car on the front. Inside it said, *Happy birthday to the best son a father and stepmother could ever have.* It was his father's handwriting, and the sentiment got to Mick a little more than he expected. He closed it quickly. "Nice card," he said. "Thanks."

"Recognize the car on the front?" his father said.

He didn't, not really. "Old Beemer 2002," he said. "Don't know what year."

"It's a '71," his father said. "Two hundred four thousand miles. It belonged to a lady in Chittenango, but it was towed into the shop with a cracked block. When she heard the tab, she decided to sell it."

Mick was listening. He had the feeling this story might be going somewhere.

"I'd been telling Essa I was looking for a fixer-upper," his father went on, "so he gave me first shot, and I got it. I've been working on it during lunch and after work." He reached down to give Foolish a scratch. "I figure it'll be ready to bring home in a week or two."

His father stopped talking and took a long sip of coffee.

Mick said, "So what are you going to do with it?"

His father grinned. "Oh, that ain't the question, Mick. The question is, what are *you* going to do with it?"

267

Mick could hardly believe it. "Really?"

His father nodded. "Really."

Mick said, "Joking about this would be cruel and unusual."

A chuckle from his father. "Yeah, it would. Which is why I'm not."

Mick propped the card in front of him during breakfast and could hardly take his eyes off it—the car was a beautiful deep green and it had a sunroof and it seemed beyond anything remotely imaginable that he, Mick Nichols, might own this car, and better yet that he, Mick Nichols, might drive around in it with Lisa Doyle, in the summer, with the sunroof open.

Mick, brought up from his reverie, was suddenly aware of movement. Nora and his father were moving around, piling dishes into the sink, grabbing coats and keys. "Where're you going?" Mick said.

His father grinned sheepishly.

Nora said, "Church. Wanna come?"

Church? Neither of them ever went to church. Mick shook his head. "Naw. Maybe next time."

His father had laughed and said, "Who said there'll be one?" and then they were gone.

They'd driven off at nine-thirty, and it was nearly one now. Mick had burned the morning looking up 2002 clubs on the Internet, had eaten lunch, and then when he'd been in the backyard looking up at the ladder, decided to climb it. From the garage it was a short leap to the house. The north side of the roof was too cool, so he climbed over the top ridge to the sunnier slope, which was pleasantly warm. He took off his coat and then his shirt, and rolled them behind him for a pillow.

A pleasant, trilling *fee-bee, fee-bee* floated in the air. Mick walked to the chimney end of the roof, lay flat, and stared down over the eave.

From below, the phoebe looked up, stared at him a second or two, and flew off. In the nest, the five white eggs were still together and intact. Good, Mick thought, and was pushing himself up when he heard car doors closing out front. He peered over the roof ridge to the street.

It was his father and Nora, back from church. As they opened the front gate, he started to call out, but didn't, and a few minutes later, when his father came into the backyard and called, "Mick?" he didn't answer then, either. He didn't know why. He just wanted to be alone up here.

He sat still, and a while later the front door screen door banged open and closed, and Nora and his father emerged in their casual summer clothes and headed toward the 320i. He was carrying a picnic basket and she was talking in a cheery voice Mick couldn't quite hear, but when his father bent to put the picnic basket in the backseat of the car, Nora did something shocking. She pinched his father on the bum, and when as a consequence he jerked up his head, he conked it on the car door, and pretty soon they were both laughing like maniacs.

Who could possibly understand the adult mind? They want their kids to act like adults, but then when they think no one's watching, they act like kids. The 320i rolled off with his father at the wheel and, out of sight, Mick could hear him expertly downshifting at the State Street stop sign.

Mick went down the ladder. He grabbed a root beer from the refrigerator, called Lisa and hung up when he got the machine, and did the same when he got Reece's machine. He took a Twinkie from the box and went back up the ladder. When he was settled again, he peeled back the Twinkie wrapper and smelled it. The smell didn't get to him, so he took a first tiny bite, and that was okay, too. In fact, it was pretty good. In about a minute, he'd finished it off, then took a deep breath and looked around.

Down below Foolish found a sunny patch of grass, circled a few times, and tucked himself into the napping position.

Not so foolish, Mick thought.

He reached into the pocket of his folded jacket, felt his way past the floppy disk to the birthday card, and brought it out. His eyes feasted on it, couldn't take it all in fast enough. *His*. He actually laughed out loud to think of it and was still smiling when he noticed movement at his front gate. When he saw who it was, he could hardly believe his eyes.

CHAPTER THIRTY-NINE

Kiss Me, She Thought

State Street. That much Lisa remembered, and how it had been close to 2468 State Street because she'd made that feeble joke about the house having its own cheer, except it didn't, not quite.

Was it 2467 or 2469?

She slowed her bike slightly at 2467, but there were two Buicks in the driveway and Mick had said his parents drove old BMWs. But when she pulled up to the gate of 2469, there were no cars in the driveway at all. She was wondering if it might've been 2465 when she heard someone say, "Hey."

She looked side to side, and front to back, and began to feel a little silly.

"Up here."

There, perched on the second-story, green-shingled roof, was Mick Nichols. She laughed. "What're you doing?"

He shrugged. "Sittin'. Watchin'." He stood. "I'll be right down."

But that wasn't what Lisa wanted. "No. Let me come up."

Lisa didn't have a particular fear of ladders, but she was glad all the same that Mick stood at the top steadying this one. And she was glad to have his hand to grab when she made the little leap from the garage to the house, and again when she pulled herself from the top height of the first story onto the low eave of the second. He had his shirt off, and he gave off a mingled smell of soap and sweat that she liked.

When they got near the second-story ridge, Mick said, "Sun or shade?"

"Shade," Lisa said, smiling. "I burn."

They sat in the shade and gazed out. Everything looked green—the trees, the yards, the valley and hillside beyond—everything. In a voice meant to sound husky but kind, Lisa said, "Someday, Simba, all this will be yours," and got a laugh from Mick, which allowed her to look at him. He'd always seemed average sized, but he was surprisingly wide chested and narrow waisted. "You pump iron or something?" she said.

Mick shook his head. "I ought to," he said, "but . . ." and his voice trailed off. He gave her his jacket to use as a pillow, then laid back on his rolled shirt. "Pretty nice, huh?"

It *was* nice, Lisa thought. Nicer than anything she'd felt in a long time. "You hear about Maurice?" she said.

He hadn't, so she gave him the whole story, except the Lizette Uribe parts she'd promised to keep secret. When she finished, Mick let out a low whistle. "Wow," he said in a low voice. "Somebody shot him who was Maurice."

A second or two passed and Lisa said, "Janice is pretty crushed."

Mick didn't say anything.

Lisa said, "I thought she was stupid to fall for him and in a certain way she was, but she saw something in him that was, you know, redeemable, and I couldn't. I've been raised to believe that every person is capable of redemption. Deliverance from the bondage of sin. But really all I saw was a sleazeball."

Mick said, "Maybe because that's all he is."

"No," Lisa said, and the vehemence in her voice surprised her. "No, I don't believe that anymore."

A second or two passed and Mick said, "Maybe that's because you're so nice."

"I wish," Lisa said.

She'd propped herself on her elbows to tell about Maurice, but now she lay back and closed her eyes.

A bird called *fee-bee, fee-bee, fee-bee*.

The drone of a small plane came and went.

A small child bawled, "Where's Sam and Henry?"

The touch and then the soft clasp of Mick's hand.

Then his soap-and-sweat scent was closer and he was slowly smoothing a finger from her open wrist up her bare arm.

Kiss me, she thought, and he did.

CHAPTER FORTY

The Last Time He Saw Myra

A week had passed. It was Sunday again, and Mick was cycling toward Promontory Point, where he'd agreed to meet Myra. Which was fine, because Lisa had some big family reunion thing all day, but had more or less invited him over afterward, in the evening. "There'll be cookies in it for you," she'd said, and Mick had said, "You just made an offer I can't refuse."

Myra had been more mysterious in arranging her meeting with Mick. *Promontory Point at 1:30 P.M.*, her e-mail said. *Picnic. Wear jacket. Myrakins.*

Wear jacket? Why wear jacket? It was breezy, but sunny and warm. He didn't mind wearing the jacket, though. He always wore the jacket. The jacket had gotten him through the tough time.

He spotted her green Civic parked near an old oak with low, long-reaching branches. Myra was sitting on one. Beneath her, a red-and-white-checked tablecloth was spread on the ground. A basket sat on the cloth.

"I thought we were going to sit on the ground," she said as he drew close. "But those oak leaves are prickly little guys."

She'd brought croissant sandwiches and apples and two bottles of Mike's Hard Lemonade, which Mick was careful to drink slowly. It was pleasant under the canopy of the tree, protected from the sun and wind, almost a shady room. They chatted, but Mick noticed that Myra didn't mention Pam, and, for that matter, he didn't mention Nora.

Finally, when they were done eating, Myra slid off the branch and walked over to her car, which seemed to be filled with colored balls. When she stood upright again, she was holding what looked like a dozen helium balloons, all printed with messages that Mick could read as she got closer. GET WELL SOON! HAPPY BIRTHDAY! WELCOME, LITTLE ONE! The strings were tied to a cluster of jingle bells, which Mick supposed kept them from flying off.

"Fun exclamatory balloons," Mick said deadpan.

Myra grinned. "You're kind of funny. Not fall-down-and-laugh funny, but, still, kind of funny."

"Fewer bruises that way," Mick said, and eyed the balloons. "So what're they for?"

Myra smiled, set the cluster of jingle bells on the grass, and withdrew a small paper bag from the picnic basket. The bag had a small handle. Then, from her backpack, she took out an envelope. On the front, in Myra's writing, it said *Pam*.

"That *the* letter?"

Myra nodded and, almost ceremonially, set the letter into the paper bag.

"What're you doing?" Mick said.

Another smile from Myra. "Sending it skyward."

Mick was trying to get this straight. "Unopened," he said.

"Affirmative." She smiled at Mick, and suddenly she looked like her old self. "Here's what I decided. This letter would just make Pam feel uncomfortable and mad at me and sorry for me and all sorts of basically bad stuff." She waited. "Why put her or me through that?"

275

"So what're you going to do?"

Myra shrugged. "Maybe chat with a counselor. That's what they're there for."

The breeze made a soft hollow whistle in the trees. Myra wetted a finger and held it aloft. "This letter's going east," she said, then turned to Mick. "Still carrying a pocketful of secrets?"

"I've still got the disk, if that's what you mean."

Myra let her eyes sink into his. "How's about sending it up with my letter?"

Mick expected something inside him to recoil from the idea, but it didn't happen. It was as if he felt his whole body relaxing. "Sure," he said.

He unzipped the pocket and handed the green disk to Myra.

She set the disk alongside the letter in the bag and, while Mick held on to the strings, she untied the jingle bells and replaced them with the bag. "Does it feel too heavy?" she asked.

Mick gave the strings a jerk. "Naw," he said.

"You want to do it?"

Mick shook his head and handed the strings to Myra, who paused for a second, then let go. The balloons dipped for just a second, sank, then caught a breeze and floated straight. It looked for a moment as though the whole bunch would wind up in a tree ten yards away, but they swooped up and floated free. Myra and Mick stood watching the balloons and bag grow smaller and smaller, and then the balloons were gone.

They were both quiet for a time. Then Mick said, "You were right. It went east."

They walked back to the oak tree and gathered their stuff to leave. But as they were about to part—Mick on his bike, Myra in her car—Mick said, "I was thinking."

Myra laughed. "That can get you in lots of trouble."

Mick grinned and waited for her to see he was serious.

"Okay," she said. "What were you thinking?"

"I was thinking I don't really want this jacket anymore. I mean, I like it and everything, but it's warm now, and summer's coming, and besides I've never really gotten over how great it looked on you that day."

He shrugged free of the jacket and held it out. Myra stared at him. Her face was soft and calm and undeniably beautiful.

"I offered you the jacket then," he said, "but you wouldn't take it. Only now, we're, you know, friends. So maybe you will."

Myra smiled and took the jacket. Then she leaned forward and while hugging him put her lips to his ear and whispered, "Bye, Mick as in mittens."

CHAPTER FORTY-ONE

The Last Chapter

On the ride home from the Doyle family reunion picnic, Lisa sat silently in the backseat while, up front, her parents compared notes about various relatives—who'd lost weight, who was learning Chinese, who was taking a barge down the Danube in the fall. Lisa only half listened, which was about right, she figured, because she only half cared.

It was not quite dusk—the last angling sunlight threw long shadows and turned white buildings a soft, buttery yellow. When the Camry pulled up to a signal, Lisa found herself staring straight down the long sidewalk adjoining Cumberland. It was a long block, and at the far end of it, someone was riding a bicycle. At first, she couldn't tell if it was coming or going, but then—the bike and rider were gaining size—she saw they were approaching. And there was a dog jogging alongside. They were silhouettes, then they were dark forms, and then they were an average-sized boy and a thin black dog.

"I'll walk the rest of the way," Lisa said suddenly to her parents, and jumped out just as the light was changing. "Bye-ya," she called. "See you back home!"

As they drove off, she realized it was the first time she'd felt alive, really alive, all day. She waited on the corner as the boy and dog drew near. Her heart was galloping. It was Mick, of course, and Foolish, on their way to her house. He swung off his bike and coasted the last few yards. "I don't know why," he said, "but from way far back, I thought it might be you."

He was beaming. So was Lisa. She glanced down the street to make sure her parents were out of view, then leaned forward and kissed him on the mouth. Afterward, she ran a hand through his tightly curled hair. "You know, if you let that grow out, you'd have actual ringlets."

Mick asked how she felt about actual ringlets.

Lisa laughed. "I've always wanted some."

"Then maybe I'll dodge the barber for a while," Mick said.

They stood smiling for a time and then, in the low tone of complicity, Lisa said one word: "Cookies."

Mick grinned. "Pfeffer-nougats?"

Lisa laughed and with each new mistake—"Pfeffer-doodles? Pfeffer-hooven? Pfebber-noogles?"—she laughed louder. Finally, when he gave up, she said, "Pfeffernusse, and don't you forget it."

They'd turned now, and were walking along the path in the warm, buttery light. Lisa said, "They don't come cheap, you know."

"What don't?"

"The pfeffernusses. They're going to cost you."

Mick said he wasn't a wealthy man. "What do they go for?"

"One kiss per pfeffernusse," she said. She gave him a saucy look. "And that's cheap."

"Tell you what," Mick said. "I'll pay double that."

Lisa grinned. "That was a good answer."

They walked another half block and Mick said, "So what about Foolish? How many kisses does he have to pay?"

279

Lisa glanced down at the dog. "I like Foolish," she said. "In fact, I like him so much, I'm going to make his free."

An easy laugh from Mick. They had each other's hands now, and were talking easily, and walking slowly, in no particular hurry to get home.

EPILOGUE

Six Months Later

Tony Cruso, seeking a fresh start, accepted a teaching position in Baton Rouge, Louisiana, and traded in his vintage Porsche for a late model Dodge pickup. In August, just before he left, he received a mysterious letter from the Jemison Chapter of the National Organization of Women acknowledging an anonymous contribution "in honor of Tony Cruso" for $2,375. He presumed it was not coincidental that this was the exact amount of money he'd paid to repair his vandalized Porsche.

Nora Mercer-Nichols finished the sweater she'd been working on and gave it to Mick's father just before Thanksgiving. The sleeves are slightly different lengths and the neck is tight, but he wears it nearly every night when he gets home from work. He also tags along with Nora to church every Sunday.

Winston Reece took ownership of his uncle Arnold's VW bug, formally declared himself (through mass e-mail) "a passive resister to all conventional thought," and is growing a wispy beard, which he considers "the correct facial accoutrement for a person of my age, gender, and attitude."

Joseph Keesler resumed his classes, with Kara, at Duke University in the fall, but as a summer intern with the Prudential Group, he outsold many of the veteran agents.

Donald Pfingst completed his mission on August 30, and married the former Marie Tomlinson in the St. George, Utah, temple in September.

From the Onondaga County Department of Corrections, Maurice Gritz wrote Janice Bledsoe a letter proposing marriage. Her reply was three words long: *Can't. Love, Janice.* When paroled, Maurice enlisted in the U.S. Air Force with the hope that he could train in the recovery of downed pilots in enemy territory.

Genevieve Bledsoe, when given Maurice's letter by Janice, had read it and said, "Sweetie, I'll kill myself before my daughter marries a jailbird." A week later, the two of them began back-packing the John Muir section of the Pacific Crest Trail, which was supposed to take three weeks (and which Mrs. Bledsoe thought might make a salable story), but on the second day, Janice stopped, sat on a rock, and would go no farther. "You go ahead," she said, but her mother wouldn't, and they returned to the trailhead. They drove to Morro Bay, found a comfortable motel, and spent the next week playing card games in their room or walking along the beach, where Janice would look for stones or shells and throw them into the low, curling waves.

During the summer, Lizette Uribe took a precalculus class with Lisa Doyle at Jemison Community College. Lizette still works at Village Greens on Saturdays, but no longer does cater-ing jobs during the week. She earned a 3.7 the first quarter of her junior year at Jemison High and hopes to go into law.

Myra Vidal transferred to Reed College in Oregon, where during summer classes she met a girl named Maddy. Every so often she sends four-word e-mails to Mick. They say, *I'm well. You well?*

In late August, Mick's mother telephoned Mick from San Francisco to say that her accountant had recently told her that

282

Mick had finally cashed five of her five-hundred-dollar checks and, not that it was any of her business, she was wondering what for? "A worthy cause," Mick said. There was a silence on the line then. His mother said, "Would you care to elaborate?" and Mick said, "Not really."

Lisa Doyle and Mick Nichols could be seen around Jemison all summer long, driving the forest-green 2002 his father restored, or just talking and walking, usually with Foolish trotting happily alongside. With the first snows in late November, they switched to cross-country skis and are a regular sight on the trails of Pipsissewa Wood. Foolish likes that, too, and follows along in their tracks.

All five of the phoebe's eggs hatched in mid-June and in early July the fledglings flew away.

Laura Rhoton McNeal graduated from Brigham Young University and then Syracuse University, where she received a master's in fiction writing. She taught middle school and high school English before becoming a writer and journalist.

Tom McNeal received a master's in fine arts from the University of California at Irvine and is the author of many short stories and an adult trade novel, *Goodnight, Nebraska*, winner of the James A. Michener Memorial Prize.

Laura and Tom McNeal's first novel for young adults, *Crooked*, won the California Book Award for Juvenile Literature and was named an American Library Association Top Ten Best Book for Young Adults. The McNeals are married and live in Southern California with their two young sons, Sam and Hank.